The Portraitist

The Portraitist

A Novel of Adélaïde Labille-Guiard

Susanne Dunlap

Published 2022
Printed in the United States of America
Print ISBN: 978-1-64742-097-0
E-ISBN: 978-1-64742-098-7
Library of Congress Control Number: 2022904036

For information, address:
She Writes Press
1569 Solano Ave #546
Berkeley, CA 94707

She Writes Press is a division of SparkPoint Studio, LLC.

To my companion in all the arts, my champion, my cheerleader, and my best friend, Charles Jackson.
7/15/1943–11/20/2021
I miss you.

One

Paris, August 1774

Whenever sleep eluded her, Adélaïde would gaze out the window of the third-floor apartment she shared with her husband and think about colors. She'd stare hardly blinking for hours, noticing all the subtle variations of hue that, to a skilled eye, gave the sky as much movement and character as a living creature. Even as a child, she had understood that nothing was fixed, that light changed whatever it touched. Take the human face: Skin was not one color, but many, and never exactly the same from one moment to the next. She knew, for instance, that if Nicolas ever discovered what she was going to do that day, his face would take on one of the shades of thundercloud that had become more and more familiar to her as they drifted apart, and then she would be obliged to cajole him back to a placid pale pink.

He lay in the bed next to her, sprawled on his back, snoring open-mouthed and dripping saliva on his pillow. With a snort, he rolled away from her, and Adélaïde eased herself out from between the sheets, nudged her toes into her slippers, and stood.

"You're up early," Nicolas said, making her jump.

She pulled on her dressing gown as she walked into what served as kitchen and dining area. "I'll wrap up some bread and cheese for you."

Nicolas threw off the covers and shook himself from shoulders to toes before whisking his night shirt over his head and dressing for his job as secretary to the clergy. Adélaïde handed him the parcel of food as he strode by on his way out. He turned before leaving and stared at her. "You've stopped even making an effort to be attractive. You could at least put your hair up." He let the door slam behind him and thumped down the stairs.

He's right, Adélaïde thought. But she didn't have time to worry about that now. As soon as she heard the heavy outer door of the building open and close, she hurried down to the courtyard, filled a basin of water from the fountain, and brought it up to the apartment so she could bathe. When she was finished, she put on her one good ensemble—the one she wore to church on Sundays with bodice and sleeves that had been trimmed with Mechlin lace in her father's boutique. Her plan was to leave and come back without anyone noticing before Nicolas returned for dinner.

After waiting for two women who lived below her to finish their conversation in the stairwell, Adélaïde tiptoed out of the house and took a circuitous route to the Rue Neuve Saint-Merri and the Hôtel Jabach so no one might guess where she was going. She passed as swiftly as she could along the crowded thoroughfares with their boutiques and market stalls selling everything from leather goods to live chickens, picking her way around piles of dung and flattening herself against buildings as carriages clattered by. Such strange turns her life had taken, she thought. If she had waited—as her father begged her—until someone more worthy asked for her hand, she might have been the lady she'd just seen pressing a scented handkerchief to her nose as she flew past in a handsome *calèche*. But at the age of eighteen, her mother dead the year before and all seven of her siblings buried, Adélaïde had been desperate to get away from home, to leave the memories behind and start a new life. Enter the dashing Nicolas Guiard, who courted her passionately and made her feel wanted. Then, she couldn't believe her good fortune. Now, she realized she'd made a terrible mistake.

It was only ten o'clock when she arrived at the iron gates that opened into the courtyard of the Hôtel Jabach. She stood for several seconds and stared, taking in everything, fixing the image of this moment in her memory. She, Adélaïde Labille-Guiard, was about to enter the first exhibition where she would not just be a spectator but a bona-fide, participating artist. Two of her pictures hung in one of the galleries within, her entries in the annual salon of the Académie de Saint-Luc—not the Académie Royale, but nearly as prestigious. Her teachers—François-Élie Vincent and Maurice Quentin de la Tour—had put her up for membership years ago, before she married, and she would be one of only two women exhibiting that year. It was a bold step, a leap in fact, beyond the trite watercolor miniatures she sold in Monsieur Gallimard's shop to make a little pocket money. Those were not art.

As she passed through the gates and crossed the courtyard to the entrance, sweat ran down her back under the layers of stays and bodice and petticoats, pooled at her waist, and trickled down her legs into the tops of her wool stockings. She took the printed catalogue the concierge handed her at the door and started fanning herself with it before she even opened it.

The murmur of polite commentary echoed around her. Smartly dressed men and women sauntered in twos and threes, facing the walls and pausing occasionally to admire what caught their eye, then turning to examine the portrait busts and figures that dotted the middle of the floor on pedestals at regular intervals. From her earliest childhood, Adélaïde had been to many exhibitions like this one, in rooms that had been stripped of some of their furnishings and given over to the contemplation of art. She wanted to savor it all and take her time to feast her eyes on everything, to give herself a chance to appreciate the honor of having her own work displayed alongside that of more established artists.

It was in the second of the main galleries that Adélaïde first noticed a small group comprising a slight, dapper man, an older woman who could still be called attractive, and two young ladies of startling beauty.

One of them had a face of such exquisite proportions that Adélaïde wished she'd brought a sketch pad and a pencil so she could take her likeness then and there. The other one, although not quite as pretty, exuded sensuality and was clearly aware of the power she had over men in general and the gentleman in their party in particular. She cast her eyes down, her long lashes fluttering against cheeks rosy with what might have been embarrassment if they hadn't been carefully painted with vermilion stain. That was when Adélaïde overheard the gentleman say, "No, I insist. Your allegories are perfection, Mademoiselle."

Adélaïde froze. *Her allegories?* That lady had pictures hanging in the exhibition? The only other female member of the Saint-Luc she knew of was the elderly Mademoiselle Navarre, a pastellist and miniaturist who painted still lifes, not allegories. This lady, whoever she was, must have been elected very recently. No others were on the roster of exhibitors the last time Adélaïde had seen it. She held her breath, willing herself to blend into the crowd, standing sideways to the group and pretending to examine a rather voluptuous rendition of Leda and the Swan. Her ears tingled as she strained to hear the rest of the conversation despite the ebb and flow of casual comments as visitors moved through the gallery.

"Do you really think so?" the lady said.

"I believe the world will be forced to acknowledge that the young Mademoiselle Vigée has made her mark and is ready to take her place among the most talented portraitists in Paris today."

Vigée. It was a familiar name. Adélaïde associated it with an artist but not a lady. Then she remembered. The pastellist and fan decorator Louis Vigée had belonged to the Saint-Luc. He had died some years before. Could this be his daughter? She must be very young.

The voices faded as the group moved on to another gallery. Adélaïde opened her catalogue, hands trembling. The artists were not listed alphabetically, so she had to scan the entire booklet before she finally found the name Vigée along with that of another unfamiliar lady artist, Mademoiselle Bocquet. More than eight works by Mademoiselle Vigée were listed, several of them oil paintings. And Mademoiselle Bocquet showed three large pictures and a number of smaller portraits and *têtes d'études*. The two women were at the end of the listing of regular members, immediately before the *agréés*, the apprentices, and must therefore have been a very recent addition—a guess that was confirmed by the fact that both of them had donated the most significant of their paintings to the academy. So, they were full members, not apprentices. She, Adélaïde, was still just an *agréé*.

Several of Mademoiselle Vigée's sitters had titles—*comte, duchesse, baronne*. Adélaïde hadn't had time to examine the artist's clothing, but she had the impression of silk and lace, of an extravagantly trimmed hat—evidence of affluence. She herself could hardly afford gum Arabic for pastels and the most essential pigments and was forced to execute works on inexpensive paper. This young lady artist had the luxury of working in oils on the much-more-costly canvas.

Adélaïde's stomach churned. Why, oh why had she waited six years to show her work in an exhibition like this one? How could she hope to compete with someone like Mademoiselle Vigée, who it seemed had the further advantage of entrée to lofty social circles? Adélaïde braced herself to examine the allegories Mademoiselle Vigée's gentleman friend had praised so extravagantly. Perhaps they weren't very skillful. Perhaps family and friends engaged Mademoiselle Vigée out of kindness to indulge a whim, and she would exhibit this year and then disappear to marriage and children.

Yet as soon as Adélaïde stood before the three oval canvases, she knew the man she had overheard had not spouted empty praise. Mademoiselle Vigée had a tendency to emphasize prettiness in the shape of a face, but the flesh tones and drapery—exquisite. Adélaïde had studied enough about oil painting to appreciate the subtle use of glazes to bring the model's skin to life. Because she must have had models. No one could paint the musculature of a female back and arm

so accurately by trying to look in a mirror or relying on imagination.
And the attention to detail, the fine brush strokes, the composition—it
all indicated a high degree of skill and the best training.

Models. Oils. Training. Hope drained from Adélaïde's heart. How
could her two modest offerings compare to these? A miniature watercolor and a pastel, with only herself as model in one and an engraving
as the source of the other. Perhaps it was too late for her. She'd waited,
hesitant, doubtful of her own worthiness. But why? Her teachers had
pressed her again and again to display her work in public, but she
resisted for reasons that had nothing to do with her desire or ability.

They had to do with Nicolas. At least, the idea of him, the thought
that his regard for her diminished every time she picked up a brush
or a crayon and that he disdained the one thing that mattered to her
more than anything else. At first she'd tried to draw him into her ambitions, asking him to sit for her. He'd refused. He'd told her it was child-
ish to pass her time in that way and that he was too busy earning her
keep to indulge her. That was when she started hiding her work from
him, pretending she'd given it up or at least given up any serious idea
of becoming a painter. He had little regard for art anyway. The only
pictures he truly appreciated were the erotic drawings he bought on
occasion. He tried to hide them, but in their small apartment, nothing
escaped her notice. When she discovered a sheaf of titillating engrav-
ings in a folio under their bed, she hadn't been so much disgusted at
the subject matter as at the crudeness of the execution.

What was so shameful about sexual pleasure anyway? Many of
the pictures sanctified as art by the academies were blatantly erotic.
Adélaïde took a long look at the dozens of portraits gazing down at
her in attitudes of pride and coquetry and thinly veiled desire; the
mythological subjects of rape and seduction; the fecund landscapes
inviting her into distant vistas; the still lifes where exhausted flowers shed their petals in a constant state of incipient decay; the grand
history paintings that froze men in attitudes of action and women in

simpers of adoration or weakness. No, she thought. She would not be intimidated. She belonged here as much as anyone. She'd been told she had talent and knew she had a limitless capacity for hard work. This Mademoiselle Vigée and her friend—what did it matter if they were artists too? The world had an unlimited supply of paint and canvas and subjects. There was room for all.

Yet, in the back of her mind, Adélaïde suspected that there might be less room for women artists than men and that if Mademoiselle Vigée continued to paint, a day would come when they would be considered rivals. Right now, Mademoiselle Vigée had the clear advantage of training and resources. No matter. That situation could be remedied. Adélaïde would take steps to narrow that gulf, something she knew she would have to do sooner or later. So, it would be sooner. She had put off owning her place in the art world long enough in deference to Nicolas's *amour propre*. He must learn to accept who she was. If he didn't—well, she would cross that bridge when she had to.

Adélaïde took a few steps toward the gallery where she thought she'd find her own pictures, then changed her mind. She was too preoccupied, too unsettled, to view them dispassionately. So she left the Hôtel Jabach without looking for them and made her way back to the apartment, her mind galloping ahead. She'd return the next day, or possibly the day after, when she'd thought it all through and would be calm enough to face her pictures and judge them as a visitor might.

Two

Adélaïde hadn't had time to change out of her Sunday *habillement* before she heard Nicolas enter the building and pound up the stairs two at a time. *Courage*, she thought. She would tell him straightaway. Perhaps he would surprise her and be glad. Perhaps the prospect of lucrative portrait commissions that would result from the exhibition would soften him, and he wouldn't accuse her of preferring painting to spending time with him or of being unwomanly for pursuing a career that would put her in the public eye. She smoothed down her hair that still bore traces of powder and took a seat at the table, raising her cup of tisane to her lips as Nicolas burst through the door.

"What is this!" His eyebrows were drawn together, and his eyes flashed as strode over to her and waved a booklet in her face.

"I-I don't know." There it was. The thundercloud—darker than she'd ever seen it. He didn't even look like himself. And of course, she did know what *it* was. The exhibition catalogue. Her own copy remained tucked in the pocket tied around her waist beneath her petticoats.

He leaned down toward her. His eyes were red, as though he'd been crying. For an instant, shame washed over Adélaïde. She should have told him, been more honest. "I'm sorry, I should have . . ." She couldn't think in that moment exactly what she should have done, knowing that he likely would have forbidden her to exhibit. Most husbands would have done so in the same circumstances. She'd been naïve to think otherwise.

Nicolas took two steps away and then wheeled around to face her

again. "Do you know who gave this to me? Do you know? The miniatures you sold were bad enough. I had to laugh them off, claim they
were nothing more than a harmless whim."

So, he knew about the miniatures. "But, I told you when we
married—"

"You tricked me! You and your father. All along you were just waiting to humiliate me."

A harsh sob escaped his throat, and he gripped her upper arm and
yanked her out of the chair, sending it tumbling backwards. Adélaïde
felt his fingernails through her sleeve and bit her lip to keep from
crying out, afraid to struggle against him.

"I should have annulled the marriage the very next day! You couldn't
give me children anyway. All you wanted me for was to support you so
you could indulge your precious painting." He kicked a nearby chair
and sent it across the floor. "Who did you have to sleep with to get
your pictures in this salon?!"

He threw her away from him. She lost her balance and fell. He
began ripping pages out of the catalogue and crushing them in his
hands.

"Nicolas! You forget yourself!" She tried to scream the words but
they came out strangled and husky.

"I? I forget myself? You're my wife! You're supposed to love and
obey me! Instead you make me a mockery!"

Before she could scramble away, he grabbed her again and raised
his fist. It was the last thing Adélaïde saw before the world went black.

⌒℮つ

At first, when Adélaïde awoke later, her eyes wouldn't focus. She
blinked hard, and gradually her surroundings began to take shape.
But everything was in the wrong place. She wasn't in her bed. She lay
on something hard and was surrounded by broken china and smashed
bits of wood. *The floor*, she thought. She pushed herself up on one

elbow. "Arghh!" The pain in her arm was so intense she couldn't suppress her cry and fell back down. *Don't push yourself up*, she thought, and clenched her stomach muscles to raise herself to a sitting position. Her head pounded as if it were about to explode with pain on one side of it. She bit her lip to keep from crying out again and surveyed the scene around her.

It was the apartment. But it looked as if some whirlwind had come through and hurled every item she owned around the room, smashing it to bits. Even the bedding was torn in shreds. She lifted her right hand to the sore on her head and touched something sticky. She smelled her fingers. Blood. Then she looked down at her left hand and swollen wrist. When she tried to move it, pain shot all the way up her arm. Where was Nicolas? There was something . . .

Bit by bit, she remembered. She'd been in the apartment, just returned from the exhibition. Footsteps pounded up the stairs from the street. The door flew open. Nicolas, his face purple with anger.

And she had hoped he wouldn't mind. How foolish.

She was still wearing her good dress, but it was torn and dirty. Her head had cleared, although pain pulsed in one spot. Adélaïde rolled onto her knees and pushed herself up with her right hand. Her right hand. Thank heavens. He hadn't injured her painting hand. She went to the small mirror in the bedroom and examined the nasty bruise that half closed her right eye. She took a scrap of linen and soaked it in water, wincing as she patted the bruise and cleaned up the blood on her head as best she could.

She and Nicolas might have become distant and prone to arguing over every little thing, but this—to injure her. She would never have foreseen it. She didn't know him at all, it seemed. Now the apartment that had been her home for six years felt perilous, like a foreign landscape with monsters hidden in the corners. There might as well be. It contained so little of her. She'd erased herself from her home gradually over the years, as she drew herself in, folding her wings for protection.

She thought it had been only to protect her soul, her heart. Now, it seemed she would have to protect her body as well.

Whatever was to happen in the end, she needed to be away from Nicolas now. But how? If she left to find a room somewhere, the police would simply return her to her husband with an admonishment that she should behave better and maybe he wouldn't hit her. The only option was her father. But would he take her in? Their relations had become strained ever since she married against his wishes. He would no doubt congratulate himself at how right he'd been about Nicolas. But it didn't matter now. He was all she had. She'd never cultivated female friends, always too busy with her art in every spare moment, and whatever other distant relations she had lived far away in the provinces.

Adélaïde found a shawl and wrapped it over her head and around her shoulders, although it was hardly the season for it. With great care, discovering new sore spots and aching muscles with every step, she gathered all her hidden art supplies and packed them into a satchel. She paused in the open doorway and took one more look around the apartment she and Nicolas had entered so joyfully six years ago, then walked out of the building, never to return.

౿

That evening, after her father's companion Jacqueline had cleaned the gash on her head, put a cool cloth over her eye, and wrapped her wrist, Adélaïde sat sipping wine at the kitchen table in the capacious apartment.

"You have every right to feel triumphant," she said to her father. "But as I said, Nicolas has never behaved this way before. You didn't really know him. He could be very kind." Even as she uttered the words Adélaïde knew she was stretching the truth, although she wasn't certain why she would bother to do such a thing.

Claude-Edmé Labille reached out and patted his daughter's good hand. "Why would I feel triumphant that my only surviving child has been hurt? Do you really think me so heartless? And the fact that he hasn't beaten you before changes nothing. Now you know he is capable of it."

Adélaïde gazed at her father in his scarlet silk dressing gown, still looking well-dressed enough to serve one of his wealthy customers although the shop was closed for the evening. It had been months since she'd visited him. The last time, she had pretended everything was well with Nicolas. Her visit hadn't been long enough to discover that Jacqueline, whom she knew only as the head seamstress in the workshop, had become much more than that to her father.

After Jacqueline discreetly retired to another room, Adélaïde said, "So, Jacqueline—" and smiled.

A delicate pink—no more than a drop of carmine mixed with lead white—suffused her father's cheeks. "None of that now," he said. "We must speak of you and your predicament. What will you do?"

Adélaïde's mind whirled, thoughts chasing each other too fast to be spoken. After a time, though, she managed to catch two threads that circled back and back, demanding her attention. She had a simple choice: She could return, Nicolas would apologize, and she would go back to hiding her ambition and try to be careful not to put him in that position again or to provoke him in any way that would goad him into violence toward her. That would be the easy thing to do. It would be what most would expect of her, a married woman.

But perhaps his actions had given her an excuse to make the other choice. The difficult choice. She stood on a threshold between her past and her future. To go one way would be to go backwards. But to go forward—was she brave enough? Brave enough to take charge of her own life, whatever that meant? The thought sent a shudder through her. She looked up into her father's eyes. Smile lines stretched from their corners and disappeared somewhere under his silk cap. He kept his gaze steady, giving her time to answer.

And then she knew. "I will not go back to him, to that apartment. We have to separate."

The words echoed in a silence filled only by the tick of the mantel clock, drilling into Adélaïde's aching head saying *tsk, tsk, tsk* over and over. More fool she was for ever expecting to be married and continue painting in the first place. Her father had warned her, but she wouldn't listen. Marrying Nicolas had turned out to be more of an ending than a beginning. It had ended her lessons in watercolor with François-Élie Vincent and pastels with Maurice Quentin de La Tour. It had ended her Sunday strolls in the Tuileries or the Palais Royale gardens with her father. Nicolas demanded she promenade with him on Sundays and complained about any expense of which he did not approve. That was why Adélaïde started selling miniatures in Monsieur Gallimard's shop—so she could make some money to purchase her art supplies. But that was all over now. "I cannot go back."

Claude-Edmé spoke at last. "You are welcome to remain here as long as necessary. You must know that."

Did she know that? Not many fathers would take in a disobedient daughter without scolding, without insisting that the law said she must return to her husband come what may, that Nicolas had been within his rights to beat her, that she had made the decision to marry him and must face the consequences. Her eyes burning with unshed tears, Adélaïde said, "I don't deserve your kindness. If I stay it would be at most a temporary arrangement. For one thing, I need a studio."

"*If* you stay? My dear, where else would you go? And this dream of yours, to be a portraitist. Are you certain that is what you want?"

Adélaïde hadn't told her father about the salon. He was not a connoisseur of art, and he'd never complimented the few of her pictures he'd seen. His was the world of fashion, of rapidly changing styles that dominated society for a month or two and then vanished. How could he be expected to understand her desire to create something of beauty that also endured? She searched in his eyes for an answer. All she saw there was affection, tinged with sadness. It was enough. She reached out and took her father's hand. "Yes. More certain than I've ever been of anything."

"I confess, you aren't like any other lady I know. The ones I serve in my boutique care only about what the queen wore to the opera or to the last ball. But you—" He smiled as he waved a hand at her now-disheveled gown and disarranged hair.

Adélaïde looked down at her dirty bodice and put her hand to her head. The absurdity of it all struck her, and she laughed, letting the tension of the past few days—of the past six years—spill out in gales of uncontrolled mirth. It hurt her sides and scraped her throat, and helpless tears rolled down her face and plopped onto the linen of her fichu before being absorbed as if they'd never fallen.

Adélaïde's father stood and went to a cupboard in the corner of the kitchen next to the stove, which at this time of year was only lit when the daily serving girl was cooking. He bent down and opened the bottom drawer, withdrew a small metal box, and brought it to the table. Adélaïde stopped laughing, her breath coming in hiccups, and watched him as he pulled a tiny key on a silver chain out of his pocket, fitted it into the lock on the box, and opened it with a click. She was still too stunned, too thrown off balance, to wonder much what he was doing.

He pulled out a velvet pouch that clearly showed the outline of coins. "Here," he said, taking her hand and placing the pouch in it. "I wish I could do more, but I have had to invest in some very costly lace recently."

Adélaïde looked down at the pouch. All at once, she realized what he'd given her, and what it meant. She teased open the cords that held it closed and upended its contents on the table. One, two, three . . . The gold coins tumbled heavily onto the polished wood. Ten Louis d'Or. She gasped. It was enough to secure her own apartment and purchase many art supplies. "It's too much!"

"Nonsense," her father said. "What else should I spend it on? If you'd married differently, it would have been part of your dowry."

"This is freedom," she said. "Thank you."

"Freedom for the moment. But as you appear to be certain you will not go back to your husband, we must get you a legal separation. And until then, you are not safe. You had best remain here for the time being. We must ensure that Guiard has no right to your assets or to your companionship. I will send word to my *avocat* in the morning."

Just like that. Her father wanted to end the marriage as much as she did. Until that moment, Adélaïde hadn't fully understood the depth of her father's animosity toward the handsome, self-absorbed Nicolas. She supposed that if a child of hers had come to her beaten by someone who should have loved her, she would have felt exactly the same.

Adélaïde stood and walked around the table to stand next to her father, put her hand on his shoulder, and bent down to kiss his cheek.

He patted her hand and smiled. "You must be very tired. Jacqueline has made up your bed by now."

Adélaïde took a candle and made her way to the bedroom that had been hers as a child, with its narrow cot, small cupboard, and nightstand. A clean shift had been laid out for her and a basin of fresh water waited on the stand. She splashed her face, unpinned and untied all her clothes and donned the shift, then slid beneath the light covers. She'd thought she'd never come back to that room, but here she was. *No, I won't cry.* This wasn't the end, it was a beginning. From now on, she would make sure that no one could deflect her from her purpose. She had wasted enough of her life being distracted by a beguiling, selfish man. From now on, if she wanted to make up for her six fruitless years chasing a kind of happiness she didn't really want, she would have to keep to a steady path, her eyes focused ahead on her goal. A life as a portraitist awaited her. Now all she had to do was reach for it.

Three

Adélaïde wrote to the Académie de Saint-Luc to tell them to send any communications to her care of her father at À la Toilette, his boutique. The last thing she wanted was for Nicolas—who she assumed remained in their apartment—to intercept any potential communications about portrait commissions. That, after all, had been one of her reasons for taking the chance and exhibiting in the salon—and the one she thought her parsimonious husband might actually appreciate. Now, he would certainly see them as what they were: her ticket to freedom. Without such commissions, she would never move past creating pretty miniatures to sell in a shop and never have enough money to survive on her own now that she was pursuing a separation. She ultimately agreed with her father that it would be best to wait until the separation was legally binding before getting her own apartment and studio because until that time, Nicolas would be within his rights to drag her back home or rape and beat her. Adélaïde didn't really think he'd do that. But how did she know? The man who had attacked her two days ago bore little resemblance to the man she had fallen in love with.

She had little time to fret over such things if she was going to start moving forward. She would at last be able to get to work without any interference. There was the matter of completing enough pictures to be advanced from her position as *agréé* at the Saint-Luc, something that never would have been possible while she lived with Nicolas. She still had the catalogue and had looked again and again at the entries for Mesdemoiselles Vigée and Bocquet, experiencing anew every time a flood of piercing envy as she read of their portraits in oil of aristocrats and nobles, imagining they had studios stocked with all the materials they needed and had room for sitters too.

Adélaïde returned to the Hôtel Jabach as soon as she could wear a hat without pain and the swelling around her eye had gone down. She needed to see her own pictures there, to see if they belonged among the others, truly, or if she'd been deluding herself that she was good enough to take her place among professionals. She walked through the galleries slowly and examined every single oil painting, pastel, watercolor, drawing, and sculpture, making notes in the catalogue about each one. She did not hurry to see hers. She wanted her eyes to be full of everything around them first, to be saturated with all that a dispassionate observer would see.

And then she turned a corner, and there they were. Her shoulders unclenched. She allowed herself to smile and looked around to see if anyone else was near. A couple had just entered the chamber and walked over to her two entries, stopping in front of them. Adélaïde pretended to be examining a portrait bust on a plinth in the middle of the floor, her ears tingling to hear what, if anything, they would say.

"He's so alive!" the woman whispered. The man mumbled his agreement. And then they passed along and out of the gallery.

Adélaïde supposed it was enough. Her portrait of the magistrate did give him life and presence—La Tour had counted her among his best students. And now she could honestly see that her work was just as good as the others in the salon. Better than some.

She passed swiftly to Mademoiselle Vigée's allegories to look at them again with her own pictures in her mind. Her first impression was confirmed. This was the work of a formidable rival. As to Mademoiselle Bocquet—she did not possess quite as much talent and ability as Mademoiselle Vigée or Adélaïde herself, but she, too, had been admitted as a full member. Why? What influence did they have?

On her way out, Adélaïde stopped to talk to the guard on the pretext that she might be interested in commissioning a portrait from Mademoiselle Vigée but that she couldn't decide between her and Mademoiselle Bocquet. "She was elected as a member to the Saint Luc recently, wasn't she?" Adélaïde said to the old man who'd been dozing on a chair by the main door.

"Ah yes." He leaned forward and lowered his voice. "It was quite unexpected. Bit of a scandal, really. You know officers from the Court of the Châtelet raided her studio in July. They confiscated everything she had."

"How distressing!" Adélaïde said, caught between genuine outrage and secret glee. "What for?"

He leaned yet closer. Adélaïde could smell his pungent breath and had to will herself not to back away. "They said she'd been painting professionally without a license from the Guild."

"Hah!" Adélaïde said, taking a step back. "And how would she have gotten such a thing? Women can't belong to a guild."

The guard shrugged. "*Beh.* She had everything back in a few weeks anyway. And as you see, she's well connected. Her godfather Gabriel Doyen got the officers of the Saint-Luc to vote her and her friend in with a special session. It doesn't hurt to be so nice to look at either."

Adélaïde wanted to ask if a man's looks were taken into consideration when being elected to the Académie de Saint-Luc but thought better of it.

The guard prattled on, furnishing all the information Adélaïde could possibly want. The older woman she had seen with them at the opening was apparently Mademoiselle Vigée's mother, who as a widow had married a jeweler named Jacques Le Sèvre. And yes, Mademoiselle was indeed the daughter of Louis Vigée. As to Mademoiselle Bocquet, her mother taught drawing to ladies and was quite well known. Her father owned a bric-a-brac shop not unlike that of Monsieur Gallimard.

Adélaïde jotted this information in her catalogue before pressing a coin into the guard's hand and taking her leave.

While she had been indoors, a brief rainstorm had washed the Paris air clean and left behind puddles that carriages splashed through to the consternation of pedestrians. Adélaïde took deep gulps of air as she walked, choosing a route off the busiest roads that would enable her to pass through the gardens of the Palais Royale. Her heart was full of art and ambition, and, passing by the palace that held one of the finest collections of paintings in France and therefore probably the world, it somehow seemed a fitting way to end her momentous day.

cᴏᴏ

Summer faded and autumn sped by in a blur of ceaseless work. Freed from the necessity to pretend for the sake of Nicolas, Adélaïde spent every possible moment in the studio she'd set up in the best-lit corner of her bedroom, sometimes working until the light went and she had to use candles. She hardly paused to celebrate Christmas and barely noticed as the days grew shorter. She rarely went anywhere except to deliver miniatures to Gallimard to sell or to replenish her art supplies and to go to the homes of the people who had commissioned portraits from her after the Saint Luc salon. She spent as little money as possible, purchasing only the items that were absolutely necessary to her purpose, wanting to conserve as much of the money her father had given her and that she'd earned since then for the day when a legal separation would make it possible for her to rent her own apartment and studio.

And in eight months, just as spring was returning to Paris and brightening everyone's eyes, Adélaïde decided it was time to put another of her ambitions in play. She had enough set aside to buy a roll of canvas, a palette, brushes suitable for oil painting, and the basic pigments and linseed oil she would need to finally take up the serious study of painting in oils. She had been wanting to do this for years, and now, having taken nearly a year to focus on her art, she could not progress further without this vital step. For one thing, oil portraits sold for much more than watercolors. They also had the added advantage of being less liable to damage than pastels, whose delicate surfaces had to be either shown behind glass or treated with a varnish that would darken the vivid colors. Few serious portraitists lacked expertise in oils. Most importantly, Madame Le Brun used oils so expertly her portraits glowed. If Adélaïde was ever to compete, she would have to find her own style, something that would mark her out as unique, where people would look at one of her oil portraits hanging in a gallery and say, *Ah! Another Labille-Guiard!*

Adélaïde knew enough of the basic techniques to make a start on her own, but trial and error would take time—and more money than she wanted to waste on experimentation. So her only option was to seek training. The cost of the lessons would be a worthwhile investment in her future. But who would teach her? She couldn't afford someone like Joseph Vien, one of the most popular instructors at the Académie Royale. Briard was a fool, and she'd gone far beyond him in skill already anyway. And not all of the others she knew of would take female students.

After a moment, Adélaïde smiled. *Of course.* If anyone knew who might take her on as a student it was her old tutor, the man who taught her everything she knew about watercolors: Élie Vincent. She owed him thanks as well. He had sent a very kind note about her pictures in the salon. That settled the matter.

⌒℮⌒

Two hours later, Adélaïde walked to the apartment building near the Louvre where Vincent lived. She pulled the bell at the door, but when it opened a few moments later, instead of the wizened concierge Adélaïde expected to see, a man in a green velvet coat who looked to be about her age burst out in such a hurry he narrowly avoided knocking her down.

"*Je m'excuse, Madame!*" he said, splotches of red blooming in his cheeks. He reached out to steady her. "You were coming to see someone in this house. Allow me to fetch the concierge."

"Please, I would not keep you from your obviously urgent business." Adélaïde couldn't help smiling. The stranger's curling brown hair rested on sloping shoulders, and dark, blue-gray eyes that brightened when he smiled peered out from under long, languid eyelids.

"I insist."

"Very well, if you would tell the concierge I am come to call on Monsieur Vincent, I would be most grateful."

"Monsieur Vincent?" The young man paused, brow furrowed, hand on the door handle, and then a moment later said, "Oh! You mean my father."

His father? It was Adélaïde's turn to be confused. Then she remembered. This must be Élie Vincent's son, just come back to Paris after three years at the Académie de France in Rome, his reward for winning the coveted Prix de Rome. Before she could say anything else, he'd disappeared into the building, returning a moment later with the concierge, who was still wiping crumbs from the corners of his mouth. He must have been in the middle of his lunch.

"Please conduct this lady up to my father's apartment, Cédric," he said with a gracious smile. He tipped his hat to Adélaïde before hurrying away.

⌒e⌒

As soon as the serving girl had brought in a tea tray and they were settled comfortably near the heating stove in the parlor, Adélaïde told Élie the reason for her visit.

His eyes lit up, and he clapped his hands together. "You must become a student of my talented son, François-André!"

Adélaïde didn't mention that she'd encountered him only moments before. "Oh? Is he accepting lady students?"

"He won't charge you as much as someone like Vien—he's just starting out. It will be to his advantage as well. Having one student—and one as brilliant as you are—will surely lead to more. His lodgings and studio are in the Louvre. You know he won the Prix de Rome, of course."

The pride shining from her mentor's eyes made Adélaïde forget that he had just called her brilliant. It seemed that Francois-André, although granted a studio in the Louvre, was still just an *agréé* of the Académie Royale, but his acceptance was assured once he'd completed the required number of canvases. Unlike his father, whose success was entirely in the realm of miniatures, André—so Élie told her—painted huge, ambitious scenes on historical subjects—supplementing his efforts with portraiture so he could earn money for materials and models.

"The free accommodations are most welcome. But even those not yet fully accepted to the Académie are forbidden to pursue commercial endeavors, which means he cannot be seen to sell his paintings or even to display them other than at the official salons. A silly convention, if you ask me. Students are another matter, though. That is seen as advancing the cause of art."

Adélaïde and her former teacher finished their cups of tea, and she rose to leave. "Thank you, Monsieur Vincent. You have helped me immeasurably."

Vincent cocked his head on the side and looked Adélaïde up and down. "There is something different about you. You seem more serene. In recent years, it seems that every time I've seen you, your shoulders have been up around your ears and your eyebrows drawn together. Now, you look young and pretty, as you should. What has changed?"

Adélaïde blushed. Was it so obvious how unhappy she'd been? "I-I'd rather not say. Not just yet."

Vincent leaned back in his chair and raised one eyebrow. "As you wish."

Although she cared little for the opinions of her neighbors, Adélaïde wanted to postpone as long as possible the inevitable questions about her decision to separate from Nicolas. She didn't want to waste time or energy satisfying people's curiosity when she had so much else to do. And as much as she didn't want to admit it to herself, a tiny corner of her heart kept doubting that she had made the right decision.

Four

The next day, Adélaïde took several wrong turns in the twisting corridors of the Louvre before she finally found the door with a pasteboard card on it that said, "F-A. Vincent." She smoothed down her skirt and straightened her hat before knocking. At first, there was no response. But she knew he was in there because when she put her ear to the door, she could hear male voices rise and fall in indistinct conversation. She knocked again. She had come without any art supplies of her own, intending only to discuss the terms of her study with him. Adélaïde wondered what exactly Élie Vincent had told his son about her and even whether the prizewinning artist would agree to teach her. She knocked a third time, more loudly still.

"*Entrez!*" came a call from beyond the door—a call tinged with unmistakable vexation.

Adélaïde opened the door and stepped inside, immediately struck by the cloying smell of turpentine and the light bouncing off the white-painted walls. She didn't know where to look—at the shelves full of every pigment and brush a painter could ever need, at the partially finished canvases leaning against one wall, at the workbench splashed with colors from mixing hues of every variety. It took her a moment to notice the studio's two occupants. One was André himself in his painting smock, with his back to her, standing before a large canvas and using a delicate brush to daub in a shadow on the underside of a very muscular arm. *Yellow ochre*, Adélaïde thought.

The second man was the owner of the arm, a strapping fellow

standing naked on a pedestal in the middle of the room. He smiled at Adélaïde without altering his position or making any attempt to cover himself.

"You have a visitor," the model said. "A pretty one."

André made a sudden movement with his brush hand that spoiled the line of the shadow. "*Merde!*" He swished his brush in the glass of turpentine on the table next to him and turned.

"Should I come back at another time?" Adélaïde couldn't help but smile.

Red-faced, André spoke to the model, "Please rest a bit, Marc."

Marc slipped a loose robe over his shoulders, walked to a chair and sat in it, the smile never leaving his lips.

"I'm so sorry . . . It's Mademoiselle—"

"Madame. Guiard."

"Sorry, Madame Guiard. My father said you were interested in studying oil painting. I didn't expect . . . well, no matter. My studio is not so large, but you are welcome to come and learn whatever I can teach you. Father says you are already very accomplished in watercolors and pastels."

"You call this not large?" Adélaïde said, with a sweeping gesture that encompassed what must have been forty square yards.

He smiled a little sheepishly. "I suppose it's large enough for most purposes. But my canvases, you see—"

He looked back at the painting he'd been working on. At least ten by six feet, Adélaïde thought. He was certainly ambitious.

"I see," she said.

They stood looking at each other in silence for a moment. That was it, Adélaïde thought. That's what it was about his eyes. They really were the most remarkable dark blue, like the Seine on a rare day when it reflected the sky. Or perhaps it was simply that his lids hung over and cast a shadow, darkening the irises. To paint them, she would have to mix ultramarine and black, perhaps a little ochre.

She forced herself back to the matter at hand. "I can't afford to pay you much. I hope your father mentioned that."

André slipped his smock off and tossed it over a stool, wiping his hands on a turpentine-soaked rag as he approached her. "He said that you would excel as my pupil and that the future students you would inspire would make it well worth the investment of teaching you for free."

Adélaïde turned to the side, unable for a moment to continue gazing into André's eyes. "Ah no. I did not ask for free, only for a reasonable amount. Shall we say two livres per lesson? I would come every day if it suits you, or less often, if not. When should I start?" She'd prepared all that beforehand, not certain she would be able to say what she meant on the spot, and not wanting to give him the opportunity to mention a fee she could not afford.

He shrugged. "If that is your wish. Every day would be agreeable."

Adélaïde nodded, then looked past him and approached the unfinished canvas. "Belisarius begging, it appears." It was a common enough subject for a history painting.

"Yes. I hope to enter it in the August salon. I would like it to be my reception piece."

How marvelous, Adélaïde thought, to know that all you had to do was paint a certain sort of picture and you'd be admitted to the most prestigious academy of art in the world. She looked back at André, suppressing her impulse to say something to that effect. It wasn't his fault he was a man, after all. "I'll come tomorrow. What should I bring?"

"A smock."

"No brushes? No palette?"

He laughed. "You think you'll actually start painting on the first day? In a month, perhaps. Before then, I will teach you everything I know about mixing colors, the right oils to use with which pigments, and how to encourage or discourage drying, depending on the time of year, how to prepare a canvas—and then there are the glazes and washes. Also, which brushes to use, what they're made of, and how to clean and condition them. It's a great deal more complicated than pastels and watercolors."

Adélaïde's cheeks warmed, and she was conscious of reacting perhaps too defensively. She longed to tell him that La Tour had counted her his quickest pupil ever, and that she had already read a treatise on painting in oils and there was little he could tell her about the properties of the different oils and pigments that she didn't already know. But what would that accomplish? He would soon enough discover the extent of her ability. So she simply smiled. "Tomorrow then."

ⸯⸯ

With only her smock, as instructed, Adélaïde returned to André's studio the next day to begin her lessons.

"I've lined up the pigments for you. Most of them are sold as powder, although some come in solid blocks and require you to scrape them or melt them down," he said.

She knew all this. It was the same with watercolors and pastels. Only the preparation differed. *Patience*, she thought.

"Later I shall be painting the skin tones in the faces of my figures for Belisarius. For these I shall use—"

"Vermilion, light red, and light ochre." Adélaïde didn't really intend to interrupt him, but her mind had raced on from theory to execution.

"Those would be good colors to mix for a fair complexion, but my figures are weather-beaten old soldiers. Therefore, I use carmine and burnt umber—with the light red."

She nodded.

"I suppose you're going to tell me which oils to use for mixing, which for drying, and which to avoid for these colors, and how to use glazes to give skin tones their subtlety?"

Adélaïde went cold. He was angry. She'd embarrassed him or annoyed him. At the beginning, he had stood immediately next to her, but had now taken a step away. "I-I'm sorry. It's just that—"

"My father says it was you who approached him about learning to paint in oils, so I presume that means you acknowledge that you need instruction. Let me assure you, reading a treatise is not the same as working with the materials. Now, if you intend to let me teach you in a methodical manner—the way I learned—I would be happy to continue. Otherwise, you must find another instructor."

This was a disaster. In no way did Adélaïde think she knew everything! It was just that she had so little time. How could she mend things?

After a moment, she laid her hand on his arm. "Please, forgive me. I had to teach myself everything I know about watercolors and pastels, only receiving instruction concerning composition and form from masters like your father and La Tour. I feel time is racing on, and I must gain the knowledge I need to paint portraits in oils so I can earn a living. I meant no disrespect. I am not some dabbler looking for a way to pass the time." She held his gaze and thought she saw something shift behind his eyes before he looked down at his hands and nudged a jar of powdered lake to a different position.

He said without looking up, "I, too, am to blame. You are not a naive youth who thinks he can take a few lessons and master an art that has taken centuries to perfect."

"Nor, like a youth, can I depend on my abilities alone to assure my success. I must not simply be as good as a man. I must be better."

In the silence that followed her words, Adélaïde heard the gentle rhythm of André breathing, without thinking matching her own breaths to his. He said nothing. She thought, with anguish, that he didn't want to teach her after all, and she started to remove her smock in preparation to leave.

But he touched her shoulder and turned her toward him. His

expression had softened. "Shall we start again? Perhaps you can tell me what you already know, and we can go on from there."

Relief washed over Adélaïde. It was all right. And this young man— he not only listened but actually heard what she said and valued it enough to amend his own actions because of it. In that moment, her view of the world slipped a little sideways, tipped off balance. The feeling wasn't altogether unpleasant. Perhaps, over time, she would become used to it.

◌◯◌

Adélaïde was still thinking about her first lesson with her former teacher's son as she climbed the stairs to her father's apartment. Something made her pause before entering and listen. Two men talking. One was her father, and the other was—Nicolas. His voice, even through the door, sent a shiver through her, damping the cautious joy she still felt after her hour with the young Vincent. Adélaïde took a step down and started to turn around, intending to go away again. She hadn't seen her husband since the day she stumbled out of their apartment, bruised and bleeding. She had no desire to see him now. Yet what could he want? The legal machinery of their separation had been grinding away for almost a year. If he objected, surely he'd have tried to contact her a long time ago.

Courage, she thought. What harm could he do her now? Before she could change her mind again, Adélaïde climbed back up to the top of the stairs and crept into the apartment's vestibule. She'd be able to hear better from there and gather her wits to face him.

"I'm not sure what the point is," her father said.

"It's just . . . I don't want that to be what she thinks of me. I am not that man. I don't know what happened. She'd just pushed me so . . ."

Adélaïde held her breath. First he sounded sorry. Then he was blaming her?

"You must know she is becoming a professional portraitist," her father replied. "You can't stop her."

She listened hard for his answer, but he spoke too quietly for her to hear through the door. She wanted to know what he thought about this. She needed to know what he really believed, why he had lashed out at her so violently that one time. She had guessed, had formed her own opinion. But was she right? Adélaïde opened the door quickly and strode through into the parlor.

Her father and Nicolas stood at exactly the same moment and faced her. Her father's eyes were hard. Nicolas would not get anywhere with him, Adélaïde could see. And Nicolas—his soft brown eyes gazed at her with an expression she remembered from before they were married. Had she misinterpreted it then? Did it not mean everything she thought it meant, that he loved her, that he wanted her?

Claude-Edmé pulled his watch out of his pocket and frowned at it. "A customer will arrive soon. I was just saying goodbye to Monsieur Guiard," he said, gesturing in the direction of the door, which Adélaïde blocked at that moment.

"Go tend to your boutique, Papa. I'll see Nicolas out." Her father walked past her, squeezing her hand briefly on his way. Adélaïde stayed where she was. Nicolas took a step toward her. She put up her hand to stop him. "Perhaps you'll tell me what you came here for."

Nicolas looked down at his feet, passing his soft cap back and forth between his hands. He licked his lips, which Adélaïde could see were dry. He was nervous. "I want you to give me another chance."

Could he possibly be serious? "Another chance for what? To stop me doing the one thing that brings me joy and that could make me wealthy in my own right?" Just saying the words reminded Adélaïde of how everything had been. She'd been ready to melt just a little when she saw Nicolas, looking so like he had when she first met him. Her heart was ready to betray her all over again, once more subduing the good sense in her head.

"It would be different. I would be different. I need you." He searched her eyes.

What was he hoping to find? "Why? Why do you need me?" It wasn't enough for him to utter those words. He must say the ones that meant something to her. He must tell her she could be an artist, he would not stop her. And more. She wanted to see how hard she could push him, whether he would say what she wanted to hear, that he was sorry and that he still loved her.

He ground his teeth and opened and closed his mouth. "You see it's . . . It's just that . . ."

Say it, she thought.

"I simply can't withstand the shame of a legal separation." He blurted out the words as though they'd been forced up from his stomach. "It was you who pushed me away. Don't say you don't know that! You'd come to bed too tired because you'd been drawing or painting all afternoon."

Adélaïde, angry, opened her mouth to say something, but Nicolas spoke before she had a chance.

"You thought I didn't know. I saw your crayons and brushes, hidden, you thought. You couldn't keep that secret."

And yet, he'd said nothing. How long had he been nursing this anger in his heart? All at once, his reaction made sense, in a twisted sort of way.

"We were both young," Nicolas said. "Perhaps we shouldn't have married after such a short courtship. But we're older now. I'm ready to give it another try. We both need to give in a little, not be so rigid."

He'd turned things around. He wasn't sorry. He was still angry. Nothing would change. And as always, he was clever, manipulative. At first, he asked for forgiveness. Or did he? Not in so many words. Now he wanted compromise. Just when she was poised to take the next step in achieving everything she'd always dreamed of, when he finally wasn't standing in her way anymore. Adélaïde remained silent for a long moment, which emboldened Nicolas to step forward until he could reach out and touch her arm.

She felt the pressure of his fingers in the very same place where he'd grabbed her and hurled her to the floor nearly a year ago. Adélaïde jerked herself free. "I'm afraid I'm not prepared to, as you say, 'give in a little.'" What was she thinking? "*Adieu*." She stepped aside to let him pass through the door.

He squashed his hat on his head and turned to her, still holding the door open. "You think you're different. You think you're special, that you don't have to behave like other women. Well, you're welcome to your lonely life. No one will want you under those conditions." He whirled around and slammed the door shut behind him.

Adélaïde sank into the nearest chair, her heart pounding. Nicolas was angry, yes, but she could also see the hurt in his eyes. He was right about one thing: she had pushed him away. And perhaps he was right, too, that no one would ever want her again, not like that. No one would want to be with a woman for whom art took first place in her passions. Because that was how things were. That was how they'd always been, although she'd tried to hide it. There was no going back, because going back would change nothing.

When she put her hand up to her cheek, Adélaïde felt tears. It was the first time she'd cried since the day she moved into her father's apartment.

Five

Paris, January 1778

"Is this really true? Is it over?" Adélaïde traced the red seal on the document with her fingertip as she sat at the supper table in her father's apartment. After four years, the court had made a decision. She was free, with conditions, which applied to Nicolas too. They could never divorce, so neither of them would ever be able to marry again—unless the law changed, which in that tradition-bound country was unlikely. There would forever be a slender cord tying them together.

Nicolas had not returned to her father's apartment after that one time. He hadn't written to her or tried to communicate with her in any way during the remainder of the separation proceedings. His lawyers talked to her lawyers whenever anything needed to be discussed. But Adélaïde had heard rumors in the neighborhood. She heard that he'd boasted of looking forward to the finality of a separation, because he would be able to dally as much as he liked with women and have an ironclad excuse not to marry them.

"So, the two of you will be rid of me at last," Adélaïde said as she, Jacqueline, and her father toasted the outcome with champagne. Yet not all of Adélaïde's thoughts were joyful. Like it or not, she had loved him once. He was part of her history and could not be so easily erased. This piece of paper with the elaborate scrolled writing was a sorry end to something that had once promised more.

"There is no cause for you to rush away," her father said. He covered her hand with his and looked to Jacqueline for confirmation.

"Of course not," she said and smiled.

"You are very kind. But I need a larger studio. I need to be able to paint in oils elsewhere than at the Louvre as a student, and if I subjected you to the pervasive smell of turpentine you would soon toss me out anyway!" The comment made them laugh, as Adélaïde intended.

Adélaïde had gotten to know Jacqueline somewhat after living together, even though she was busy from dawn until dusk in the shop and with the seamstresses and Adélaïde hardly left her studio except to eat and go to the Louvre for her lessons. Jacqueline was always kind, always gentle, but Adélaïde couldn't help but catch the glances between her father and his lover. She wondered why they didn't marry but felt it wasn't her place to ask.

One day, though, when she stepped out of her room to fetch some water, not expecting either of them to be in the apartment, she heard hushed voices in the parlor and crept to put her ear to the door.

Jacqueline was weeping. "He won't let me go. I don't understand!"

"Hush, ma chère, it doesn't matter. Aren't we happy as we are?"

Jacqueline's muffled sobs continued, and Adélaïde tiptoed away. So, she thought, that's why they are understanding about my position. Jacqueline herself is tied to someone, and they cannot marry.

By the time they all met again for supper, Jacqueline was her old self, only a slight pinkness in her eyes showing any evidence of her earlier distress. When she put the bowl of soup down in front of Adélaïde, Adélaïde touched her arm and looked up into her eyes and nodded. She nodded back and smiled.

Nothing was ever said about it.

Adélaïde was truly happy her father had found this new life, this love. But that didn't change the fact that each night, before she blew out her bedside candle, a tiny ache dragged at her heart. Witnessing their tenderness toward each other made her yearn for something similar. She hoped that, once she was living alone, she would no longer notice it. And soon it would fade away so she could get on with her plans, turn her back on love, and work toward the future she had purchased at such a heavy price.

⌒℮つ

It took Adélaïde a few weeks to find the right studio, one that had enough room so she could live there as well as work. Her limited budget forced her to move farther away from the Louvre and the center of things to less expensive lodgings on the Rue de Grammont. Curiously, she didn't mind the longer walk to André's studio, even in winter. Her drafty room—with its small heating stove that doubled as cooking stove in the corner and broken shelves near a soapstone basin she filled with water from a pump outside—felt like luxury, because it was hers. Her father gave her a bed with a sturdy straw mattress, an armoire for her clothes, and a few cooking pots and dishes—enough so that her only unmet needs were for the studio half of the room. She bought a larger easel and additional brushes and pigments. The mended shelves furnished plenty of room for all her art supplies, which she took great pleasure in organizing. Most miraculous of all, the room had three windows. This made it colder in the winter, but the light was good enough for painting even on the most overcast days.

Although her domicile had changed, Adélaïde's schedule stayed much the same as it had been for the three years she'd been part of André's studio. She worked on her own in the mornings and walked to the Louvre every afternoon except Sunday, when she would go to Mass at Saint-Eustache with her father and Jacqueline. Her apartment was nearly twice as far away as her father's atelier had been, but she hardly noticed the difference. The icy wind brought fire to her cheeks, and she strode along with her shoulders back and chin high.

It amazed her that she reached the Louvre in nearly the same amount of time as before.

⚭

One day in February, when the natural light left the skylights in André's studio and all the students who had gradually come to study with him over the years began cleaning their brushes and putting their materials away, André approached Adélaïde as she wiped the remnants of paint off her palette. "Stay a little after the others leave. I want to talk to you about something that may help you get more notice and more portrait commissions."

As she'd progressed in her skills and gained confidence in André's presence, Adélaïde had talked to him a little about the difficulties of being a woman and an artist. She wasn't always certain he fully comprehended, though. Or perhaps he did but could not understand that it was more than simply the lack of opportunities that were beating her down. It was the constant need to validate her own desires, to overcome the feeling that everyone else was right and she was wrong. He could not imagine her daily struggle to keep going, to look beyond all the obvious obstacles—not enough money, almost no recognition, the belief among many that it had been her artistic activities that had driven her husband away from her, that he didn't deserve what he got from his unconventional wife. That struggle alone threatened to wear her away to nothing, apart from her constant doubts that she would ever amount to anything. Sometimes she felt as insignificant as a drop of rain, or a cobble on a busy thoroughfare.

And yet . . . And yet was it truly being a woman that made it all so difficult? After all, she had read in the papers that Elisabeth Vigée was now married to the art dealer Pierre Le Brun, and she managed to continue to pursue her thriving career as a portraitist, numbering those among the highest rungs of society as her clients. How was it that another woman could rise so easily in that closed world and she could not? What did Madame Le Brun have that made it possible for her to thrive in that manner? In her heart, Adélaïde didn't believe Madame Le Brun was a better painter than she was. So why, then, did commissions, opportunities, money flow in her direction instead of Adélaïde's?

When the last of the other students had gone, André went to the workbench to clean his own brushes, his back to Adélaïde, and said, "You seem different lately, somehow."

"How different?"

He shrugged. "Happier? Calmer, perhaps?"

"What you notice is more relief than happiness," she said.

"Relief about what?"

Adélaïde had not told him anything about Nicolas, unwilling to complicate their simple relationship of teacher and pupil, as well as because she would rather simply put it behind her. She kicked herself for letting anything slip now. Yet he was bound to find out eventually. She was surprised he hadn't already. "My husband and I—we're legally separated."

She felt rather than saw him stop what he was doing. "I'm sorry. I didn't know. I thought—"

Adélaïde said, "You needn't be sorry. Nicolas and I—we weren't suited to one another."

She hoped he wouldn't pursue the matter. For a few moments, the silence was broken only by the sound of brushes swishing in liquid and the faint whistling of the wind from outside. But Adélaïde could feel the questions piling up.

When André finished and had washed his hands, he walked to the cupboard, took down two glasses that were almost clean, and fetched a bottle of wine from the crate on the floor. "I feel so foolish," he said as he poured them each a glass. "I never thought to ask why you often seemed unhappy."

"I'm glad you didn't. It would have been hard to explain. And I had left my husband's home before I became your student. I lived with my father for a few years, above his shop."

André paused before saying anything else. "And now?"

"Now I have my own lodgings, with my own studio. I am a free woman. Or as free as I can be when dissolving a marriage is not legal."

André gazed at her in the fading light. "He must have been a fool indeed not to value someone like you."

Someone like me—what is that? Adélaïde longed to ask him, but the space around them that was normally so easy and simple had become complicated. "You said you had something to tell me, something that might lead to more portrait commissions?"

"Oh, yes," André said, clearly relieved at the change of subject. "I realize that, since the disbanding of the Académie de Saint-Luc and the end of the Colisée exhibitions, you have had no opportunities to show your work." He pulled a chair away from the table in the corner and nodded at her to sit in it.

Both of those exhibitions had been directed to cease operations by the prudish and power-hungry Comte d'Angiviller, the director of the *bâtiments du roi* and therefore the ultimate authority controlling all artistic production in the realm. With no way to put her work in front of the public, Adélaïde had had no commissions for nearly a year. What money she had left from her father and the sale of miniatures in Gallimard's shop would not last longer than a few more months.

André refilled her glass and walked over to the workbench, where he picked up a copy of a pamphlet. "Have you heard of this fellow, Pahin de La Blancherie? Here's a copy of his newsletter."

Adélaïde put her glass down and took the pamphlet, which called itself *Nouvelles de la République des Lettres et des Arts*. It made the grandiose claim of being the only forum for discussing the art not only of France but also of Europe, as well as covering the latest developments in science and agriculture.

"Turn to the last page. I've marked it."

Adélaïde read the passage and understood immediately. It said, *Within the year, this body hopes to secure an adequate exhibition space to display fine examples of the works I have briefly mentioned here and to offer such for sale to interested parties.*

"I cannot exhibit anything there; the rules of the academy won't allow it. But you can." André downed the contents of his glass and poured himself another one.

The glimmer of hope that kindled in Adélaïde's mind soon faded as she read on. When she finished, she put the pamphlet down and picked up her glass. "It's still months off, if it ever comes to pass. And all I'd be able to show would be pastels." Adélaïde was unwilling to spend too much on art supplies. The pastel crayons and the materials to make them were less expensive than oils and could be executed on paper rather than the costly canvas. She had thought of teaching, but she did not have enough renown—or space—to attract students. If only there were some other way to turn her skills to ready cash. If only . . . "Of course."

"What?"

"Oh, nothing. I just remembered something." She hadn't meant to say anything aloud. Especially not to this young, attractive artist while they were alone in his studio. But the idea for a solution burst upon her so suddenly and with such urgency that she had let the words slip out. She could embark upon a project, she felt sure, that the sweet, prim and proper, married Vigée Le Brun would never think of, but that she, as a legally separated woman who lived by herself and whose morals were already questionable, could undertake with little risk. And little expense, since she needn't use her new skills as an oil painter. Pastels on paper would be more than adequate. The money that would result from the drawings she had suddenly decided to make would enable her to live and work in comfort until her career as a portraitist was established.

The market Adélaïde planned to exploit didn't show itself in the galleries. People spoke of it in hushed tones, of pictures intended only for private collectors, pictures that would never be shown in the light of day but would be brought out from their secret hiding places to be enjoyed by select—mostly male—company late at night, after much brandy had been consumed. Pictures like the ones Nicolas had hidden from her, tucked away under their bed. She, a woman, would produce and sell erotica. It was daring—and dangerous.

"What are you smiling about?" André asked.

"Was I smiling? I suppose I must have been."

"Aren't you going to tell me why?"

"It's nothing, I assure you. Just a silly thought." She finished her wine. "Thank you, and now I must go before it is fully dark and I am set upon by thieves."

André laughed. There was little risk of that between the Louvre and the Rue de Grammont.

She stood, and André brought her cloak to her and draped it over her shoulders. He rested his hands there for a moment before brushing away some imaginary lint. When he lifted them, Adélaïde wanted to grab hold of them and put them back, two warm points of contact with a man she so admired. Would he continue to think well of her if he ever discovered what she was about to do? She would never find out because if she had anything to do with it, he would never know.

Six

Paris, March 1778

Anonymity was essential. Adélaïde knew for certain that she must not use her own face and figure in her miniature, private pastels, nor could she sign them or give any information that would trace them back to her. No one would know who the artist was, and—the other practical matter—they would be sold through an intermediary. The trouble was, who could that be? It was the flaw in her plan. One person, at least, would be bound to know. It would have to be someone well outside the rarefied world of the Académie but who nonetheless could appreciate the quality of her work and its potential for profit. And so she settled on Monsieur Gallimard, the proprietor of the knick-knack shop where she sold her miniatures. Something told her he might be persuaded to trade in such things—and to keep her involvement a secret. She would no doubt need to give him a higher percentage of the money collected, but as she saw it, there was no other solution.

First, she needed a model. To be effective, these pastels would have to be as realistic and fleshly as possible. The best models were expensive, but she didn't need the best. Models of every size and shape, every degree of loveliness or otherwise, came and went to the studios in the Louvre every day. She must simply find one of them who was attractive enough and willing to come and sit for her for an hour or two before going home.

Dressed in her soberest, most respectable garments, Adélaïde waited at the end of a dreary late-winter's day a discreet distance from the door that led to the studios in the Louvre. She wasn't alone in the shadows. A few men waited as well—whether for their lovers or in hopes that one of the girls leaving would be willing to earn extra money on her back, she couldn't know.

A short while after the sun dipped too low to be of any use to an artist, models of both sexes started to dribble out onto the Paris streets. Adélaïde approached a woman who paused to pull her cloak closer around her. "Excuse me—"

The woman looked her up and down, frowned, and hurried away. She wasn't right anyway, Adélaïde thought. Too haughty.

Next came several small groups of chattering women, leaving en masse for their own protection, probably. But a group would not do; she needed only one. Before long, the stream of departing models slowed to a drip. One older woman slinked away with one of the men, and the other men waiting gave up and wandered off. Just as Adélaïde was ready to abandon her search for that evening, a young girl with an ordinary, pleasant, Parisian face—wide brown eyes, an up-tipped nose and sensual lips emerged, wrapped herself in a threadbare cloak and started her brisk walk to her lodgings. Adélaïde took a deep breath and hurried to catch up to her.

"Mademoiselle? Mademoiselle?"

The girl stopped and turned toward her.

"I wonder, would you be willing to sit for me for an hour or two this evening?"

"Who are you?" the girl asked, looking Adélaïde up and down with suspicion.

"I'm an artist, a pastellist. I have shown at the Académie de Saint-Luc."

"A lady artist? I thought they weren't allowed."

Adélaïde smiled. "Those fellows in there don't like us much, but we exist, and some of us are good."

"You one of the good ones?"

"One of the best." She had to say it, whether she believed it or not. It was an innocent enough falsehood, and it might even be true.

A spark of interest lit the girl's eyes, yet she huddled in her cloak against the brisk breeze and took a step away. "I should go home before I'm chilled to the bone."

Adélaïde saw her opportunity slipping away. "I don't live far from here, my apartment is warm—warmer than the studios in there, at any rate—and really, I just need an hour. I'm tired of the look of my own face, and you're very pretty."

The suggestion of a smile brightened the girl's expression and made her more attractive than she at first appeared. "How much?"

Before embarking on her search for a model, Adélaïde had casually asked André what he paid the women who sat for his history paintings. She offered the girl half. "It's only for an hour, remember."

⁓

The girl's name was Paulette, and she lived in a poor neighborhood on the Left Bank near the university, sharing a room with three other models. She shed her clothing without inhibition and let Adélaïde pose her lying back on the faded chaise in her apartment, one arm up with her hand behind her head, the other holding a bit of drapery between her legs. "I want you to think of something delicious. A pastry."

Adélaïde sketched by the light of six candles—an extravagance that she hoped would pay off. In an hour, she had the contours and coloring she wanted.

"That's all," she said, and the girl dressed with dispatch, clearly as accustomed to putting on her clothes as taking them off. Adélaïde gave her the coins. "If you'd like to earn the same again, or if you have other model friends who would welcome a few extra *sous*, I'll be outside the Louvre in three days at the same time."

"I'll think about it," Paulette said, eyeing the coins in her palm. "Three days, you say?"

She'll come back, Adélaïde thought.

The enterprise was off to a promising start. Her goal was to have ten finished pastels within a month. Each of them would be small enough to be hidden in a drawer or an unassuming box or to be slipped between the pages of a large book. She would make a series showing the female body in provocative poses that would lead a male viewer to become aroused. Once she finished them, she'd take them all to Monsieur Gallimard's shop on the Rue Neuve des Petits Champs, across the street and down a bit from her father's more elite establishment, and try to work out an arrangement with him.

⟶⟵

It turned out that Adélaïde was right. Paulette liked earning that little extra money.

"I'll buy myself a new hat," she said, looking over her shoulder provocatively three weeks later as Adélaïde glanced up and down from the roughened blue paper tacked to her table. "Or maybe some of those crayons you use there. I used to draw lots of pictures when I was little. My *maman* said they were quite good."

After their session, when Paulette was dressed, Adélaïde said, "I have completed the series. Would you like to see them?"

Paulette shrugged. "I guess."

Adélaïde lined up the finished pastels in a row on the floor against the wall so they could be viewed as one group. Even she hadn't looked at them all together like that. She smiled. She'd gotten the light and flesh tones perfectly, with the suggestion of candlelight caressing the tantalizingly hidden places, and with Paulette's eyes and mouth—mischievous, innocent—she fairly jumped off the heavy paper, she was so vivid and alluring.

Paulette studied each one in silence for a long while. "What will you do with these? Will they be in an exhibition?"

"These I must sell. An artist—like a model—has rent to pay and food to buy."

She nodded. "You were right."

"What do you mean?"

Paulette looked up at Adélaïde and cocked her head on one side. "You're one of the best."

Adélaïde smiled. Although not a connoisseur, the girl must have seen a lot of pictures in her days of modeling at the Louvre. She had a basis for comparison. "You're an excellent model. I'd like to do a larger pastel of you that I could exhibit, if you're willing to continue. I'm afraid I can't afford to pay except at the same rate, which I know is quite low."

Paulette took another long look at the pastels. "I tell you what. I'll sit for you if you show me how to do that." She pointed.

"You want to learn to draw and use pastels? It takes an immense amount of practice, and I've never taught anyone before. I'm still learning myself, learning to paint with oils so I can get more money for my pictures."

"If you don't teach me, who else will?" Paulette put her hands on her hips and lifted her chin.

Adélaïde laughed. "I'm willing to try. But you must not expect too much. I have no way of knowing if you have any talent until after we've worked together for a while."

"If I could just do it well enough to make pretty flower pictures I could sell in the market instead of freezing my tits off posing in front of crusty old men, it would be worth it." She smiled.

Adélaïde's first student agreed to start her lessons the following week.

Seven

Paris, May 1779

Monsieur Gallimard had been delighted to sell Adélaïde's erotic pastels, although he took fifty percent—an outrageous commission that she had no choice but to accept. And it seemed his customers had an insatiable desire for them. Over the past year, she'd had to crank the drawings out at the rate of ten a month. It all made her faintly uneasy, but the coins began to pile up in the jar she hid beneath the floorboards in her apartment, which soothed her conscience as she began to feel more financially secure.

Still, she couldn't entirely relax. Something else had robbed Adélaïde of her composure, something she'd tried to dismiss but that kept teasing at the edge of her mind. *Nicolas.* Every time she took another folio of pastel drawings to Gallimard, she thought about the erotic pictures her estranged husband had hidden deep in a drawer or under their bed—anywhere he thought she would be unlikely to find them. That was the only kind of art he appreciated, and not for its artistic merit. What if Nicolas purchased one of her drawings from Gallimard? Did he know enough about her style to make the connection? Apparently, he was sometimes seen on the Rue Neuve des Petit Champs, although he had given up their old apartment and moved nearer to his office. But it was too late to worry about it now. She had already opened that Pandora's box.

When André noticed that she began to come to her lessons with more supplies, better brushes, and a small roll of canvas, she explained it by telling him her father had given her the money. Fortunately he did not pry further, and at least for now, her secret was safe from her teacher. Besides, she told herself, the arrangement with Gallimard was temporary. She would end things as soon as she had enough money. But how much was enough? Adélaïde had to face the fact that she might have to continue to supply the ambitious shopkeeper until she had some other way to generate the same income. At least she no longer had the cost of hiring a model, thanks to the bargain she'd struck with Paulette—who at that very moment was beside her, hard at work on a still life of a pile of books and a candlestick.

"Madame Guiard, why do you frown so?" Paulette asked, looking up before using a small knife to sharpen her pencil.

"I'm not frowning, I'm just concentrating," Adélaïde said, but she knew it was a lie, and relaxed her face.

"That's better," Paulette said. "I don't know what evil thoughts go through your head, but sometimes you look at me as if you wanted me to disappear in a puff of smoke!"

Adélaïde smiled. "Rest assured, I am very happy that you are here in the flesh!" They both laughed at the private joke and went back to work.

A short while later, Paulette stopped what she was doing and held up her drawing, tapping the pencil against her lower lip and cocking her head this way and that. "When will I use the colors, not just a pencil?"

"Soon." Adélaïde set aside her brush and palette and wiped her hands on her smock as she stepped closer to examine Paulette's progress. "You've come a long way already. I can see you have an eye."

The girl smiled. It seemed to Adélaïde that Paulette had grown in both confidence and beauty since she started coming to her to model. She'd lost her edge of bitterness and become more open. From some of the conversations they'd had, Adélaïde could guess why that was so. Paulette trusted Adélaïde to believe in her desire to be more than she was, to transcend the expectations that poverty and a pretty face had attached to her. With a little more work, Paulette would be able to support herself respectably selling miniatures in the market instead of becoming an artist's concubine at best, a prostitute at worst.

"Before you can use the colors, you need to see them. I've explained to you how to notice the gradations in shadow and depth when you look at your composition. Now try to see the different hues, shades, and tones in all the varied surfaces."

Paulette peered at the books. "I see brown and black and white mostly, with a little gold lettering on the spines."

"How many different browns and blacks? And is the white really white? I spy a little green there, as well as in the leather book covers. And what colors and shading would you have to use to render the metallic sheen of the gold lettering—which is not a single color, but changes according to how it catches the light?"

Eyebrows pinched together as she stared hard at the subject of her drawing, Paulette went quietly back to work.

As she watched her student transferring the image before her eyes to the flat paper in front of her, giving it substance and form filtered through her own individual way of seeing, Adélaïde had to admit she was pleased. More than pleased: gratified. She hadn't thought she would want to teach, but here she was. And she liked it.

Not more than her own work, of course. That was still her passion. Which was why whenever the chatter that abounded among the artists in the Louvre turned to Madame Le Brun, the knot in Adélaïde's stomach rose into her chest. Adélaïde had not seen her rival since that day at the Saint-Luc salon. But she was there, always, a shadow that peered over Adélaïde's work and assessed it with a critical eye. *You'll never be like me,* the shadow said. And then, Adélaïde had to ask herself if being like Madame Le Brun was what she wanted. Madame Le Brun had recently painted portraits of the queen and other members of the court. Nobles and aristocrats clamored to sit for her. Judging by her rumored output, Madame Le Brun either spent nearly every hour of the day painting, or she could work very fast. Since the lady was married and had a child, Adélaïde thought it must be the latter.

Adélaïde knew herself well enough to believe she would never be able to paint so fast. She was still, after all, a student herself in many ways, even though she was older than Madame Le Brun by eight years. She was not fast, but that didn't mean she couldn't match her beautiful rival in all other ways, the ones that mattered most. Match—and surpass. But how? Adélaïde's primary concern at the moment was earning enough money just to survive and buy the expensive oil pigments and rolls of canvas. But despite everything she did, she hardly moved forward. She felt as if she were constantly reaching out to grab the trailing sash of one of Madame Le Brun's fashionable gowns, but every time she got close, the lady quickened her pace. Adélaïde had heard that Madame Le Brun had become a great favorite with the queen, no doubt hoping someday to be named official portraitist, with the stipend and connections that went along with such a prestigious appointment. Adélaïde was very far from gaining that kind of renown. She had had only a handful of portrait commissions to boast of, and all were pastels, which sold for a fraction of the thousand or more livres Madame Le Brun could command for each of her portraits.

She could do something else to gain more renown, though. She could develop her studio, become a famous teacher. There were few enough good artists who would take on lady students, and many ladies eager to acquire the genteel skills of painting miniature family portraits or decorative still lifes. Would that be enough to make the sacrifice of time worthwhile? Would it be worth having to lower herself to the level of the dilettantes to attract the occasional serious student, someone who could be a true acolyte? And with her limited output and nowhere to exhibit anymore, how would she find more students of either kind?

A drip of chartreuse oil paint plopped from her brush onto the floor. She had stopped working, brush poised, as she pondered her predicament. She loaded her brush again and tried to resume her painting, but she kept distracting herself. The problem was that this small studio of hers simply wouldn't do. To attract more students, she needed more space. Yet to afford more space, she needed more students. Adélaïde cast her eye around her familiar room. She had two easels for herself. Paulette sat drawing with sheets of paper tacked to a board on her lap. What else could she fit in such cramped quarters? Perhaps one—maybe two more small easels and a chair for a student not yet ready to use an easel. They'd be quite crowded together, but maybe she could accommodate four students, if they didn't all come at the same time and if she only used one easel for herself. She could teach in the mornings and go to André's studio in the afternoons. That wouldn't have to change.

Still, it felt impossible. Adélaïde expelled her breath in a long sigh.

"What is it?" Paulette asked.

"I was just thinking that I need more students, but I don't know where to find them."

Paulette put down her pencil and paper and stood, hands on her hips as though she were ready to scold Adélaïde. "Truly? You can't think how? You need an advertisement, of course. Put notices in the *Mercure de France*, and the *Journal de Paris*."

"Advertise myself? It's very unseemly."

"I don't see how it's any worse than selling those naughty pictures."

"Those 'naughty pictures' do not bear my name or my place of residence." Adélaïde spoke more sharply than she intended. "I'm sorry," she said. "You're quite right. I suppose that's what I'd have to do."

But the idea of advertising filled her with misgivings. What if Nicolas saw the advertisement? What would he think? She'd heard from the baker that he'd been seen with an older woman, a wealthy widow, and that he was dressed quite handsomely. He would congratulate himself that she was the loser in their separation if he deduced from the advertisement that she was struggling financially, not knowing about her income from that other, secret source.

"I don't know," Adélaïde said as she walked over to the stove to put a kettle on for tea. They both needed a break.

"Everyone advertises," Paulette said. "Here." She shuffled around in the satchel she brought with her to carry her lunch and a few stubs of pencils and pulled out a crumpled bit of a weekly paper. "See?" she said, pointing to a line that said a lady was giving lessons on the clavecin to young girls seeking to acquire this genteel talent.

Adélaïde read the papers every day and had never noticed such advertisements. Perhaps just one would pass by unseen by anyone except those looking for instruction in painting. It was still a risk, and with her precarious position, it could miscarry by calling undue notice to her. "No, I don't think I can consent to that. I shall have to think of something else."

"Suit yourself," Paulette said and went back to her drawing.

As always, after Paulette left for the day, Adélaïde sat down to her cup of tea and unwrapped the linen napkin from around the morning's loaf of bread, cut herself a piece, and put it on a cracked plate. And as always, she took only two sips of the tea and one bite of the bread before the thought of going to André's studio, the delicious anticipation of spending time in his company, robbed her of her appetite. She would eat later, she thought, and snatched her hat and cloak off the hook, put a few brushes and a palette into her satchel, and ran out the door.

Eight

One morning a few weeks after she and Paulette had spoken of placing an advertisement for more students, there was a knock on Adélaïde's door at about the time Paulette should be arriving. Adélaïde had given her a key, so she was surprised at the knock, thinking it might not be Paulette after all. She always worried about the possibility that Nicolas would reappear and discover where she lived. She crept to the door and put her ear to it before calling out, "Who's there?"

"It's me, Madame Guiard."

It was Paulette after all. Had she forgotten her key? Adélaïde opened the door wide, a greeting on her lips that never materialized. There indeed was Paulette, but not alone. Behind her stood three other young women, two of them with portfolios tucked under their arms.

"Come in," Adélaïde said, and opened her eyes wide at Paulette.

"Madame Guiard, this is Jeannette, Laure, and Geneviève." Each of them curtseyed to her in turn. "They went to the Louvre to find a drawing teacher and were told that the only one who would teach ladies had no more room for students at present. I just happened to be on my way out after a sitting, and I took the liberty of talking to them about you."

Adélaïde looked around her small studio in alarm. However would four of them fit, with easels and materials? "I'm very flattered," she said, and began to protest, but Paulette cut her off.

"I told them lessons were five livres, and they are all prepared to pay."

One of them spoke up. "I have heard of you. And I saw your work in the salon of the Académie de Saint-Luc but didn't know you took students. I'd rather learn from you than Briard anyway."

The other two nodded in agreement.

"Well, I don't have much room, I'm afraid."

"But as you said"—Paulette squeezed Adélaïde's arm and nodded—"you'll soon be taking a larger studio, to accommodate your students and work on bigger paintings."

Shrewd Paulette. And how surprising that here were three young ladies who had actually heard of her and wanted to learn from her— even though she hadn't done anything to make it known she was a teacher. "Of course, you're right, Paulette. I've found the location but haven't moved there yet." She felt the lie was justified, in the circumstances. "For the moment, things will be a bit tight."

It didn't seem to matter to the students, who in the next weeks came regularly, paying their money until Adélaïde had accumulated enough extra cash to move to a studio with more space and more light.

Word spread, and more and more women of all ages turned up at her door, until she had eight—including several from well-to-do families. Her growing fame as a teacher also led to portrait commissions, and soon Adélaïde was thinking about how to break the news to Monsieur Gallimard that she would no longer provide him with a supply of lucrative pornography. A word in the wrong place, and everything she was now building would tumble to the ground.

In particular, Adélaïde thought about one of her students, Marie-Marguerite Carreaux de Rosemonde, who although a member of the aristocracy had real talent. But her family didn't support her ambitions and considered her lovely pastels little more than a feminine accomplishment.

"They want me to marry well," she said one day to Adélaïde as she and Paulette helped her tidy up the new studio, a well-lit, high-ceilinged space closer to the Louvre. "But I shall not marry. I don't think I'm strong enough."

At first, Adélaïde thought she meant strong enough for the social and mental strain, but that wasn't the case.

"You see, I have a weak heart. I'm not supposed to exert myself too much. Sitting in front of an easel is about the extent of my ambition. A marriage bed would be too . . . taxing."

Adélaïde and Paulette laughed, as Marguerite intended, but the revelation struck Adélaïde and explained some things she'd noticed. What she'd thought was simply aristocratic ennui when Marguerite's eyes glazed over and she would stop painting and leave early on some excuse or other must have been her weakness asserting its demands. After that, Adélaïde vowed to be more vigilant and make sure Marguerite didn't tire herself too much.

After a time, Adélaïde's life settled into a comfortable routine. She taught her eight students in the morning, then went to André's studio for lessons in the afternoons. She had tried to convince herself at one point that she could continue learning on her own, that the cost of the lessons with André was not worth it now that she had grown so much in her abilities. But she always found a reason not to stop. After all, she now earned more than enough to justify the expense. And to be honest with herself, she would be sorry to miss the company of men—especially André. Not that she was unhappy with the state of her domestic affairs, but she liked the different tenor of the conversation—the comforting baritone voices, so solid and sure compared to those of young women. Well, mostly it was André's voice she liked to hear. And that troubled her a little.

Although it had been a year since Adélaïde's legal separation from Nicolas, somehow, rather than free her to be more herself with André, things had become more complicated. She was all too aware that she'd been impulsive when she and Nicolas first met. She'd been smitten in a way that went against reason. The last thing she wanted was to

make the same mistake again. She was older now and less susceptible, she thought. She congratulated herself on how she'd been able to
work side-by-side with a kind, attractive young artist in his studio for
nearly five years and maintain a friendly but professional relationship.
She persuaded herself that anything she felt beyond pure admiration
for André was simply the comfort and camaraderie of a teacher who
treated her with respect. Adélaïde tried her hardest to believe that
when she looked up from her work and met André's eyes before he
quickly reached for a different brush or mixed a new pigment on his
palette, it was merely an accident of timing. She paid him money for
the lessons in oil painting, and he taught her.

Continuing to be a part of André's studio also gave her opportunities she hadn't anticipated. The figure-drawing classes in the Louvre
were closed to women. But behind the door of his own studio, André
could hire models and allow them to pose in any state of dress so his
students could learn the finer points of anatomy and practice rendering the musculature and skin tones that were necessary to any figura-
tive painting. The models were usually female, which suited Adélaïde
in a studio filled with seven men and herself. She had to admit one
thing, though: gazing at a naked body in mixed company was somewhat unsettling. Perhaps in that one respect, the administrators of the
Louvre were correct.

It was all part of her grand scheme, though. She may not have
the wealth or the connections of Madame Le Brun, but one day, she
would have her own studio, choose her own models, and exhibit in
the Académie salons, and people would pay thousands to commission her to paint their portraits. Her pictures would hang on the walls
of the Salon Carré next to Vien's and Robert's and, yes, André's. She
would show the world that she could paint as well as any man—no,
better. Because she had the soul and sensibility of a woman.

Indeed, she was a woman trying hard not to let her heart interfere
with her ambition. Adélaïde mostly succeeded and kept her eyes on

her own work on the occasions when André brought a male model in to pose. That's exactly what happened the second time she saw Marc, the model who had been there when she came to André's studio the first time to inquire about lessons. André's *Belisarius Begging* canvas had long since been completed, but he had told Adélaïde he planned to start working on something else to be the reception piece that would enable him to become a full member of the academy, *The Rape of Orythia*, and for that he needed a male model. It made sense to combine the purpose and halve the expense by starting his own work while instructing his students.

"Ah!" Marc said. "I see you have kept the lady around."

Adélaïde had been mixing powdered lake with a few drops of nut oil, counting them so the resulting paint was the right consistency. She looked up quickly just as Marc began taking off his clothes and caught André putting his finger to his lips in a signal that Marc shouldn't say anything more. Before André could glance in her direction and realize that she had witnessed this silent communication, Adélaïde went back to mixing her pigment, afraid her own cheeks had turned a noticeable shade of pink. To add to her dismay, she'd continued to drip oil in the powder, and the blue she'd planned to use to experiment with shadows was now too runny. No matter, she thought. Better to simply sketch the figure in pencil. She wasn't working on a composition that included a male nude anyway, but on a modest portrait of a woman. She meant to practice her use of glazes in executing the gauzy fabric of a fichu, the texture of hair, and the skin tones. The drawing exercise that day would be purely for technique.

In her usual fashion, once she began, Adélaïde soon lost all sensation of where she was and how much time passed. She submerged herself in the effort to transfer the lines and shapes and volumes that her eye perceived in all their complexity onto a flat sheet of paper. She'd started out using a pencil, but soon became frustrated with its limitations for rendering volume, and instead took a selection of pastel crayons out of her satchel. As she drew and smudged and softened the contours of the model's chest and arms using her fingertips and the heel of her hand, she let her gaze drift lower to his loins and the thatch of dark hair that hid most of his genitals. It made her think about drawing her erotic pastels of Paulette. How different this hard, angular body was from Paulette's gentle curves. As different as her intent in this exercise—to reproduce, to record—compared to the deliberate effort to titillate in those other pastels. She smiled.

"You've had practice, I presume?"

André's voice was low and close enough to her ear that she could feel the warmth of his breath. He often spoke quietly when critiquing the individual students' work so as not to disturb anyone else. But he'd rarely stood so near to her. She stayed utterly still, resisting the reflex to straighten up from her hunched-forward position, which might make him move away. Or perhaps he did not realize how intimate it was, this gazing over her shoulder as she ran her fingers over the arm and chest muscles of a male nude. She had gotten to the point where she needed a different color crayon, so she slowly sat back, lifting her chalk-dusted fingers off the surface of the paper. André did not move away until her back touched his torso, and then, as if she were a burning ember, he took a quick step toward the next student.

"Excellent," he said.

Adélaïde wasn't certain whether he was referring to her drawing or something else.

⁕

Years later, when Adélaïde tried to piece everything together, it wasn't entirely clear to her exactly when she finally acknowledged that she was in love with André. They'd spent nearly five years in almost daily proximity, sharing a passion for painting that came from somewhere deep inside each of them. She'd thought during those times that perhaps there would never be anything more between them. Perhaps it was enough.

Yet by the summer of 1780, Adélaïde knew it wasn't, not for her, and she was beginning to suspect not for him either. She couldn't be certain when or understand exactly why André, too, began to look upon her with more than the interest of a teacher for his pupil. But whatever the cause, there could be no doubt that for a few months at least and possibly much longer they'd been like a pair of moths flitting around each other, wings almost touching, only the fear of destruction keeping them at a distance. Still, they circled closer and closer as the days went by.

All this teased at the edges of Adélaïde's mind one warm June Sunday at Mass at Saint-Eustache. She went through the motions of standing and kneeling and crossing herself and taking communion as she did dutifully every week. She kept up the relationship with religion primarily because it linked her in some nostalgic way with her late mother and the siblings she never really knew, not because she believed a word of it.

And attending Mass took up at least part of the day. Sundays were the only days André did not teach, so she had to find other ways to fill the empty hours. Often, she would return with her father and Jacqueline to their apartment after Mass. She liked spending time with them. The ease with each other that had formed when Adélaïde lived with them while waiting for the legal separation continued during these more sporadic visits. She could have chosen to go there on that Sunday too. The day was lovely enough for strolling through the gardens of the Tuileries, which they often did, where her father and Jacqueline would nod to the many ladies whose ensembles he had furnished, all the while telling Adélaïde how they'd missed some important detail or had become too fat to wear a gown altered for them only the previous year.

But Adélaïde didn't choose to go home with them, not that particular Sunday.

On that morning, she had awoken so restless that by the time the church bells tolled the end of Mass, she kissed her father and Jacqueline and then rushed out of Saint-Eustache and into the sunlight like a bird being freed from captivity. She walked back to her apartment the long way, postponing her arrival in order to eat up the time, yet the day stretched ahead of her with no end in sight, and nothing she turned her mind to or thought about doing appealed to her.

She sat down to work on a pastel portrait commission, thinking she could finish the drapery or the background, but she could not settle to it. Adélaïde was never one to mind her own company, yet alone in her studio that day, the emptiness oppressed her. She felt a lack, an absence of something, a cold, barren void just on her left side—where André normally placed his own easel in his studio, and from which direction the faint odor of masculine sweat emanated every day, growing more pronounced as the hours passed.

Adélaïde shook her head and picked up her crayon and mahlstick again, willing herself to concentrate.

It was no use. Laughter and chatter floated up to her window on the silky breeze, and golden sunlight spilled in through the windows, teasing her, tempting her, until she could no longer stand it. She must go out, no matter where. She told herself she would not seek out André, who undoubtedly had his own plans on a Sunday. She would only walk toward the Louvre, perhaps wander over the Pont Royale and down along the left bank of the river. The summer rot had not yet poisoned the air by the Seine. She could occupy herself alone—she was perfectly capable of that—and watch the promenaders go by in couples and families and imprint their expressions on her mind to ponder later, when she sat in front of an easel. She could, she was certain, spend a day without André, just not in her studio where the act of drawing brought him to mind with such force.

Yet the closer she drew to the Louvre, the more her resolve faltered. What would it matter, after all, if she did seek him out, if she did try to see if he happened to be there and they could work side by side as if it were any other day of the week? He wouldn't have to talk to her or even acknowledge her presence especially. Surely he wouldn't mind.

Adélaïde smiled up at the cloudless sky as she approached the grand entrance to the Cour Carré, warmth suffusing her at the thought that she might soon be in André's studio, near enough to touch him— although she wouldn't, of course.

She let herself in through the door to the galleries and the grace- and-favor apartments. She knew the way so well she could have closed her eyes and let her feet guide her down the long corridor and up the stairs to André's studio and lodgings.

When she reached his door and lifted her fist to knock, she paused with it inches from the wooden surface and listened. Not a sound any- where. The artists were all either out or sleeping. No one would see her and know she'd come to André's studio without an appointment on a day when he would not be expected to teach. She prepared herself for the possibility that her knock would remain unanswered and she would simply have to leave and make what she could of the day. At least, she thought, she would have tried. Of course, she had no way of knowing what André did when he wasn't teaching. Suppose someone was with him? A woman? Well, then she'd know. She knocked and held her breath.

Silence. Adélaïde's shoulders relaxed, and she shook her head at herself behaving like a giddy schoolgirl. But as she was about to turn and find her way out, she heard André's familiar, light footsteps approaching the door. She hardly had time to compose herself before he opened it, a look of puzzlement on his face at first, then a broad grin of welcome.

"Adélaïde!" He flung the door wide. "Did you leave something behind yesterday?"

He stood before her in a loose blouse, no wig, his brown hair falling over his shoulders. She'd come before he was fully dressed, and the knowledge sent a delicious shudder through her. So, he hadn't gone to Mass, not that morning anyway. Perhaps she should excuse herself and come back later. But now that she was here . . . "No, I . . . On a Sunday I have little to do, and thought I'd see if I might spend some time working on my painting. The light is perfect."

And it was. At that particular time of day, late morning, the skylights and high windows let in just the right amount of sunlight so subjects didn't cast sharp shadows yet blazed with their true colors.

"Of course," he said. "You are welcome. If you don't mind . . ." He looked down at his casual state of dress and gestured, palms up.

"Not in the least," she said.

Adélaïde donned her smock and went to work immediately, aware of André's movements but not looking in his direction. She imagined he continued to dress; perhaps he planned to go out somewhere. Perhaps he would sit at his desk and write letters. Or perhaps, she hoped, he had planned all along to paint and would remain there next to her in the reverent silence of the studio. When she heard the creak of the ladder he stood on to tackle the sections of his large canvas that were too high to reach from the floor, she smiled. He was going to stay.

Time slid past Adélaïde as she worked, at last able to focus, her heartbeat calming to a normal rhythm in the companionable serenity of the studio. Only the subtle change of light marked the hours. Her still life of multi-colored, fading peonies and roses in a dusty porcelain vase challenged her still-developing skills as an oil painter, and she focused on the canvas as if nothing else in the world existed. She did not feel hungry or thirsty or tired, only possessed with the desire to capture those decaying flowers so perfectly that anyone who saw them might believe the petals would fall off if only they watched long enough.

"One day, you'll bite off the tip of your tongue."

Adélaïde dragged herself out of her painting and turned toward the sound of André's voice. It took her a moment to adjust her gaze to recognize his mischievous face and to realize he'd climbed down from the ladder and had been staring at her—she didn't know for how long. She had a habit, when she was concentrating very hard, of putting the tip of her tongue between her teeth. She pulled it in quickly and covered her mouth, embarrassed. When André's cheeks dimpled with an impish smile, she didn't know what possessed her, but instead of blushing, she stuck her tongue all the way out at him with a saucy toss of her head.

He opened his mouth and laughed, and his normally serious eyes sparkled. Adélaïde couldn't help smiling back at him. His laughter died down, and it was quiet, and they continued to stare at one another, each of their gazes leading to a question neither of them dared to ask.

"I-I must go." All at once, Adélaïde panicked.

She put her brush aside and reached for a rag to wipe off her palette, but André was already handing it to her. Their fingers met. Adélaïde didn't pull the rag away, and André let his hand linger on hers, just the lightest touch. A warm shiver washed through her body. She took the rag slowly, turning her hand up so that her fingertips traced his palm.

Nothing more happened, not that day. But a door had been opened, and beyond it lay a beautiful, perilous landscape saturated with intoxicating scents and vibrant colors she knew she would be unable to resist.

Nine

What had started in June with André continued through the summer in small ways—a touch now and then when the other students weren't looking; a glance that lingered a little too long. He would stand close to her when she cleaned her brushes at the end of the day or happen to go to the workbench to mix pigments at the same time she did. And every time, a glow would spread from the middle of Adélaïde's body, from just beneath her ribs, and radiate outward until she could feel its tingle in her fingertips. As she and André approached intimacy with small gestures, tiny steps, stolen glances, Adélaïde felt as if she were holding her soul up to the light and letting warmth seep into every corner.

Still, they kept their distance. Some reticence held them apart. Adélaïde wondered if perhaps André now had a lover or had recently had one and was either in a state of inner conflict or had been bruised by experience. She had heard no gossip to that effect, though, and the art world was small enough that news of that kind had a way of skittering from ear to ear like a summer breeze.

And then, one dreary, late-August morning, when the threat of a storm made the light in Adélaïde's studio too feeble for painting, she sent her students home early after a lecture about drapery. A few hadn't bothered to come that day, including Marguerite, who often stayed at home in foul weather to protect her delicate health. Those who had braved the certain rain cast nervous glances out the window as the sky grew darker and the wind kicked up, banging loose shutters and whistling through the gaps between the limestone buildings.

Once they had all left, Adélaïde closed the windows in her apartment and her studio despite the stifling heat. It would have been wise for her to simply stay at home, but something about the impending storm made her restless—and curious. The light had changed so drastically. She wanted to be in it, to feel it so she could conjure up that image when she was painting. The impending storm charged her with energy that had nowhere to go. It wouldn't be wise to go out just for a stroll so she could be amid the wild wind and driving rain. It would be insane. Yet if she had a purpose, a reason . . . The only thing she could think of—her default action whenever in doubt—was to go to André's studio. He had become accustomed to her arrival at odd times, never making it awkward for her. In fact, Adélaïde realized that he always seemed to have been expecting her, as if a filament stretched between her mind and his and he knew at all times what she was thinking.

But that was absurd.

After a quick glance to make sure it hadn't yet started raining, Adélaïde tied on a plain straw hat, draped a light shawl over her shoulders, and set out for the Louvre. Surely there was enough time for her to outrun the storm and still capture the eerie light in her mind to store away for when she needed it. Half a mile was no distance.

Once outside, Adélaïde passed shopkeepers hastily moving their wares inside and closing shutters, all the time glancing up at the sky, which had turned a sickly greenish gray in the west. Carriages clattered by, their horses snorting and whinnying in fear as they headed toward mews and courtyards to deposit their occupants safely at home. Everyone who remained outdoors scurried to find shelter. Everyone except Adélaïde, that is, who hurried faster and faster along swiftly emptying streets.

When she was more than halfway to the Louvre, a flash of lightning seared the sky, followed by a crack of thunder that sounded as if the heavens had split apart. *Merde!* Adélaïde pulled her shawl over her head. Fat raindrops began to fall, in spurts at first, and then in a sudden torrent. The few people left outside dashed for cover, but Adélaïde kept going. It was too late to turn around and go home. *How foolish*, she thought, leaping over puddles and covering her ears against the constant thunder. As she ran past the gardens of the Palais Royale, a thick bolt of lightning struck a tree, which erupted in flames. Adélaïde paused to see it, her heart skipping with the surge of electricity. *Stay calm*, she thought, fascinated as the fire devoured the branches, shivering with fear. *Could this be how I die?*

Another crack of thunder jolted her out of her trance and set her running again. Terror had deadened her to the fact that she was soaked through from her hat to her toes, and she was surprised when she finally burst through the door of the Louvre that led into the artists' studios to find herself standing in a puddle of her own making.

Heedless of the wet footprints that followed her, Adélaïde ran along the corridors and up the stairs to André's studio and entered without knocking, her heart pounding and her breath coming in gasps.

André said nothing when he saw her, only grabbed a clean towel from the cupboard and ran to her, wrapping it around her shoulders and squeezing her to him until the towel soaked through and dampened his own clothes. "What on earth were you thinking?"

Adélaïde shivered, but not because she was cold. "I-I wanted to be in the light, to feel the storm. Isn't it magnificent?"

André shook his head, a smile tickling the corner of his lips. "Sometimes I think you are a strange creature," he said and pulled her a little closer, rubbing her back along its length, from the nape of her neck to the curve just above her buttocks.

"I am," Adélaïde said. "But I think you are too."

She wanted to wrap her arms around him, but they were pinned to her by the towel. So she pressed herself into his body and turned her face up to his. He looked down at her, his eyes darkening with desire.

After a hesitation no longer than a single breath, the world changed. The space between their lips closed and soon they were teeth to teeth, tongues twining and tasting, salt that may have been tears and the wordless language of tiny gasps of pleasure. The thunder might have continued to roll, there may have been rain drumming on the sky-lights, but all Adélaïde knew for certain was that she and André would never be the same again, that the bridge had been crossed, and there was no way back from there.

᠆᠆᠆

For three hours that day, they talked, laughed, and made love. No awk-wardness, no hesitation. Always touching each other, letting moment merge into moment punctuated by bursts of passion that echoed the storm raging outside. Adélaïde thought she knew everything there was to know about intimacy and pleasure. But to open herself so com-pletely, to let André touch her body in ways she had never dreamed of, coaxing her to ecstasy over and over—before he allowed himself to take his own pleasure—was the most delicious agony. When they lay together, spent and drowsing, the world fell into place for Adélaïde. André had accepted all of her, all at once, because he already knew who she was. How could she ever have been fooled by the heedless infatuation that had made her cling to Nicolas and make the disas-trous decision to marry him?

When the storm subsided and it seemed that André had drifted off to sleep, Adélaïde looked up at the skylights, now washed by the rain and letting in oblique streaks of sunlight. The day was nearly over. It was time to leave. She could not stay all night, not yet anyway. She stretched first one leg then the other out from under the tangled sheets, then sat up slowly, trying not to disturb André. Her clothes were scattered around the studio on the other side of the privacy screen and no robe was at hand. The idea of walking naked through that room, wending her way around André's canvases, both thrilled and terrified her. How would she concentrate when she next came for a lesson? She would manage somehow, she thought. And so she stood and, as quickly as she could without making a sound, gathered up the elements of her dress—petticoats, stays, bodice, over-skirt, fichu. The skirt and bodice were still damp from her dash though the rain, as were her stockings and shoes. No matter, she thought. It was warm enough that they would probably dry by the time she got home.

André stirred when the door latch clicked as she lifted it. "Come back!" he murmured, reaching an arm out and then letting it fall back on the covers with a soft thump.

Adélaïde blew him a silent kiss and then hurried down the stairs and out into the mild evening, walking home hardly knowing how she got there. The storm had washed the sky clean, and the setting sun touched all of Paris with fire, even gilding her modest studio so that it looked to her like a palace. She hugged herself and spun around like a child with a new dress, catching a glimpse of herself in the small mirror. *Who is that woman*, she thought, *with her face so bright and joyful?*

She was new, inside and out. At the age of thirty-one her life started over. Perhaps now she could go on without fear, without hesitation.

⚬

She and André were no good at keeping their affair a secret. The artists in the Louvre were too involved in each other's business not to notice the way they acted with each other, the way they touched every chance they got, the fact that André took to spending nights away from his lodgings in the Louvre and would creep in quietly in the early morning hours. It was no more than a few weeks before everyone they knew treated them as if they were a married couple, knowing that—because divorce was illegal—Adélaïde would not have been free to marry André even if he asked.

This new relationship had the peculiar effect on Adélaïde of both allowing her to forget Nicolas completely and raising the specter of his continuing existence at odd moments. Perhaps naively, she hoped he had truly disappeared, truly let go of her at last, or let go of the idea that she was his property, at any rate. But no matter how hard she tried to pretend to herself she had come to André as a virgin, as someone unsullied by anger and disappointment, the shadow of Nicolas always lurked around a corner, ready to leap out and depress her at her happiest, most contented moments.

That shadow remained only in her imagination until one late August evening. As Adélaïde had almost finished tidying everything in her studio away so she would be ready to leave and go to supper with André, someone knocked on her studio door. The only person she was expecting was André, so she called over her shoulder, "*Viens mon cher!*" Adélaïde waited for her lover's arms to encircle her from behind, for him to kiss her earlobes and whisper about how he'd missed her since they parted early that morning.

But whoever entered stopped after stepping through the door, and said, "I didn't expect you to be so delighted to see me."

Nicolas! Adélaïde whirled around, knocking a bladder of precious ultramarine paint to the floor. "What are you doing here!" She stooped to salvage what she could of the pigment, keeping her eyes on Nicolas as much as possible, wary of what he might do finding her alone like this. "You'd better leave. My friend will be here soon."

"Your friend. That would be François-André Vincent, if I have been accurately informed." He took a step toward her, and Adélaïde flinched. Nicolas smiled, but stopped. "I'm not going to hurt you. Although I suppose I should expect you would fear it. As I tried to tell you, before—I'm not really that person."

Was he going to apologize? "I hear you have a new amour yourself. I trust you treat her with more dignity than you treated me." Adélaïde stood and wiped her paint-covered hands on her dress, forgetting that she'd already removed her smock.

His face darkened. For a moment Adélaïde worried that she had awakened the brute who had rendered her unconscious all those years ago. But he said nothing and stood still. Only his nostrils flaring and his hands clenching and unclenching the brim of his hat revealed any suppressed fury. "She is a good woman."

"And she could walk away if she chose to. Something I could not do." Adélaïde knew she was playing with fire, but something drove her on. All the anger she had suppressed for the sake of peace and quiet threatened to tumble out of her mouth. She pressed her lips together and breathed for a moment or two. "What is it you want?"

Nicolas's face regained its mask of composure, and he curved his lips into a smile that did not extend to his eyes. "It must be reassuring to know you still have a vestige of attractiveness and that you can still wield your charms to ensnare another man—another man to support you so you can dabble in painting." Now he began strolling around her studio, touching items Adélaïde had recently put away, nudging them out of place, casting quick glances in her direction to gauge the effect of his actions. "I hear rumors you've been doing quite well lately. That somehow you've managed to turn a profit on your money-wasting hobby."

"That is no longer your affair. I have the document to prove it."

"I suppose it is not my affair, as you say. But I have also heard that your finances have seen a miraculous improvement, and yet you have sold few pictures of late. At least, not that anyone knows about."

Adélaïde felt as if she had been doused by a bucket of icy water. Was it possible? Could he somehow have found out about her commerce in erotica? "I-I have many students. They pay to learn from me, as you see."

Nicolas stopped and examined an unfinished pastel of children playing tacked to Marguerite's easel. At that stage, it looked like not much more than formless shapes. He made a face as if he had tasted something sour and turned to look at her. "Not much of a teacher, are you."

He was baiting her. He wanted her to lash out. He was clearly angry that she had managed to make a modest success of herself and that the world would see that she didn't need him, that possibly she never had. Adélaïde couldn't really comprehend how a man in his position might feel. But it was no longer her affair. "You'd better state your business and then leave." Adélaïde crossed her arms over her chest and glared at him.

"Very well. I find myself a bit short of cash lately. And, as I said, you seem to be doing quite handsomely. For old time's sake, you might spare someone you once cared for a little of your newfound wealth. Only a few livres, say, a hundred?"

This she did not expect. If he were in dire straits, his animosity about her ability to thrive was all the more understandable. "You must know I don't have that kind of money to throw away!"

"Really? That's not what I've heard. Monsieur Gallimard led me to believe that the drawings he sells for you are so popular he can hardly keep them in his shop."

Adélaïde's heart stopped for an instant. What she had most feared may have come to pass. Stay calm, she told herself. Even if Nicolas had one of her drawings in his possession, surely he couldn't know for certain it was her work! Gallimard would not have been so stupid as to say anything to him. Although when she thought about it, she hadn't directly told him not to. Secrecy was understood between them, so she thought. He, like everyone else on the street, knew of her separation from Nicolas and probably knew how he had treated her. But they also might be tempted to pity him as they blamed her for not being a proper wife. He could play on that sympathy, perhaps pretending to take an interest in his estranged wife's activities. And at that moment, Adélaïde could hardly ask him what he knew without giving herself away. "He's exaggerating. My miniatures sell for a pittance."

"Oh, I think you know otherwise. And I'm more than willing to keep my counsel about the ways you choose to earn a living, with the right incentive. I suppose it's a step up from earning it on your back. Or is that what you do with Vincent?"

The blood rushed into Adélaïde's ears, and her whole body quivered. So that was it. If she had had a knife in her hand, she would have rushed at him and gladly thrust it into his heart. But the power at that moment was all on his side. She would have to acquiesce to something in order to get rid of him. "I'll give you fifty, and no more. And you must swear you will not return. If you do, I'll have you arrested." It was a hollow threat, and she was sure he knew it. Although she suspected this wouldn't be the end of his requests, she just needed to make him go away now so she could think it through, figure out a way to keep him quiet in the future without paying him.

He shrugged. "I suppose that will be enough. For the moment." He didn't move.

"This 'good woman' you speak of. I had heard she is quite wealthy," Adélaïde said. "And that looks like a new coat and jabot."

"Yes, she is generous with me in all ways." He let his comment settle a moment, giving Adélaïde time to fathom its entire significance. "But I need to buy her a present, one that will impress her, and I can hardly ask her for money for that."

"Don't you earn enough from your work?"

"Oh, I left my position. It was not convenient to remain when Gloriande wanted to travel and wished me to accompany her."

So, he no longer worked, yet wanted to profit from her, Adélaïde's, labors. The thought infuriated her, yet he'd backed her into a corner. "Wait downstairs. I'll bring you the money." The last thing she wanted was for him to see where she kept it.

"You think I'd stoop to burglary? I assure you, I am not a thief. But have it as you will. If you don't come out in five minutes, I have a printer ready to start his presses on a pamphlet that details the virtuous Madame Guiard's private enterprise, complete with an illustration."

"*Fils de pute!*" she muttered as he turned and walked out.

She had no way of knowing if his threats were real, or if he'd made up most of them, but he was fully aware she couldn't take that risk. Perhaps he'd gone to Gallimard to purchase something akin to her drawings and had seen his chance to slander her. He could claim she was the artist even if she wasn't, and the damage would still be done.

She took the coins out of the locked cabinet, ran down the stairs, and threw them at him where he stood on the street.

Ten

Paris, March 1781

To Adélaïde's relief, Guiard had gone abroad with his wealthy widow soon after their encounter in her studio the previous autumn. She had no idea how long they would stay away, so every day she worried that he would return to plague her again about the drawings. She hoped that, if he'd really had something to hold over her aside from suspicions, he would have pressed her for more money.

For now, her secret was safe, even from André, although it was harder and harder to hide those activities from him as they spent so many hours and days together. Would André be shocked if he found out? Did he—like most men—have a hidden store of images not suitable for female eyes? It hardly mattered. She was confident that she had made the right choice not to involve him in any way whatsoever. They hadn't been very successful at keeping their relationship quiet as it was. André assured her that the artists they knew wouldn't judge them for it. But Adélaïde knew that, as she became more accomplished and had more commissions, many would seize upon the opportunity to imply that André—because of his love for her—was the real author of her work. And there could be other unanticipated consequences, for her teaching, for instance. Yet so far, having her name coupled with André's had had no ill effects. Her students were loyal and serious, some more talented than others. If they had heard rumors, none of them mentioned it or threatened to leave because of it. Besides, women had few enough opportunities to learn drawing and painting.

Adélaïde figured she'd have to be overtly immoral to frighten most of them away.

The trade in erotica was another matter. She wanted to end it, but the money was extremely useful. In the first year, the series of drawings and its copies had sold so quickly, Adélaïde started experimenting with putting two female figures in each picture, having them tease each other in ways she knew would arouse a male viewer. These sold even better, and she found herself making copies late into the night at times. She could have refused to continue supplying them, but it was such a luxury to afford the best pigments and fine canvas from Antwerp and to dress more like the respectable teacher of painting she had become.

She put her worries about the titillating pastels out of her head as she addressed the young women eagerly waiting for her instruction one early March morning. "Today we'll concentrate on skin tones," she said, and turned her easel so the eight eager women could see it.

Before she could continue the lesson, though, someone knocked on the door. She was not expecting anyone, and as always, the specter of Nicolas raised her alarm, so she went herself to open it and see who was there.

A young woman in rumpled traveling clothes, with a small portfolio clutched to her chest as if for protection, stood in front of her. She looked as if she hadn't slept all night.

"Yes?" Adélaïde asked.

"My name is Marie-Gabrielle Capet. I have come from Lyon overnight in a *diligence*, and I would like to study painting with Madame Labille-Guiard." At that point, the woman's eyes closed, her face lost all its color, and her knees buckled.

"Marguerite! Paulette! Come help."

The two students rushed over, each taking the young woman by the arm. She could barely put one foot in front of the other. They led her to the chaise where models posed and made her sit and put her feet up.

Adélaïde patted Mademoiselle Capet's face. "Have you eaten?" She asked.

She shook her head. "Not since yesterday morning."

By now, the other women had clustered around. "I have brought some bread with me—she can have that," said one.

"There's cheese in my satchel," said another.

Adélaïde reached in her pocket for some coins, handing them to Paulette. "Go and buy a sweet pastry and bring it back. Marguerite, put the kettle on." She lifted her head to address the others. "Please, take your seats. We'll have our tisane a little early today." She went herself to get a glass of potable water from the jug and brought it to Gabrielle. "Rest a little and drink this, and after you've had a bite to eat, we'll talk."

Something about this girl who had taken it upon herself to travel from Lyon to Paris for the purpose of studying with her and becoming an artist touched Adélaïde—and surprised her as well. Could her fame as a teacher have spread as far as Lyon? She'd find time to ask Mademoiselle Capet later how she came to know of her.

"May I see your work?" Adélaïde asked once the girl was seated comfortably.

Mademoiselle Capet nodded, handing her portfolio to Adélaïde. Adélaïde untied its closure and drew out a dozen sheets of paper, all sketches in pencil. Rather than the genteel still-lifes or portraits of family members she expected, the drawings depicted peasants at work—in the fields tying wheat into bales; drawing water from a well; scrubbing pots in a kitchen—even a butcher slaughtering a calf. Rendered using only lines and shading, the girl had captured the distinct characters and personalities of each individual and given them a sense of movement and effort.

"These are very good," Adélaïde said. "Where did you study before?"

Somewhat revived after a glass of water and a crust of bread, Mademoiselle Capet said, "Only with my mother, who is not a real artist, but who took pains to listen in and remember the lessons given to the high-born ladies she served."

Remarkable, Adélaïde thought. "How did you know you wanted to draw?"

The young woman shook her head. "I don't know. But my mother took me to some exhibitions when she had a few hours off, and after that all I wanted was to create beautiful pictures."

Adélaïde knew without question that here was an extraordinary talent. Such a student could make her name as a teacher.

The studio had gone exceptionally quiet, Adélaïde thought, and when she looked up she saw that the other eight students had stopped working and stared at Mademoiselle Capet and her drawings, eyes wide. Even Paulette, who never lacked for conversation, had not said a word since returning with the requested pastry, half of which Mademoiselle Capet had already eaten.

"Please continue your work, ladies," Adélaïde said, and then turned her attention back to Mademoiselle Capet. "Do you have someone to stay with in Paris?"

"I have only a little money—of course to pay for the lessons, and also for accommodations. I don't know how long it will last, though."

"Mademoiselle, you say your mother encouraged you—what of your father? Does he support you?"

"Please, call me Gabrielle." She looked down at the floor. "Papa thought I should go into service, just like him and Maman. But Maman understands that I don't want that. She knows of my dreams. I've promised to send drawings home to her when I can, and she says she'll come to Paris whatever the cost if my pictures are ever shown in public."

A mother like that. How wonderful it must be, Adélaïde thought. "And how long do you intend to study?"

When Gabrielle lifted her eyes, all trace of reticence had vanished. She leaned forward, her gaze steady and strong. "I intend to remain in Paris for the rest of my life. I want to be an artist. I want to learn everything you can teach me. I'll work harder than anyone—I'll help you in any way you wish. I can cook and clean, sew—whatever you need."

Her gaze was so intense Adélaïde had to look away. "Welcome to my studio. Let us make a start right away, if you're not too tired. The others will show you around while I prepare what we shall do today."

Eleven

Gabrielle more than repaid Adélaïde's generosity. She showed signs of brilliance and had progressed enough after less than a year to exhibit in the annual outdoor Exposition de la Jeunesse, along with Marguerite. She'd sold a few pictures and gotten a commission or two. And in only two years, she had become so much a fixture in Adélaïde's life that Adélaïde couldn't imagine not having her there. Soon after her arrival, Adélaïde had been able to rent a small apartment for herself separate from the studio so she could create more space for her growing cohort of students. The studio became Gabrielle's home, where she happily functioned as general caretaker and factotum and would retire to a cot in a corner to sleep at night. Most surprising of all, Gabrielle and Marguerite had become close friends, despite the difference in their stations.

Although Adélaïde's teaching career grew and thrived, she was still not attracting the commissions she hoped for, even as she watched Madame Le Brun's rise in popularity and prestige grow exponentially. Most of the time, she tried not to think about her rival. What was the use of making a comparison? Besides, Adélaïde's life was too full to let petty concerns disrupt her equilibrium. Most of the time.

But one day in André's studio, after she had cleaned her brushes and taken off her smock and was waiting for André to finish, she happened to pick up a discarded copy of the *Journal de France*. She perused it without much interest until she spotted Madame Le Brun's name. The article said Madame Le Brun had been appointed official portraitist to Queen Marie Antoinette. "Did you know this?" She asked André, her normally soft voice shrill with indignation.

"Know what?" he asked, not taking his eyes off his work.

"She's official portraitist to the queen. How in God's name does she do it?" Adélaïde spat the words out as she crumpled the paper in her hands.

André finished the highlight he was painting on Orythia's breast, a finishing touch on his Académie reception piece, *The Rape of Orythia*. He stepped back and squinted at the painting before saying, "It's because she plays the game."

Adélaïde's stomach knotted. He must have known. He didn't have to ask who *she* was. And Adélaïde didn't have to ask what game he was referring to. For a year at least, André had been trying to persuade her that if she wanted to be successful, to get lucrative commissions, she had to do the very things that angered Adélaïde about Madame Le Brun. She would have to spend money on fashionable gowns and attend tedious salons, pay obsequious calls on potential sitters who would expect a free portrait on the understanding that they would display it prominently for all their friends. She would have to go to the opera and visit people in their boxes and listen to gossip instead of listening to the music. What was the point?

André took his brush over to the workbench and swished it in the jar of turpentine. "I know you dread it, but I don't entirely understand why. Everyone does it. Do you know I heard that Madame Le Brun commands at least a thousand livres for a single portrait?"

Adélaïde picked a bit of lead white paint off her thumb. "You know what I think about all that."

"But it's so foolish, your reluctance! What harm can it do?"

What harm. He didn't know, and she wasn't about to tell him. He didn't know that Nicolas might have discovered her illicit trade and would likely make her life hell if she suddenly became very successful or put herself too much in the public eye. André didn't know that Nicolas had already tried to extort money from her merely on suspicion.

"You could at least submit to the Salon de la Correspondance and get your pictures out in public again," André said. "I don't understand why you didn't do it the first year they opened the salons. You know you're twice the artist she is, if you'd only let the world see what you can do."

That was another step she'd been resisting. Every day he would bring up the subject. She wanted to do it, how she wanted to! But she was afraid. She couldn't tell him why. Her fear was all tied up in Nicolas and the erotic drawings. She changed the subject. "And what about you? You deserved to be elected a full member of the Académie years ago. Far more than did Jacques-Louis David."

David, the darling, the blazing hope for the future, the genius—she had heard all these descriptions of him as she wandered the halls of the Louvre or listened to André's students' chatter. David was only a year older than Adélaïde, and unlike André and most other artists had not had to undergo a period as an *agréé* before his election. She suspected that was thanks to his influential family connections. After winning the Prix de Rome (three years *after* André, Adélaïde had been quick to point out), he was immediately elected, with all the respect and privileges that entailed.

André wiped the clean brush on a rag and went to the basin to wash his hands. "I don't grudge him his success," he said. "He has other disadvantages that I would not wish upon anyone."

He was referring to the tumor in David's cheek, which caused a deformity that could not be disguised. Madame Le Brun, however, had no physical disadvantages. In fact, she was a beauty—far more beautiful than Adélaïde. No wonder she painted so many self-portraits, Adélaïde thought, a little uncharitably.

She didn't look up as André came to her and took her by the

shoulders. "You know what you have to do. I still don't understand your reluctance."

He was right. She should get over her fear. What power did Nicolas have over her, after all? He didn't know any other artists. He couldn't spread ugly rumors about her to anyone who really mattered. She took a deep breath. "All right. I'll do it. But I don't know what to submit. They will have to be pastels. I'm not ready for oils."

"You'll think of something," André said.

☙

Adélaïde did think of something and, after submitting a series of pastel portraits of some of the artists she knew to the monthly Salons de la Correspondance, she submitted three more important pictures, one of them a self-portrait, as a way of putting herself forward. She had gotten used to her growing renown and in a few months had already received commissions for both pastel and oil portraits. But unfortunately, more was required. The price of having one's work displayed at the Salon de la Correspondance was to attend at least one discussion, to participate in a debate about art. She wasn't afraid she would have nothing to say, but putting not only her art but her person so obviously in the public eye felt doubly dangerous. Added to that, the spirit of the discussions was honesty. Would her work be criticized to her face? She had never had to submit to being so openly judged.

On the day the debate was to be held, Adélaïde dressed in her finest ensemble and hired a carriage to take her across the river over the bridges crowded with buildings, not wanting to arrive in a spoiled dress or with her shoes covered in muck. The spring mud in the gutters and between the cobbles hadn't yet dried, but the milder weather brought people out in droves to enjoy the end of a dreary winter. In the press of traffic, the ride took almost as long as walking, but that gave her time to think.

Adélaïde was aware that a crossroads in her life and her career lay ahead of her. For all of her thirty-three years, it seemed, she had had only one goal in mind: To draw. To paint. To be known as a painter. And now, she was known—at least, by many who mattered. It was a bonus that she had a studio full of talented women who challenged her and gratified her with their own progress as artists. But how was she to take the next step? What could she do to get a royal appointment of some kind or—even more unlikely—be elected to the Académie?

She hadn't come up with an answer before the carriage arrived at the exhibition rooms. It was still a little early to join the invited guests for the discussion and debate, so Adélaïde wandered through the interconnected galleries. Her pictures had only been hung the day before, along with all the other new entries, and she wanted to see where they had ended up this time and what the idiosyncratic La Blancherie had decided to display next to them. He had a knack for provoking controversy—which, she had to admit, often translated to sales. Mind buzzing with anxiety about the coming debate, Adélaïde meandered around the objects placed in the middle of the floor— some of them were sculptures, but many were strange mechanical devices whose functions she could only guess at.

She entered the main gallery and there they were, all together, hung so they faced the viewer on entry. Her own face, the self-portrait pastel in a straw hat that André intended to purchase at the end of the exhibition—he refused to take it as a gift—flanked by the head of a young man on one side and the portrait of the Comte de Clermont-Tonnere on the other. She'd done the portrait from an engraving, hoping it would plant the idea of a commission in the mind of one of his friends. She entered to get a closer look, passing by a highly efficient kitchen stove, a pair of waterproof shoes, and several other mysterious items.

Only when she was well into the room did she look to see what pictures were on the wall next to hers.

Her breath caught in her throat. *No, he didn't.* It was unthinkable.

And yet, clearly La Blancherie had done the one thing that she dreaded more than anything about exhibiting her work. Just a few feet beyond her pictures was an oil portrait of a woman—also in a straw hat. She had seen that face only once or twice, but it was seared into her memory. If she'd had any doubt at all, it would have been erased by the full-length portrait of Marie Antoinette immediately next to it. Adélaïde opened her exhibition guide, madly flipping to the page that described the objects in that particular gallery and gasped when she read, "Two lady artists—together for the first time."

Ice trickled through Adélaïde's veins. Not since the Académie de Saint-Luc salon eight years before had she been forced to see her work in direct comparison to that of Elisabeth Vigée Le Brun. Of course, she knew why La Blancherie did it. It was a novelty, something to stir up interest. She braced herself to read more of what he said in the catalogue, fearing that he had set her up for ridicule.

But no. To her relief, La Blancherie praised both of their works, commenting intelligently about their contrasting styles. He noted the use of color and shadow in Madame Le Brun's pictures and the strength and realism in Adélaïde's—virile was the word he used, a direct contradiction to the criticism normally leveled at work by female artists, which was often described as too soft and feminine. Adélaïde wondered how Madame Le Brun felt about the comparison or indeed if she had read it yet. If her self-regard matched her popularity, Adélaïde imagined she might feel diminished by it. Who was Adélaïde, after all? Only a teacher and a pastellist with no royal appointment.

After gazing at the five pictures a while longer, forcing a degree of objectivity into her eyes and mind, Adélaïde decided that far from being shown up by the comparison, her own work indeed stood up to it. Her style might never make her popular among those seeking a flattering portrait painted by a popular *saloniste*. But she was true to her vision and would not compromise.

Like it or not—and mostly she liked it—Adélaïde had stepped up to a new rung on the artistic ladder. It remained to be seen whether it would protect her in a sense or further expose what might be seen as her moral weaknesses. Her liaison with André was common knowledge now. She didn't think it could do her much harm at this point. Only the existence of those erotic pastels was a hazard. But no one need discover them, ever.

It truly was time to move forward, whatever the consequences.

Twelve

Paris, September 1782

"I'd like to do a portrait of you, in your honor," Gabrielle said to Adélaïde one afternoon, "to thank you for your many kindnesses."

Gabrielle had continued to improve following the Exposition de la Jeunesse. She gained confidence knowing that someone with taste thought her work worthy of purchase. That exposition and Adélaïde's own showing at the Salon de la Correspondance had the added effect of making the studio even more popular with aspiring lady artists. Adélaïde had nine regular students—her nine muses, she liked to tell herself—and a few others who came occasionally for help with specific aspects of their painting or drawing or to one of the master classes she gave. No one, as yet, could compare to Gabrielle.

"I would be honored, but it would serve you better to do one of yourself," Adélaïde said touching Gabrielle's cheek with affection. She understood that when someone hired a lady artist for a portrait, the appearance of the artist was as much a factor in the choice as the quality of her work. It seemed men could be as ugly or as old as they liked, but women must be young and attractive—but not too attractive. At least, that applied to everyone except Madame Le Brun, it seemed, whose beauty somehow managed to be an asset. There were those who said it was the determining factor in her elevation to being Marie Antoinette's portraitist.

But that same day was an important one for Adélaïde. Despite her resolve following her success in the Salon de la Correspondance, it had proved more difficult than she thought to wean Gallimard off the erotic pastels she supplied. And André had been hinting at something—something so wonderful that she hardly dared imagine it. If it came to pass, she must ensure that she severed all ties with Gallimard and that no one ever connected her with this secret commerce. She would deliver her final series of pastels to Gallimard that morning and inform him that there would be no more forthcoming, no matter how hard he argued with her.

She stood and addressed the studio. "I have go out for a while. You ladies all know what to do. When I return I expect to see some improvement. And Paulette, try not to make your first layer too heavy, or you'll end up having to scrape some of it off."

Adélaïde picked up the portfolio containing a sheaf of four additional pastels of Paulette in provocative poses, plus some monochrome copies of others for Gallimard to sell at a lower price. All the way to the shop, she rehearsed what she would say to him. She knew he'd become accustomed to the lucrative trade in her pictures and wouldn't want to cut off the supply.

"Ah, Madame!" Gallimard greeted Adélaïde warmly, threading his way through the crowded shelves of knick-knacks and ornaments. "Please, come to the parlor and have a tisane with me." He nodded to his assistant and directed her toward a lady customer who was examining a china dog.

Once they were settled in the small, windowed office at the back of the shop and the serving girl had given them their tisane and left a plate of pastries on the table next to them, Adélaïde opened her portfolio to show Monsieur Gallimard her final pastels of Paulette. He examined them one by one, licking his lips as he did so. "Magnificent. Might I say, luscious."

Adélaïde squirmed and cleared her throat. "Thank you. But I am afraid these will be the last."

Gallimard tore his gaze away from one of the pictures and stared at

Adélaïde in disbelief. "But they cannot be! I have customers waiting. They will be most displeased."

"You can easily get an art student to copy the ones I have already executed. And no doubt he would be glad of the extra money."

Gallimard pursed his lips. "The quality of the work, the brilliance of the colors, especially the flesh tones—that is what my customers will pay for. I am not a seller of cheap imitations."

He meant to flatter her, she knew, but she was resolved on ending the association. "All the same, you will have to find another artist. I cannot continue to draw these. I have my students to think of and some commissions I have had to postpone because I didn't have time." That was a lie, but Adélaïde didn't care.

He stood and walked away a little, one hand on his hip, looking around as if trying to pull an idea out of the air. Adélaïde noted the fine quality of his coat and jabot, and that he wore what looked like a ruby ring on his pinky finger. She had no doubt her hard work had contributed to his newfound affluence. "It is unfortunate," he said. "I have received a request from someone in the highest position at court for a series of pictures. But you would have to find a different model."

"I just told you I will do no more of these for you."

"He is willing to pay a thousand Louis d'Or for six pastels."

Adélaïde caught her breath. That was an obscene amount of money. And it probably wasn't the true sum. She guessed that Gallimard charged his clients more than double what he gave her.

"I see I have surprised you. You would have to find a young girl to model for you, though, one who has not yet blossomed into a woman. I'm certain you could pick one up in the Cour des Miracles." He smiled as he said it.

Adélaïde was stunned into silence for a minute. She didn't know whether it was the suggestion of having a young girl pose or that someone at court had requested it that offended her more. "I'm afraid you have mistaken my nature, if you think I would subject a young girl—even a beggar—to such—" She couldn't speak.

Gallimard looked down at his fingernails. "I think you might find it dangerous to ignore my request, as well as foolish. You could become a very wealthy woman, and I possess more information than you might wish to be made public about your artistic activities."

Adélaïde stood. She uncurled the fingers she didn't realize she'd been clenching. "At what cost? And what do you threaten me with?"

"Come, come, Madame. We both know you are hardly a virtuous woman, living in flagrant sin with a young man who has yet to cement his reputation as an artist of the first rank."

The very thing she most dreaded looked as though it might come to pass. Gallimard had drawn André into her enterprise, hinting that he was some manner of accomplice. If Gallimard chose to expose her, her downfall might spell André's as well. This was the last thing she needed on the eve of daring to take the long-overdue step of allowing her ambition to lead her to the financial and artistic success she knew she deserved. The fact that men like Gallimard and Nicolas held such power over her, simply because she was a woman, infuriated her. *Let them do their worst*, she thought. It's probably all toothless threats anyway.

Before she could decide against it, in one swift movement, Adélaïde reached over and grabbed the best of the pastels she'd just brought the shopkeeper, folded it in half and rubbed it together to utterly spoil the image. She had not applied a fixative so that the colors would remain brilliant, assuming it would be framed under glass either before or after Gallimard sold it. "I said I will not do it! And don't forget, if you expose me, you expose yourself." She whirled around and ran out of the office and through the store, knocking a porcelain ornament to the ground and shattering it.

She didn't stop until she was several streets away from Gallimard's shop. *What have I done?* Adélaïde forced herself to breathe slowly and wait until her hammering heart quieted. If Gallimard acted on his threats, she could lose everything she'd worked and fought so hard for. She might even lose André.

But to her surprise, by the time she returned to her studio, she felt strangely lighter, as if some invisible hand had pulled a dark blanket off her heart. Her fears of exposure, she realized, weren't the only burden she'd been carrying. While celebrating the beauty of the female body was a noble endeavor, exploiting it for the prurient interest of men was something else—something she was glad to have abandoned.

Still, every day after that Adélaïde read the *Journal* and the *Mercure* and picked up any leaflets she found, scanning them for vicious gossip about her or André. So far, nothing. Perhaps Gallimard had realized he would be putting himself in danger with the authorities if any suggestion of the illicit trade could be traced back to his shop. Adélaïde counted on the fact that he had as much to lose as she did.

One aspect of the matter, however, still disturbed her: She suspected that Gallimard was able to command premium prices for her works in part because he told the purchasers that they were executed by a woman. He as much as hinted at it several times. She could still hear him saying, *It is easy to imagine the delicate fingers that traced these delectable forms*, a reference to the pastel technique in which she used her finger to blend and smudge colors and soften shapes initially outlined with her crayon. Thinking of it sent a shiver all through her.

But there was nothing else she could do about it. The pictures were out there, being shown and drooled over in small circles, perhaps framed in a private boudoir to add spice to someone's lovemaking. She was glad there was no magic that allowed an artist to see through the eyes of her subjects as others gazed upon her work.

⌒♡⌒

A month later, André asked Adélaïde to meet him in his studio at the Louvre. As her teaching schedule and portrait commissions had become more demanding, Adélaïde had spent less and less time there. They tended to see each other only after the workday was over when they could fall exhausted into each other's arms in her apartment, so this summons came as a surprise to her.

She left her students to work on their own and walked the half mile to the Louvre in the bright Autumn sunshine. When she arrived, rather than simply letting herself into the studio, Adélaïde paused and put her ear to the door. Voices. André was not alone. She smiled, remembering the first time she'd come to see him there. She tapped on the door. André hurried over and opened it, signaling with a look that they should not indulge in their usual amorous embrace. He led her in, his hand under her elbow. "I think you and Alexander are acquainted with each other."

Adélaïde rushed forward and reached out her hands to her old friend, the portrait painter Alexander Roslin and a Swedish transplant. What could he be doing there? He and André were not close, as far as she knew. "It is good to see you! How long has it been?"

The painter smiled. "Perhaps a few years, but I have been watching you from afar. It has been a pleasure to see your progress, as an artist and a teacher."

Before Adélaïde could settle into catching up with Roslin on news and gossip, André interrupted them. "Our purpose here is professional rather than personal," he said. "We have been putting our heads together to see how we can advance your career, now that you are as accomplished an oil painter as you are a pastellist and now that you have an impressive coterie of talented students."

"All female, I hasten to add." Even with her recent successes and those of her students, no young men sought to join her studio. After all, who of those who actually had a choice would study with her rather than someone like Van Loo, or Robert, or André himself?

Roslin took her arm and led her over to the table, where a carafe of wine and three glasses had already been laid out. "It's all quite settled.

We've decided you must be elected to the Académie Royale, and I intend to put you forward. As you know, my late wife was an academician, and I see such talent in you that it seems fitting you should become so as well."

For a moment, Adélaïde thought she must be dreaming. Although it had crossed her mind as a possible reason for André's mysterious hints of late, she hadn't dared believe it. Of course the idea of being elected to the Académie had been in the back of her mind almost as long as she could remember. But she assumed she would certainly not be elected until she was much older and more well-known. "I have no suitable oil paintings to submit for consideration. I have only just started to paint portraits on canvas."

"You are among the most superb pastellists of all time—and I'm not alone in thinking that," Roslin said. "La Tour supports your nomination. You could be elected initially as a pastellist and rise to the status of portraitist as your volume of canvases increases and you exhibit your finest in the salons of the Académie."

Adélaïde fell silent. Distant bells chimed. Gulls cried as they wheeled and curved over the Seine. Somewhere a child laughed, and a street vendor called out in a jumble of indistinct vowels. She was in Paris, in the Louvre, sitting with her beloved and one of the most revered artists of the age, and they proposed putting her forward for election in the Académie, the greatest honor an artist could aspire to in that day. It didn't seem possible. "You are too kind." Her voice fell apart at the edges.

"It's unlikely you'll be elected this year. Artists seldom are the first time their names are put forward. But we must start the process. I assume you agree to it?"

⌒℮⌒

Académie salons occurred every two years. That meant Adélaïde had a year to prepare for what could be her first entries—a year to work and worry, to believe one minute she could conquer the world and the next that she deserved to have no more success than a worm in the gutter. A year, too, to make sure Gallimard did not poison her chances by exposing her former illicit trade. So far, nothing had come of his threats, but every day she dreaded reading the newspaper or hearing that one of her affluent students had received an anonymous letter.

And she had heard through her father that Guiard and his paramour had returned to the vicinity of Paris. They were living in Neuilly—far enough away that Adélaïde was unlikely to encounter Nicolas on the street. But she didn't for a moment believe her estranged husband would forgo the chance to extort money from her if he had the need—and the opportunity. Anything to bedevil her success.

If only she and André could marry. Such an official tie, something sanctioned by the church and the state, would insulate her from whatever calumnies Gallimard could concoct and allow André to sue Guiard for libel if he tried to destroy her career. But divorce was still illegal. Unless Guiard died, her situation would remain the same.

Even with no legal tie to André, she would not change her circumstances, not for all the riches in the world. All who knew them understood that theirs was true love and friendship. Adélaïde wondered, though, which of their friends would defend her against any attacks on her character and which would remain quietly in agreement with the slander should it ever come to light.

For the moment, she could do nothing but continue to work hard, redoubling her efforts to produce more canvases as well as pastels. The machinery of the nomination process went on in secret. Even André, because he was not an officer, could not intervene. She trusted Roslin to do his best, but she was also aware it might not be good enough. And she had heard the rumors that Madame Le Brun was trying to get herself elected in that same year. It would be just her luck, Adélaïde thought, that Madame Le Brun's connections would give her an insurmountable advantage, even if she herself had the support of all her artist friends.

Adélaïde hadn't told anyone except for Gabrielle about the possibility of being elected. She knew she could trust her assistant not to breathe a word of it, and she needed someone besides André himself to talk it over with, to give vent to her anxieties and uncertainties—someone who wouldn't judge her harshly if she failed in the attempt. That would be most embarrassing of all, to be put forward and rejected. She hadn't even told her father, although he'd gone to see her pictures at the Salon de la Correspondance and sent her a bottle of champagne in congratulations.

Waiting and hoping were all that was left to her at this point. And she wasn't very good at either of those things. She didn't have time to be.

⌒℮⌒

A few days later, just as Adélaïde was finishing a lesson on mixing oil colors with her more advanced pupils, someone knocked on the studio door. "*Entrez!*" Adélaïde called, assuming it might be the delivery of rolled canvas she expected. She heard the door open and rather than the heavy shuffling of a laborer, the light step of a woman made her turn to see who it could be.

The woman, whom Adélaïde judged to be close to fifty years old but still vigorous and attractive, presented her card. She was the Comtesse d'Angiviller. Adélaïde looked up in surprise. How could it be that the wife of the director of the Bâtiments du Roi, the officer who controlled all royal patronage of the arts—and who, along with the Académie's director Jean-Baptiste Pierre, was deeply opposed to women artists—how could it be that she had arrived at her studio?

"Comtesse." Adélaïde curtsied, as did all her students when they saw her. "As you see, we are not suitably prepared to receive visitors." Adélaïde couldn't imagine what had brought this unexpected guest to her door. Had she come to discourage her from allowing herself to be put forward for election to the Académie? Or perhaps she had come to prepare her for the fact that she would not be admitted?

"Never mind that!" The comtesse walked into the room, removed her gloves and started strolling from one student's work in progress to another's, peering closely and smiling at each of them in turn. "I have heard you are an excellent teacher. I know from my own experience that you are an artist of the first rank, having seen your works in the Salon de la Correspondance." She said nothing more for a while, continuing her perusal of the projects propped and tacked on easels. The students stepped away politely as she approached so she could better examine their work.

The comtesse stopped when she had seen everything and faced Adélaïde, who had not moved from her place, astonished and wary.

"You rightly wonder why I am here. I have a favor to ask of you. My husband does not approve of women learning to paint, except for things like miniatures as a genteel pastime. Yet I am a true connoisseur and cannot help wishing to discover how artists produce the magnificent works that grace the walls of galleries and palaces. In other words, I'm not interested in a genteel pastime. Would you consider giving me lessons?"

This Adélaïde did not expect. Could there be some trick in it? Was the comtesse sent to spy on her, to see if she behaved in any way immorally? "Unwomanly" was the usual aspersion cast upon women artists. But she could hardly refuse. "It would be my honor, of course!" Adélaïde said.

"There is one condition, I'm afraid. The lessons must be in secret. Since I would be joining your already thriving studio, I would ask all the ladies here to swear they will not tell a soul."

That quickly squashed a hope that flew into Adélaïde's mind at the idea of having such an illustrious pupil. Whatever the lady's reasons for being there, Adélaïde thought that news of her presence in the studio would encourage others of her class to commission portraits. Even with enforced secrecy, though, being in the good graces of the wife of the person who controlled all artistic activities in the kingdom would be no bad thing. "I accept your condition, and I know my students will as well." A chorus of *"Oui, bien sûr"* and a few dipped curtsies followed.

"Good! I should like to start tomorrow. My husband is away for a few days and will not notice my absence."

For the remainder of the day, Adélaïde's mind whirled with the potential implications of having Madame d'Angiviller as an ally. Would it smooth her acceptance into the Académie? Would the comtesse recommend her as a portraitist to her wealthy, influential friends? Perhaps she'd even send her more students—although Adélaïde's studio was full at the moment. She thought she might have to open another and rent more space to accommodate the young lady artists who would flock to her.

But she was getting ahead of herself. The comtesse had promised no such outcomes. It would be up to Adélaïde to decide how far to push the association, how much she dared presume.

Thirteen

The Comtesse d'Angiviller proved to be an enthusiastic and willing student as well as a connoisseur who wasn't afraid to put her money where her interests lay.

"I should like to commission you to make portraits of my two favorite actors in the Comédie Française," the comtesse said one afternoon in January, "Jean-Baptiste Brizard and Jean-François Ducis. And I shall pay you five hundred livres for each one."

Brizard and Ducis were the stars of the Comédie. Adélaïde had to stop herself from saying, *Are you certain you want me to do this?* Or, *That's too much money!* Instead she took two deep breaths and stood up a little straighter. "It would be my pleasure. When may I have the actors sit for me? Shall I go to them, or will they come to my studio?" She wasn't certain these were questions she should ask. A more experienced portraitist would know. But something in the comtesse's manner made her unafraid of revealing her ignorance.

"I don't want them to sit for you. I should like you to attend their performances and make sketches. I want them to be captured in their roles as brilliant actors."

Here was a challenge—to portray a man in action, not seated in a careful, studied pose. She would have to do the lion's share of the work from rapid sketches. She pursed her lips and thought for a moment.

"Do you think you can't do it?" the comtesse asked. "Because I know you can, and your style is precisely what is required for such a challenge. Vigorous, yet sensitive. Pastels will do. I don't want you to have to delay because you must wait for layers of paint to dry. And besides . . ." She cast her eye around Adélaïde's studio. Two of her students had left to get married, and her diminished income from that and no more money from Gallimard showed on the visibly empty shelves where art supplies were kept.

Adélaïde looked down at the floor, embarrassed. "Of course I will do it. You are too kind."

Madame Angiviller approached her and tipped her chin up with her index finger so Adélaïde could not avoid looking into her eyes. "You have a brilliant future ahead of you. Of that I am certain. You may not be as well connected as certain other lady artists, but I can help you with that. And you are a gifted teacher who cares about her students." She stepped away and walked over to the easel where her own work stood waiting for her to finish it. "Heaven knows, you have managed to coax what little ability I have out of me and onto the canvas. I shall finish this one still life and then allow someone with more talent to take my place. I have learned what I came to learn. And I know of several young ladies who would welcome the opportunity to join your studio."

Something in the comtesse's expression told Adélaïde that she wasn't simply talking about painting or about Adélaïde's abilities as a teacher. The two of them had become friends, and their friendship was the first stroke of good fortune Adélaïde had had for a long time. It was true that, as an art student, the lady possessed little natural talent. She approached her study with more intellectual than artistic curiosity, applying an analytical eye to everything she did. Adélaïde couldn't help thinking that someone with such a keen intelligence and knowledge of the world would have made a capable diplomat or civil servant. It was sad that such avenues were closed to women.

Before she left that day, the comtesse invited Adélaïde to sit in her box at the theater on two evenings the following week. "Once you've seen them perform, I shall introduce you to my protégés so that you may observe them at closer quarters and get what you need from them in the way of time and cooperation. I have already told them about this project. They are only too willing to oblige me."

⌒ℰ⌒

After that day, whenever she was able, the comtesse would visit Adélaïde's studio in the evening after the students had gone home—all except for Gabrielle, who either sat and listened to their conversation or retired to a corner to read. They talked sometimes for an hour or more, discussing wide-ranging topics, everything from politics to architecture to the writings of Diderot and Rousseau. It became clear to Adélaïde that the comtesse was, in her own way, teaching her something, preparing her for something. In all these conversations, she never mentioned Adélaïde's bid to be elected to the Académie Royale, a bid that would be decided in part by the comtesse's husband, the Comte d'Angiviller. Adélaïde still couldn't decide whether that was a good sign or a bad one.

One evening in the late spring, at a break in their conversation, Adélaïde asked, "Are you ever bored?" She couldn't imagine not having an all-consuming passion to occupy herself with, and although the comtesse was interested in many things, she appeared to be passionate about none of them.

"No. Never," she said.

"How do you occupy your time when you are not here?" Adélaïde felt she knew the comtesse well enough to ask a personal question.

"I have a salon, as you know, and it furnishes me with enough activity in the planning and execution as I could ever wish. Besides, if I were busy all the time, I wouldn't be able to come here and talk to you!"

Adélaïde smiled, and said, "I attended a salon once. It seemed all posturing by men and competing to see who could make the wittiest remark at someone else's expense."

The comtesse laughed. "You describe one of Madame Necker's gatherings, if I can guess."

"Yes, I think it was." It had been that one experience that had put Adélaïde off the idea of making any other attempts to infiltrate society in such a manner. Madame Necker was the wife of Jacques Necker, a Swiss official who had been minister of finance to the king. But his reformist ideas made him unpopular with the nobility, and he had been forced to resign the year before.

"You must not judge Madame Necker too harshly. She has put her energy toward a great many worthy causes and believes fervently in the education of women—a belief her husband does not share."

Naturally, Adelaide thought, and said, "Why is it? Why must men be so against women exercising their talents and intellect?"

The comtesse looked off into the distance. At first, Adélaïde worried that her question might have been taken as impertinent and prepared to utter an apology. Before she could, the comtesse said, "I believe that it has to do with power. No one wants to give up power once it is acquired, and although not all men are powerful in public life, all of them are powerful at home. Or almost all, at any rate."

Adélaïde thought back to Nicolas. It made sense. In pursuing her career as an artist, she subverted his power over her. He as much as confessed it when he'd visited her at her father's apartment. She said, "For all the advantages they have, I don't think I'd like to be a man."

"Well, then, it's fortunate you aren't!"

Adélaïde would not like to be a man, but she wished to have a man's freedom to occupy a position of importance. If she could be elected to the Académie, it would be a start. Her portraits of the actors Brizard and Ducis—both of them in their roles as King Lear—were coming along better than Adélaïde could have wished. Something about the double challenge of not only representing a man in all his complexity and reality but in the act of portraying someone other than himself ignited her imagination and brought all her skills into play. She chose

to depict them both at the moment when the blind king realizes how
he has been betrayed, highlighting the actors' different interpretations.

Those bold essays were not, however, to be her reception pieces. On
André's advice, Adélaïde chose to make the pastel of her dear friend
and fellow artist, the sculptor Augustin Pajou, serve as the work upon
which her election to the Académie would hinge.

There were so many unknowns. The comtesse had told her that
despite her connection to the Comte d'Angiviller, she herself couldn't
directly lobby Monsieur Pierre, the conservative director of the
Académie, to look kindly on Adélaïde's application. She assured
Adélaïde, however, that the combination of her undeniable brilliance and the support of some of the most revered members of the
Académie would be worth more than her own influence anyway.

Adélaïde had no doubt that, if she had been a man, her election
to the Académie would be assured. But that fact remained unspoken
between them because it was too obvious to mention.

☙

Paris, June 1783
The day of the election, the studio's atmosphere crackled with tension. Adélaïde had decided to tell all her students about it in the end,
partly to explain why she had sometimes been distracted and inatten-
tive in recent months, partly to relieve Gabrielle of the necessity for
secrecy. The knowledge that a decision was being made at that very
moment concerning their teacher's possible acceptance to the most
elite artistic institution in France—perhaps in the world—set everyone on edge. Each time one of the ladies stood or scraped a stool back
on the wooden floor, they all looked up. Adélaïde, too, was finding it
hard to focus on anything. She strolled around, hardly conscious that
her feet were moving, and peered over her students' shoulders, not
really seeing what she was looking at. When she got to Gabrielle, who
was putting the finishing touches on her self-portrait, she whispered,

"Superb," so quietly she hoped not to disturb the others. But everyone was so highly attuned to what was happening—in the studio and in the meeting of the officers of the Académie over at the Louvre—that even her barely audible comment made them all shift and look around.

The light from the north-facing windows started to fade as the afternoon drew to a close, and the nine women who entrusted their artistic education to Adélaïde rose one by one to clean their brushes or put away their crayons, covering their work either with fine paper or cloths, depending on their chosen medium. They dawdled, no doubt hoping to still be there when the news arrived. "Perhaps no decision will be made today," Adélaïde said. "Perhaps—"

All activity stopped at the sound of a man's heavy step climbing the stairs to the studio. Adélaïde held her breath, and twenty eyes turned to the door when it opened. André entered, his face revealing nothing.

Adélaïde rushed to the table on the side where a bottle of wine and several glasses stood, filled one and held it out to André. He took it from her with only the briefest smile. *Roslin's petition was disapproved—I was not elected*, she thought, and prepared herself to hear the worst. Her students would be devastated.

"We should speak in private," André said.

"Whatever you have to say, I want my ladies to hear it."

Like a tableau vivant, all nine students stood frozen in the midst of whatever they'd been doing when André came in.

"Very well. As you wish." André drank down half the glass of wine and Adélaïde refreshed it, pouring a measure for herself as well but not yet tasting it.

"The committee deliberated a long time. Angiviller and Pierre were dead set against admitting any more women. Roslin and others argued as best they could, but it seemed their minds were made up." He paused to drink again. Adélaïde had forgotten that it wasn't only Angiviller whose stance against women had to be overcome but that the director of the Académie was just as opposed. André continued,

"Yet that is not the worst of it. A message arrived from Versailles. Apparently, the queen herself wished to have her protégée admitted."

A chorus of gasps met his announcement.

Madame Le Brun, Adélaïde thought. So, the rumors had all been true. And her rival was the queen's favorite, after all. How was it that this woman kept finding ways to thwart her ambitions, somehow without effort stepping into the loftiest appointment and attracting the wealthiest sitters?

"I am afraid your character, your modesty, was called into question as well," André said, glancing at the young women who had gradually crept closer and now encircled the two of them.

Adélaïde's heart pounded. So it wasn't just another woman artist that gave them pause. They couldn't know, could they? About the erotic pastels? "Go on," she said. Better to find out at once.

"It was suggested that our association, our liaison, extended to my being the true author of your oil paintings."

Now cries of "Not true!" "Unfair!" "Preposterous!" echoed through the studio. Adélaïde sank onto a chair, more out of relief than disappointment. Her secret was still safe. The accusation about André was nothing more than she had expected to face.

André raised his voice to cut through the chatter. "But the committee was persuaded by looking at one of your pictures next to one of mine that nothing could be further from the truth. The difficulty is that, in exchange for admitting her pet portraitist to the Académie, the queen signed a document that limited the number of women members at any one time to four."

There it was. The coup de grace. Only four, Adélaïde thought, and Madame Le Brun was the fourth, because there were already three other lady members. She calmed her breathing. There was no point getting upset. What could she do? Perhaps she'd still be alive when one of the existing female members passed away. One of them was very old. Well over sixty, she thought.

"However, after Roslin reminded the committee that Madame Therbusch had left France and was unlikely to exhibit in any more salons, so that although there would technically be five members only four would be active, the committee voted to elect Madame Labille-Guiard, since she is deserving as an artist of the first rank and certainly the foremost pastellist in Paris—barring, of course, La Tour."

A roar of delight shattered the tense quiet of the studio. Adélaïde's students rushed to her, surrounding her with tears and congratulations. André backed away to let them bask in their teacher's well-earned glory.

Once wine had been poured for everyone, André raised his glass. "To Madame Labille-Guiard. Pastellist, painter, teacher—and academician."

⚬⚬⚬

Later that night, after she and André had retired to her apartment and she had time to fully absorb the fact that she had been elected, Adélaïde sat up in bed in a panic. "The salon! It's only a few months away!"

"Hush, *mon amour*." André pulled her back down next to him. "You have many works to exhibit. Everyone will be more than happy to lend you your portraits of them for such an honor. You have all the artists' portraits, and *Delightful Surprise*, among others you exhibited at the Salon de la Correspondance over the past year. And what about the actors? Madame d'Angiviller would be delighted if you showed them in the salon."

Adélaïde's heartbeat slowed. "Of course. I hadn't thought of that." But she realized in picturing them that the majority of her portraits so far had been of men, as if something within her was resisting her own femininity. And then she remembered that that would soon change. The comtesse had gotten her a commission to paint a pastel portrait of Madame Mitoire and her children. In that instant, Adélaïde decided her picture would not be another simple family portrait. It would be a celebration of womanhood, of all that distinguished them from men and gave them their unique power.

She smiled, and whispered into André's ear, "I could never have done this without you. I wish we could marry."

André stroked her hair. "You didn't need me. Your talent would have prevailed no matter what."

Whether or not that was true, all Adélaïde could think was that he hadn't said anything about the other subject, about marriage. Since it was impossible at that point anyway, she let the matter drop.

Fourteen

Paris, August 25, 1783

She wouldn't have done it for any other purpose, Adélaïde kept telling herself as she walked to her father's boutique with the intention of asking for his help—the kind of help most women would ask of their mothers. Yet Adélaïde knew that, even if her mother were alive, her father could do a better job of ensuring she was dressed as well as she could be for the opening of her reception salon at the Louvre that evening. Oh, she'd been to those salons often enough, as a spectator. She never missed one, attending every other year for as long as she could remember. It was always a crush on opening day, with people of all conditions and classes standing in line to get in, clogging the great stairwell up to the *salon carré* to see who had painted or sculpted what in the past two years, which royal portrait had been painted by whom, how many wild landscapes and vases of flowers spewed their colors everywhere. She'd seen them all, but never like this—never as one whose paintings and drawings would be hanging amid the floor to ceiling pictures, from knee height up thirty feet to the architraved ceiling.

And the critics and pamphleteers would be there in force too, looking for anything scandalous to write about. No doubt they were licking their pencils with glee at the prospect of seeing the two newly elected lady academicians try to be polite to each other, if they even crossed paths. It was therefore important that she be dressed as well as she could be, as well as her father—the most sought-after modiste in

Paris aside from Mademoiselle Bertin—could make her. It was a pity, she thought, that she and Madame Le Brun were more likely to be judged as women than artists. Rivals they might be, but both of them deserved to be taken seriously.

Adélaïde paused before opening the door of her father's boutique. It wasn't where she expected to be at that moment. What would her mother think if she'd been alive to witness her daughter's success as an artist? Adélaïde couldn't remember any conversations with her mother about art. And yet, it must have been her mother who took her to the exhibitions and salons when she was young. And her father—his business was so removed from everything she valued in life. Nonetheless, here she was, turning to him.

She opened the door and set the bell above it to tinkling.

Her father looked up from a notebook he'd been studying. "Adélaïde, my dear! I was hoping you'd come."

"Hoping?"

"You think I don't know what day it is? I hoped you'd come before today, before the very day of the opening, but it's not too late." He led her through to the workshop behind the boutique as he continued speaking. "I have had some of the girls making over a dress just for you. You'll want to look your best, of course."

Somehow, over the last few years, she and her father had grown close enough that he would guess what she needed without even being asked. They never spoke of serious matters, only seeing each other at Mass once a week and perhaps for a walk afterward where they discussed trifles. She had sent him a letter about her election to the Académie, not thinking he would care about it very much. But this. She felt the sting of tears in the back of her eyes and blinked rapidly before greeting the seamstresses, who flocked around her as soon as she entered their domain filled with color and texture.

For the next hour, Adélaïde allowed herself to be fussed over in a way she had never been fussed over before. And when she looked at herself in the mirror at the end, she knew that coming to her father had been the right decision.

"You look beautiful," her father said when he returned, a smile on his face and one hand behind his back.

"Thank you, Papa," Adélaïde said, unable to stop looking at herself in the mirror.

"Just one more thing. I thought you should have this. It was your mother's. You didn't know her well enough. She was so ill for much of your life. But she would have been proud."

He brought out from behind his back an exquisite ivory fan and opened it for Adélaïde. "See these paintings on the guards and the leaves? So beautiful."

Adélaïde took the fan and examined the stunning, detailed watercolor paintings of a miniature courting scene that continued across the delicate, rose-colored silk. The work of a master. She ran her fingers over the surface hardly touching it, just feeling the change in texture from the soft background to where the paint had stiffened the fabric ever so slightly.

Her father said, "It was painted by Louis Vigée."

Adélaïde gasped and nearly dropped the fan. Did he know that this painter of fans was the late father of her rival, Madame Vigée Le Brun? She searched his eyes, but could find no evidence of guile there, and it wouldn't be like him to be so petty. Still. Could there be such a coincidence? If he didn't know, she wouldn't tell him. In any case, it was time to go and meet André outside the Louvre. He'd advised Adélaïde that she should be seen by as many people as possible. He would take care to introduce her to everyone he knew, within the hearing of anyone he deemed famous or influential. The idea made Adélaïde queasy. She still hadn't gotten used to being recognized by those who had seen her at the Salon de la Correspondance.

Adélaïde decided not to hire a carriage to take her the short distance to the Louvre from that end of the Rue Neuve des Petits Champs.

The walk, along such familiar streets, calmed her nerves, especially on a warm, late-summer evening, when the angle of the sun cast long shadows across the cobbles and lit up the buildings as though from the inside, the reflection on the windows glowing golden orange.

She had her face tilted upward admiring the effect on the top floor of the Louvre when André's hand touched hers. "Let's go in."

They had decided it would be better not to pretend to be strangers. Their liaison was too well known to be hidden, and they didn't want anyone to think they were ashamed of it. Adélaïde basked in André's gentle presence as he shepherded her through the crowds and into the building.

⌒⌒

It took them a full three-quarters of an hour to get all the way into the Salon Carré. A current of joy washed through Adélaïde's body as she wandered slowly around the perimeter of the room on André's arm, waiting for knots of people to break apart before the two of them could move on to view the next group of paintings. They tried to take everything in, spending time examining paintings on the bottom row, then on to the ones deemed significant enough to be displayed at eye level, and up to the paintings in the third and fourth tiers above, craning their necks so as not to miss a thing. The high up paintings were hung so they cantilevered away from the wall at their tops in an effort to compensate for any foreshortening that might result from the viewing angle. Adélaïde was glad to see that most of the portraits were not hung so high, though—only the landscapes and still lifes and some very large history paintings.

André's *Rape of Orythia* was in this salon, of course, along with other pictures of his. Although he'd finished it a year before as his reception piece, it was customary to display it in the first possible salon. Knots of people, connoisseurs and commoners, nobility and shopkeepers, paused before the large canvas and savored it in all its beauty—the colors, the composition. But Adélaïde couldn't help smiling at the sight of the naked Boreas—god of wind who abducted a princess and made her his bride—whom she knew as the model Marc. She had watched André create this canvas from the very beginning, from the dead layer to the final glazes. She knew the places he had painted over, the changes he had made, the way he'd agonized over every detail, and her heart swelled with pride.

"Look," André said, nodding to a place farther down the wall.

There it was. They'd already passed the pastels she'd drawn of André's friends and fellow academicians, including her reception piece of Augustin Pajou. And across the salon she could see the pastels of the actors that the Comtesse d'Angiviller had commissioned—and that had paid her expenses for the next six months.

Ahead, though, was the pastel portrait of Madame Mitoire. Adélaïde had done as she intended, painting her as no man could ever be portrayed. She was breastfeeding her infant surrounded by her other children. A group of onlookers had stopped before it and were commenting and pointing. Adélaïde had been a little worried that the spectacle of a mother with breast exposed and infant so obviously at suck might attract the prurient interest of men, which was not her intent. But she was pleased to see that the viewers now in front of it were mostly women and girls. Their faces softened as they gazed at what may well have been a familiar enough sight, albeit with the mother more elegantly dressed than was usual. Even from there, Adélaïde could see that Madame Mitoire's skin glowed, that the composition was perfectly balanced as the mother and her three children formed an unbroken unit, a continuum of love.

Satisfied, Adélaïde continued around the gallery, hoping to see the paintings Madame Le Brun had submitted and perhaps be introduced to her rival. She had hopes that they could find a way to be friendly—or at least, not so directly competitive. Now that they were both members of the Académie, there was little left for either of them to achieve.

Still, Adélaïde had to admit that her willingness to make an overture of friendship to Madame Le Brun was in part due to the fact that she had been admitted to the Académie at a slightly higher rung than her rival. Madame Le Brun's reception piece, so André had told her, was an allegory—*Peace Bringing Back Abundance*, to mark the end of the American war in which France had invested so heavily. The gossip was that Madame Le Brun had sought admission to the Académie as a history painter, but unlike Adélaïde, she had no access to a man's private studio in order to draw from the male nude. That meant that she could not undertake any of the usual classical subjects, hence the allegory with two female subjects. Sadly for her, her attempt had backfired. The officers had not given her a category. She was not a portraitist, or a history painter, or a landscape artist, or a painter of still lifes. She was just a painter in oils. She was the only member who did not have a category. It was a subtle dig, but Adélaïde knew if it had been her, she would have felt it keenly.

Whatever envy Adélaïde harbored in her breast, she couldn't help sympathizing a little with her rival. Yet perhaps Madame Le Brun deserved it. Adélaïde suspected that if the queen herself had not intervened, the younger woman might well have had to wait another year or two to be elected.

The press of bodies was making it warmer and warmer in the center of the salon, and Adélaïde began to feel the walls around her ripple and shimmer. She staggered. André held more tightly to her arm. "Are you quite well?" he asked.

The last thing Adélaïde wanted to do was faint in such a public place. It was then that she remembered she had tucked the fan her father gave her into the deep pocket next to her shift, accessible through the openings in her petticoats. She reached in and drew it out, spreading the sticks apart to reveal the gorgeously painted scene. But she hardly noticed the design. All she cared about was its ability to stir the air in front of her face. It worked, and after a little her light-headedness passed.

The crowd moved them along like a river current, and soon Adélaïde and André had gone beyond the Madame Mitoire pastel and found themselves in front of one of Madame Le Brun's canvases, a portrait of Marie Antoinette. This portrait, however, did not depict the queen in a court gown, but in a chemise dress, a type of gown that had once been more suitable to the privacy of the boudoir than to be worn in public, fashioned as it was out of light cotton muslin rather than silk. Lately, though, the queen's modiste, Rose Bertin, had adapted it to more respectable attire. Adélaïde had heard that the queen wore nothing but dresses like it when she spent time in her bucolic retreat of the Petit Trianon.

"That's very bold," Adélaïde whispered to André. He nodded. Bold and magnificent. Madame Le Brun had done a superb job. She captured the queen's famously delicate complexion and managed to disguise the bulging lower lip that marked the Hapsburg dynasty. The drapery was subtle and flowing, with a diaphanous gold sash that lifted away as though touched by a breeze, and the queen had just plucked a nearly overblown pink rose from a bush somewhere out of sight in the deliberately undefined background.

They walked on, intending to continue to view more pictures and take a turn through the middle to admire the many sculptures, when they were confronted by a handsome couple strolling in the opposite direction. It took a moment for Adélaïde to realize that the tall, auburn-haired beauty in front of her was Madame Le Brun herself. She opened her mouth to say *bonsoir*, intending to pass along a compliment about the painting, but the look on her rival's face froze her to her place.

Madame Le Brun's eyes flicked down to the fan Adélaïde still fluttered in front of her and then back up to look directly at her, lips pressed together. Adélaïde swore she saw a glimmer of tears in the corner of one of her almond-shaped, long-lashed hazel eyes. She swept past her and André without uttering a word.

It took a moment for Adélaïde to realize what had happened. Madame Vigée Le Brun must have recognized the fine handiwork of the fan's decoration. Perhaps she herself had been in the atelier when her father was painting it. Adélaïde's heart pounded, and her palms perspired. She immediately closed the fan and tucked it back into her pocket, wishing she could run after Madame Le Brun and assure her she had not meant to hurt her or stir a painful memory. But what would that accomplish, especially in so public a setting?

Adélaïde was sick at heart. Any hope she had that this popular portraitist would allow her to exist in a state of détente, would understand that there was room in the salons and galleries of Paris for both of them, had vanished in an instant. She must surely have believed that Adélaïde had purposely taunted her with this reminder of her humble origins, heedless of the pain it might cause her. But Adélaïde would never think of being so cruel. It was, though, the kind of gesture that wasn't above many in Paris society. No doubt Madame Le Brun had been subjected to such subtle insults in the past.

And now, Adélaïde was certain she had inadvertently made a powerful and influential enemy, who might prove more damaging to her even than the petty Nicolas.

Fifteen

Adélaïde had some concern that having inadvertently created tension between herself and Madame Le Brun might turn the critics against her—Madame Le Brun was a favorite among the pamphleteers because of her beauty and her stature as a saloniste. But the first reviews of both Adélaïde's and Madame Le Brun's work were enthusiastic—Adélaïde thought they perhaps erred on the gentle side. That initial response took some of the sting away from the later commentary, where considerations other than art trickled into the articles with comments they would never dare make about male artists. Mostly these were nothing worse than Adélaïde expected. The articles gradually moved on to other news, more immediate scandals, and Adélaïde began to feel she had weathered her first salon and emerged relatively unscathed.

She was unprepared, therefore, when one morning two weeks after the opening she heard the whispery sound of paper being slid under the door, followed by quiet footsteps hurrying away. She and André were still in bed. "What was that?" She nudged André awake. It would soon be time for him to make his discreet exit from her apartment anyway.

André grunted but did not move. Adélaïde swung her legs out of bed, slid her toes into her slippers, and padded to the door. On the floor just inside lay a folded pamphlet. She stared at it for a moment, then opened the door and looked to see if whoever had delivered it was still in the building.

No one. By this time, Adélaïde's palms had started to perspire. Good news rarely came in such a surreptitious package.

She unfolded the obviously cheap paper. The ink was smudged. Someone had taken it off the press before it was even dry in order to bring it to her. Her heart pounded as she read.

It was awful. Worse than anything she'd anticipated. It made her want to go back to before, back to when no one cared that she was an artist trying to make her way because they didn't know she existed. She wanted to scream about the injustice of it. But that would wake up the neighbors, so instead she whispered through clenched teeth, "How dare they!"

At that, André sat up in bed and rubbed the sleep out of his eyes. She marched over to him and thrust the pamphlet into his hands, then watched his eyes move across the printed lines, his mouth gradually forming an astonished O. "This is slanderous!" he said.

But Adélaïde knew that fact didn't matter. "I was prepared for an attack on my art, for the cruel, anonymous commentary of the sort that claims you finish my paintings for me or that I cannot compete with the men because my pictures lack strength and virility. I was prepared for that. But not for this." She grabbed the pamphlet back from André and crushed it in her fist.

The author of the pamphlet accused her of being a whore, saying she had two thousand lovers—which was the same as *vingt-cent* after all. A crude pun at best, but not lost on anyone with the slightest knowledge of her connection to André Vincent. Was it Gallimard? She didn't think he had the imagination to write such a thing or the contacts to print it. Unsigned, of course.

And then, all at once, she knew. Nicolas. He had waited until the moment when such lies would inflict the most possible damage to her reputation. It was exactly the sort of thing he would say about her, and he was possibly clever enough to have thought of it himself. What a fool she'd been. Of course he wouldn't just go away and leave her in peace. His vanity had been wounded. Not only had she left him, had put her pursuit of a career above her duty as a wife, but she had taken up with someone else.

Perhaps this meant he'd given up on the idea of blackmail or that he lacked proof that the drawings he'd alluded to were hers. She had to admit, he'd chosen his poison well. Left to work its evil, the pamphlet would spell the end of her career. She liked to think those who knew her would realize it was calumny, but salacious rumors found their way into the remotest corners of Paris, like a damp fog in the middle of winter.

This isn't over, she thought. She might not have been able to defend herself against the charge of creating pornography if Nicolas knew enough to reveal her secret, but here was something she could address. She could take action against the intimation that she was a woman of loose morals. There were those who would defend her. Nicolas—if it were indeed Nicolas—must be made to pay for libeling her.

André had slipped out of bed and dressed in silence. What could he say? His name had not been mentioned, except through insinuation. "You know I can do nothing," he said. "It's a bit of drivel. It will all die away."

Did he really not understand that for a woman, it was so much more? "I cannot let this pass," Adélaïde said. "What parents would send their daughters to my studio if they thought I could not be trusted to set a virtuous example?" And then, she had an awful thought. What if it wasn't her estranged husband? What if Madame Le Brun had done it or caused it to be done? Could she have been angry enough about the incident with the fan to exercise such spite?

No. Adélaïde refused to believe it of her. That kind of attack reeked of a man's cruelty. A woman would be more subtle.

"What will you do?" André's voice called her out of her thoughts.

"I don't know yet. Perhaps I shall go to the courts."

"Are you certain you want the attention legal proceedings might bring? You lack standing, as a common woman separated from a husband. I am powerless to act on your behalf, legally and morally. One word from me, and you know what they'll say."

"I know. I'm not asking for your help. But I have to do something for my sake and the sake of my students."

There was only one person she could turn to who would be able to advise her. She would understand that no woman could rehabilitate her honor on her own.

She would write to her first, give her time to think about what to do. Although the comtesse had complained to Adélaïde that she had little influence over her husband's decisions and the comte himself would have to support any investigation into the matter, Madame d'Angiviller was her only option.

It might not work, Adélaïde thought. She could be made a laughing stock for reacting so extremely to a bit of drivel. But something told her it would be a mistake to let this matter fade away on its own. Whether or not it was Nicolas, whoever had written the pamphlet would be made to see that she had friends in high places and was not to be trifled with.

ⲥⲉꜟ

Adélaïde took three days to compose her letter to the comtesse. She realized she couldn't simply appeal to her because the insinuations were false. She had to word her letter in a manner that would not only arouse her sympathy but would encourage her to rally her own forces and connections to help Adélaïde take action. She appealed to the comtesse's belief in the sanctity of family, the sentiments she had adopted in her salons, where the writings of Jean-Jacques Rousseau were often the subject of discussion. Adélaïde herself did not agree with Rousseau that women belonged only in the private sphere, that they were useful only insofar as they contributed to the comfort of the home and their children. Nonetheless, his writings had recently encouraged Paris society to at least outwardly value their families more.

Not satisfied that her own appeal would be enough, Adélaïde decided she needed to add another voice her aristocratic friend would respect. She paid a visit to the actor Ducis and told him of her plans. As a man of the theater, he was well aware of the delicate balance women who dared to be artists had to maintain, of the necessity that they be as morally spotless as possible or risk being considered base harlots. Exhibiting paintings wasn't quite as bad as strutting on a stage, though, since the practice of the art took place mostly in private. But that didn't change anything.

Ducis readily agreed to help her and penned his own letter to the comtesse that very day.

$$\sim$$

The Comtesse d'Angiviller came to see Adélaïde in her apartment the morning after she received the two letters. Her expression was serious, and at first Adélaïde worried that she had overstepped the bounds of friendship in asking for her assistance. Once she had served her a cup of tea and the two of them sat in front of the long window that looked out onto the street, Adélaïde said, "I hope you forgive me. I could think of no one else to ask for assistance. I want the police to investigate, to discover the name of the author and the printer, so that I can charge them with slander."

"Madame Guiard—Adélaïde, if I may be so familiar. Are you certain you wish to take such a drastic measure? Of course I will support you in any way I can and intercede with my husband to encourage him to write to Lieutenant Lenoir so that an inquiry can begin. But do you realize what you are doing by elevating this matter to the level that will increase rather than diminish the public's attention to it?"

"Would you ask that of a man in my position? A man whose character had been impugned by lies?"

She shook her head. "But, as you know, being right isn't always enough for a woman."

"Of course. That's why I need support from those with more power and standing than I have. Will you help me? How else am I to go forward? Not just my reputation, but my livelihood depends on it. Could you imagine any young women coming to study painting with me if she or her family thought I was a shameless slut?"

"I will help you all I can but be prepared to discover that there is little I can do."

Adélaïde knew her efforts might prove unsuccessful but just having the comtesse's backing would mean something, even if whoever had produced the pamphlet was never discovered. "It will be more than I am capable of on my own, and that is enough."

"Let's start with what we know," Madame d'Angiviller said. "Do you have any idea who could have written this? Is there someone with anything to gain by destroying your reputation?"

Adélaïde hesitated. How much did she want to tell the comtesse? If they went after Nicolas directly and he wasn't the perpetrator, they'd be poking a sleeping lion. And of course, there was always the possibility that Gallimard had instigated it, even if he didn't actually execute it. "I have a few suspicions, but I don't want to pursue them until I'm more certain. However, André—Monsieur Vincent—has a notion who might have printed it, and by that means we may be able to get to the author."

"Very well. I shall write to Lenoir and ensure that my husband does as well." The comtesse stood. Adélaïde brought her shawl from where she'd hung it among her students' smocks—a gaudy splash of scarlet and gold amid the dun-colored linen. After she'd wrapped it around herself and pulled on her gloves, the comtesse said, "You do not deserve this slander, of that I am certain."

Sixteen

A délaïde's second Académie salon was just a few months away, and still, after nearly two years, the police hadn't managed to discover the author of the slanderous pamphlet. Adélaïde suspected that they had lost interest quickly after identifying the printer, who would not incriminate his customer. The printer was not deemed culpable and so was not punished in any way. When Adélaïde asked why he didn't at least have to pay a fine, Lenoir told her he could not be held liable for the content of what he printed. They'd confiscated all the copies of the pamphlet they could find and destroyed them. But how many had already made their way into people's hands, Adélaïde wondered.

There'd been no more slander since then, at least. And the actions of powerful people, who stood by her, had prevented any mass exodus from her studio and assured no loss of portrait commissions. She might not have been able to prove who penned those words, but she hoped she and the comtesse had done enough to discourage whoever it was from trying again. So much was at stake this time. The glow of her salon debut had faded. She and Madame Le Brun would no longer be given the benefit of the doubt, the soft touch because they were new. Both of them would have a lot to prove this time. And Adélaïde had decided to be bold, to dare. She still found herself struggling to pay her bills, even with a full studio and numerous commissions. Perhaps that was because despite her improved standing, she didn't dare ask more than five hundred livres for a pastel portrait and eight hundred for an oil. Madame Le Brun charged upwards of five thousand, apparently at her art-dealer husband's insistence. When she first heard of it, Adélaïde was certain her rival would lose commissions and that she herself would be the beneficiary as people flocked to her. But that didn't happen. If anything, Madame Le Brun was busier than ever, and Adélaïde had gained very few new commissions. That would have to change. She would see to it, with this self-portrait.

Standing back and gazing at the unfinished oil painting gave Adélaïde an odd, disassociated feeling, as if she had magically divided herself into two people: the working artist who stood solidly alive in her homespun dress and paint-splattered smock, and the elegant, life-size creature that had somehow been conjured up with brush strokes and pigments, fixed to a canvas that occupied an easel in André's studio. She had had to work on the self-portrait at the Louvre because her own studio wasn't big enough for such a large canvas—five feet wide by seven feet tall—at least, not as well as accommodating all her students. In the portrait, she had placed herself seated in front of an easel that had its back to the viewer, angled in the picture plane to reveal the curling edges beyond the stretchers and plain wooden supports, indicating that she was at work on a picture much like the one of which she was the subject. Adélaïde had decided to depict herself looking boldly out at the viewer, as if whoever stood in front of the painting at any time might be the subject of the painting she was working on in that imaginary setting. It was a dare. No coyness, no hiding who and what she was. Adélaïde was both painter and painted. The subject and the object. She wanted to show the world that she was not afraid, that no cowardly slanderer could disrupt her climb in the art world. It was a painterly jest with an edge: viewers who looked carefully would feel her eyes absorbing the contours of their faces, the textures of their clothing. Who was she painting? They'd never know. The strokes of her static brush would remain permanently out of sight.

Of course, rather than the homespun dress and paint-stained

smock she now wore as she prepared to continue her work that day, the Adélaïde in the picture was dressed in a gown of pale blue satin with wide lace at the décolletage and sleeves, and trimmed with flouncing silk bows. Her feather-bedecked straw hat would have been suitable for a garden party. To wear it inside a studio full of pigments and oils and still-wet canvases would have been to court disaster.

Although every detail of her own figure was complete—the sheen of the satin cascading in folds from her lap to the floor, catching the light and creating drapes of shadows, her palette and mahlstick in one hand, a paintbrush in the other—the background was still unfinished, only the dead layer and some contours sketched in. Just three months until it had to be ready. She had been working on this painting for six months already. Although not her first oil portrait, it would be the first oil portrait she exhibited in a biennial salon.

While Adélaïde waited for Gabrielle and Marguerite to change behind the folding screen into the simple brown dresses with gauzy fichus she'd had made for them and to ensure that their hair was tied up in modest turbans to keep the hair from falling forward and obscuring their faces, she thought about everything that had happened in the two years since the last salon. The Comtesse d'Angiviller had been true to her word, introducing her and recommending her to the aristocrats who attended her gatherings and persuading them that they could do no better than to commission a portrait from the brilliant lady academician. The scandal of the scurrilous pamphlet had faded, even though it still niggled at the edges of Adélaïde's mind. She fervently believed that if she hadn't persuaded the comtesse to help her get the police involved, the damage it would have done might have set her back years in her career.

And Nicolas had remained quiet too. He did not frequent the same cafes as she did, and she never saw him at the theater or the opera.

That had been something else the comtesse had insisted upon. She sent her own carriage once a month to transport Adélaïde to whichever performance was the most popular in Paris at that moment so that she would be seen—and seen to be occupying the comtesse's own box. Of course, Adélaïde invariably went without André. While unmarried liaisons were tolerated among the nobility and aristocracy, a lady artist had to be seen to be virtuous in public, if not in private.

"Where shall we stand?" Marguerite asked, startling Adélaïde out of her reverie as she and Gabrielle emerged from behind the screen.

"Behind me, behind my chair, watching me work." The velvet and gilt chair where she herself had sat now stood empty on a raised platform, like a prop on a stage. Her two best students placed themselves there, leaning on the chair back. Gabrielle, who was shorter, was in the foreground.

"Will this do?" Marguerite said, looking out past Gabrielle's face in profile, her fine features and soft eyes gazing at Adélaïde.

"Yes!" Adélaïde said. "Only don't move, Marguerite. Keep looking toward me."

The composition was perfect. If this painting couldn't gain her a royal appointment, she didn't know what would. The comtesse had been working on that as well, trying to find the most suitable member of the royal family who would be open to such a suggestion. It would have to be a woman, of course. In the meantime, Madame Le Brun had painted pictures of almost all of Marie Antoinette's ladies and several of the queen herself.

The two rivals had not encountered each other since the previous salon. Adélaïde heard that Madame Le Brun had ceased going out very much, that she had become ill with exhaustion from her social schedule combined with the unceasing demand for her portraits. When she recovered, instead of going to concerts and salons, she began hosting her own soirées, which soon became the most popular in Paris. *Let her*, Adélaïde thought. *Let her play the coquette and flaunt her beauty.* Adélaïde knew she couldn't compete in that realm, which absolved her from trying. Where she could more than compete was on canvas.

Both Adélaïde's submissions this time were oils—her self-portrait and the portrait of Van Loo. Newly elected academicians were expected to paint a portrait of one of the officers in the Académie to be hung on the wall of the gallery where they held their meetings. Adélaïde could have chosen any of them, but her reason for settling on Van Loo was because, of all the famous history painters in the Académie, Van Loo was the only one who included women in his paintings as central participants rather than decorative accessories to aggrandize the deeds of men. And André had assured her that the elderly artist admired her work and would welcome the attention. Still, she wasn't certain he'd agree and was pleasantly surprised when he did.

∽

Adélaïde met André in his studio the afternoon of the opening, two years almost to the hour after her first Académie salon.

"You have no need to be nervous," he said, pouring her a glass of champagne.

"I'm not nervous, exactly. Just anticipating." But her heart flipped over and jumped in her breast, a kitten chasing a feather. Of course she was nervous. So much hinged on this second salon.

When they entered the gallery by a side door, avoiding the crowded stairway from the street, Adélaïde said, "I'll let you go on ahead so you can react without me looking over your shoulder." And also, she thought, so that they wouldn't immediately be seen as a single artistic unit and fuel the gossip that André was more than simply her muse and lover.

André nodded and pushed through the crowds, leaving her behind. She hadn't allowed him to see the self-portrait while she worked on it in his studio, making sure it was angled away from him if they were both painting at the same time and securely covered when she wasn't there. Of course, he might have peeked under the cover, but she didn't think he would. He was more a man of his word than anyone she'd ever known. Her eyes followed him now, as he approached the large self-portrait, perfectly placed at the level just above the heads of the crowd. He stopped and gazed at it a long time and then walked on. Others took his place, heads together, talking and pointing, yet she hadn't seen him react to it in any obvious way. *Could it be that he doesn't like it?*

They had planned to meet after each of them had toured the galleries, but Adélaïde couldn't stand the wait any longer and rushed to join him, squeezing by other visitors who had stopped in clumps here and there to scrutinize the artworks. She had worn the same dress as in her self-portrait, although in deference to the crowds had chosen a less voluminous hat. The silk whispered against the floor as she hurried along, bunching the skirts in front of her to make herself as narrow as possible.

André had his back to her when she reached him. She drew close enough to murmur into his ear, "Tell me. I can take your criticism, only I have to know. Did you hate the self-portrait?" She worded her question in a way that would allow him to say he didn't hate it but also so that he would be free to temper any praise, if that's what he wanted to do.

André turned to her, eyes shining above his smile. "I knew you were talented. I just didn't know how far that talent would take you. I am in awe."

She wanted to throw her arms around his neck and kiss him, but of course, that would be unseemly in such a place. "Coming to oil painting so late, I had to do something grand," she said. "Whatever I showed at this salon, it had to justify my admittance, establish me as a serious portraitist, not just a fashionable dabbler. Don't protest, you know it did."

André drew closer to her, taking advantage of the press of the crowd to disguise their intimacy. He leaned in and whispered into her ear, "You need no justification. You are an artist of the first rank."

She wished with all her heart she could believe his words. But she knew better. "Well, let's see tomorrow what the rest of the world thinks of the painting," Adélaïde said.

"Shall we go around quickly?" André said. "I want to take you back to my studio."

Adélaïde knew that what he really meant was he wanted to take her *in* his studio. She smiled for the next hour as they battled the crowds to get through the exhibition with as much speed as possible.

⌒ℰ⌒

They'd stayed the night at the Louvre, as was their occasional practice. The subterfuge of late-night and early-morning comings and goings seemed unnecessary now that everyone in the artist community knew full well that they were a settled couple. Even the general public could no longer be deceived about their relationship, thanks to the publicity around the pamphlet. In the morning, André went out in search of copies of the *Mercure de France* and whatever pamphlets he could find to see what the critics thought of the self-portrait, leaving Adélaïde to stew and fret. When she heard the tap-tapping of his approach along the hallway, she ran to sit down again at the breakfast table, picking up a crust of bread and pulling it apart. She didn't turn to look at him when he came in.

"You'd better read them," he said as he walked over to join her and handed her the papers, folded to the reviews. Did he mean they were terrible? She couldn't always tell with André. But when she caught the twitch in the corner of his mouth, she knew he was teasing her, and she read, and read, and read.

The reviews were beyond enthusiastic. Adélaïde hugged herself as she walked back and forth in front of the windows in André's lodgings, closed against a dreary late-summer rain. *Vigorous. Strong. Sure.* Those words had been uttered by men of taste and judgment about her work, her self-portrait. One had even used the word *masterpiece.*

Those were not adjectives they applied to Madame Le Brun's elegant portraits, of which there were numerous entries in the salon that year. Her portraits beguiled, to be sure, and her technique was deft, effortless. But the male arbiters of artistic taste persisted in finding her work a little too soft and feminine, as if that in itself were a criticism.

Yet much as Adélaïde wanted to dislike her rival's portraits, she had to admit they captured the expression and essence of the sitters and then made the best of what was there. A dewy-eyed optimism overlay each one, as if the painter were determined to ferret out the good in everything and everyone. Even the supercilious Comte de Vaudreuil exuded approachability in her portrait of him. Of course, the rumors that they were lovers could explain that.

Whatever it was that Madame Le Brun did, it was continuing to make her rich. She had no students so all her prosperity must come from the portraits. That, and her husband's commerce in art.

Her husband. The word had such a complicated resonance for Adélaïde. Nicolas was still her husband, despite the papers that had legally separated their finances and their domestic arrangements six years ago. Adélaïde was afraid that, having failed to discredit her with the anonymous slander—which she still wasn't certain he had anything to do with—Nicolas would look for other ways to torment her. She feared that her newly acquired renown would make her estranged husband believe she was truly wealthy, and he would try to extort money from her again—not because he needed it, but because he wanted to. All this anxiety made her dread her increasing fame—even as she longed for it desperately.

"Aren't you pleased?" André said when she handed him back the newspapers.

She forced herself to smile. "Yes, of course. But that picture cost me a great deal of money in paint, canvas, and time. We shall see if it was a good investment. I must take advantage of this reaction to it and seize the moment to make more money, paint more portraits, teach more students."

"How can you accommodate more students? Your atelier is already crowded."

True enough, she thought. "I've had requests. With Paulette off and married, I have room for at least one more." Paulette had left off modeling and started to sell her pretty pictures in shops. It was there that she met Denis, a respectable young clerk in a lawyer's firm. He courted her, and they married. The last time Paulette came to the studio she was pregnant. Adélaïde was delighted for her, yet hoped her first student would not give up her painting so she had something to fall back on if her marriage ever went sour.

She shook the thought out of her head. Tomorrow, the Comtesse d'Angiviller had asked her to call, saying she had some interesting news for her. She hoped her patroness had managed to line up more aristocrats eager to sit for her. Whatever it was, she owed the comtesse a great deal and would never dream of declining an invitation.

Seventeen

It was a short walk to the Comtesse d'Angiviller's *hôtel particulier*, but Adélaïde knew better than to arrive on foot. To do so risked the disdain of the comtesse's servants and the likelihood that she would be ushered in through the back door instead of the grand entrance off the courtyard. Although it didn't matter to Adélaïde, the comtesse had taken her to task for it once, and Adélaïde had spent the money to hire a carriage for every visit since then.

The footman led Adélaïde into the comtesse's boudoir, where she sat at a dressing table with her maid arranging her hair. Adélaïde curtsied.

The comtesse didn't turn to look at her. "My dear! Do sit down. I have an appointment in half an hour so I must let Hortense continue wrestling with my coiffure or I will be late."

Adélaïde perched on an upholstered tabouret, her eyes following the deft movements of the maid as she back-combed hair, added a woolen pouf, and rolled curls around her fingers and pinned them in place.

"You must be wondering what I have to say to you. I didn't want to mention it until after the salon opening in case it distracted you. But at last, I have done it." She looked over her shoulder at Adélaïde, a smile of triumph on her face. "I have secured you a royal appointment."

It took a moment for Adélaïde to digest this announcement. A royal appointment. It's what she'd been hoping for from before the first Académie salon. This could secure her livelihood for a long time to come. What might the appointment be? Would protocol be dispensed with so that she could be portraitist to one of the king's brothers, the Comte de Provence, or the Comte d'Artois, perhaps? Unlikely. More probably it would be one of their wives.

"That will do, Marie," the comtesse said to her maid, who curtsied and left after dusting the coiffure with lavender-tinted powder. When Madame d'Angiviller stood, Adélaïde stood as well. Although they'd become accustomed to informality in Adélaïde's studio, in the comtesse's own surroundings Adélaïde always observed strict etiquette. Her father might not have attended to much of her education, but he did ensure she was versed in court protocol, in case she ever encountered any of his noble clientele.

"I have arranged it, but it's up to you to make something of it." The comtesse lifted Adélaïde's chin with her index finger and smiled. "Tomorrow it will be announced that you are henceforth to be known as first portraitist to Mesdames de France."

Mesdames. The king's elderly aunts. They didn't even live at Versailles.
"Thank you, Madame," Adélaïde said, and curtsied. "It is indeed a great honor." She did her best to swallow down her disappointment. It wasn't her habit to obsess over the ins and outs of court life. However, she knew that the two princesses—Madame Adélaïde and Madame Victoire—had lost much of their influence over the court when Marie Antoinette arrived, and that they were far removed from the inner circle despite their close family relation. They were the only two remaining of Louis XV's eight daughters, and they lived in their own chateau at Bellevue. "Is there a stipend, Madame?" Adélaïde asked.

"No stipend, but Mesdames assured me that they will very soon be commissioning large oil portraits from you, for which you will be handsomely paid."

The trouble with painting large oil portraits, Adélaïde thought as she walked back to her studio from the comtesse's house, was that she first had to purchase all the costly materials required to execute them and then would not be paid until some time after the portraits were finished. It wouldn't matter so much if she were already being paid thousands for her other portraits. But despite André's entreaties that she raise her fee for an oil portrait to at least a thousand, she'd resisted doing so out of fear. Her renown had grown, and she'd been pleased when the American Thomas Jefferson visited her studio and purchased a pastel, but he'd paid a mere two hundred livres for it.

The commission would, though, give her the excuse she was looking for to command higher fees. And it would perhaps attract more students. She had been working toward this honor for years. But now, realizing that it did little to change her life in any material way—at least at the beginning—was like awakening from a hazy dream and finding yourself with the blankets off and the window wide open.

Added to that was the fact that the comtesse had told her she was expected to go to Bellevue in two days and present herself to Mesdames. She would have to adhere to strict court etiquette, which meant a court gown at the very least and the hiring of an expensive carriage for the journey. And through it all, she had to pretend this appointment was the answer to her prayers.

cℯↄ

She was still feeling cheated of a true win when she walked from her apartment on the Rue de Richelieu to the Louvre after changing out of her elegant clothes, supposedly to work on a canvas she'd left in André's studio—something she often did even with her smaller canvases nowadays because she didn't have room in her over-full studio. But what she really wanted to do was to complain to André, whom she knew would listen to her patiently until she'd talked herself around to a better mood.

That day, it took Adélaïde an hour of spouting off about how unfair it all was before she could reach something that approached a sanguine state of mind. When at last she did so, she fell into silence and just watched her lover work. He picked up his palette and stood in front of his painting in progress, narrowing his eyes. Although she often worked side by side with him, she rarely simply stared at him. In doing so now, she noticed that he squinted at times and came quite close to the canvas when he was painting details. It seemed that his eyesight was weakening; she hoped it was not failing. That would be the most terrible fate for a painter. What would happen if he could no longer see? He wouldn't even be able to teach in that case. Perhaps she was making more of it than his deteriorating eyesight warranted. But still, would her work be able to support him if it came to pass that he had to stop painting?

The answer was not unless Mesdames commissioned her soon and often. She teetered on the brink of financial ruin as it was, her expenses continually rising to match her income. If only she could find a way to lower her expenses until that time.

Perhaps there was. "*Mon cher*, how did it come about that you were granted accommodations in the Louvre?" To have the privilege of free tenancy in the disused, unfinished palace would at once eliminate the necessity of paying two rents—for her apartment and her studio.

André shrugged. "I asked. It's what academicians do, I suppose."

"Who did you ask?"

He paused and rested the wooden tip of his brush against his lower lip. "I think Monsieur Pierre. No! It was Angiviller. Why?"

"I was simply curious." Adélaïde decided not to say anything about it to him just yet. She was reluctant to tell André about any effort whose success was uncertain. The fewer people who knew she tried, the fewer there would be who could see her as a failure.

And she assumed that Angiviller would turn her down for certain if she approached him directly. But now, thanks to his wife, she had another avenue to try. And she would make sure she paved the way the day after next when she visited Mesdames in Bellevue for the first time.

cℯↄ

Adélaïde composed a letter to Madame Adélaïde, the one—so the comtesse had told her—who had really decided on Adélaïde as their portraitist. Her animosity toward Marie Antoinette was how the comtesse had persuaded her that honoring the principal rival of the queen's portraitist would be both satisfying and appropriate. But of course, this fact would never be mentioned. Adélaïde knew full well that she could not bring up the names Marie Antoinette or Elisabeth Vigée Le Brun in front of Mesdames, at least not yet.

She read and reread her letter, intending to deliver it by hand tomorrow, afraid she would not be brave or brazen enough to broach the subject in conversation. But nothing she wrote felt right. She kept scratching out words, making it more polite, then more direct, then crumpling it up and tossing it on the floor and starting all over again. It all seemed so pathetic that she should have to beg for something seen as a right by the male academicians.

How did people do it, petition for favors? Everything Adélaïde had achieved in her life had been through the effort of her own heart, mind, and hands, not bestowed upon her from on high. Was it any different for Madame Le Brun? As a married woman with a child and a thriving clientele, she did not need free accommodations. Would she have demanded them if she had been in Adélaïde's position?

The whole exercise left a bad taste in Adélaïde's mouth. Yet what choice did she have? It seemed no matter how hard she tried, how true and uncompromising her work, fate placed obstacles in her way and forced her to take steps someone like André would never consider. Petitioning Mesdames for Louvre accommodations might seem of little consequence to people accustomed to the intrigues of court, those who knew how the game was played. But having to do so went against everything Adélaïde thought she believed. It should be merit, not connections, that secured her preferment. That, Adélaïde was fully aware, was a fantasy, and if she were going to fulfill her true destiny as an artist, she would have to put her principles aside occasionally.

⌒⌒

Bellevue, March 1786

Why was it that, just as you think you've reached a pinnacle of accomplishment, you see beyond it a taller peak, where you're sure something more beguiling awaits if only you could climb to *that* height? Adélaïde couldn't help wondering this as she found herself in her most elegant satin ensemble seated in a hired carriage on her way to Bellevue to accept her appointment and to make her case for accommodations in the Louvre.

After writing and rewriting just what she would say, Adélaïde had a sudden inspiration that she could persuade Madame Adélaïde to act by pointing out that no other woman had ever been granted such a privilege. Without ever mentioning either Marie Antoinette or Madame Le Brun, she would be letting her know that interceding on her portraitist's behalf with the king concerning the Louvre accommodations would demonstrate that they still had more influence at court than the queen. It was a gamble. And Adélaïde was by no means confident it would work.

By the time the carriage drove through the ornate gates that marked the entry to the grounds of the palace of Bellevue in Meudon, Adélaïde was in a frightful state of anxiety and wished she could simply turn back and come again another day, when she was more prepared. But Mesdames were expecting her. She took slow, careful breaths and smoothed her skirt before looking out the carriage window as it passed into the gardens that surrounded the chateau.

Adélaïde had expected something like the regimented, geometric gardens of Versailles, where commoners could roam and marvel at the precision of the landscaping, the straight paths angling through perfectly manicured flower beds and punctuated with effusive fountains. She had been there as a girl. But this garden was nothing like that. If she hadn't known better, Adélaïde would have thought she had entered the enclave of wood nymphs who had tamed a forest to remain wild and cultivated at the same time. Sculptures of mythical creatures and forest dwellers were hidden at first until the carriage rounded a curve on the drive that revealed them. They were so perfectly integrated with their surroundings that they might have grown up from the ground without the aid of a human hand. And the colors—shades of pale, spring green with bursts of flowering shrubs filtered the sunlight, dappling the ground. It was magical. If coming to Bellevue meant being able to get a glimpse of such an extraordinary place, she would never hesitate again.

The main chateau itself was of modest proportions, not too intimidating, although it was flanked by added buildings that doubled its size. Adélaïde reminded herself of what the comtesse had told her: within its walls, strict etiquette was observed by all. She went over the correct modes of address as she waited for the footman in royal livery to make his stately way down the stairs from the front entrance. Would he even know who she was? Would he admit her? She was no one. No one of rank, anyway. Just a servant herself, in reality.

"Madame Guiard?" the footman said when he opened the carriage door and helped her down the steps.

She nodded, and he gave her a slight bow—exactly calculated to acknowledge her precise position in relation to himself and his employers. Adélaïde followed him into the chateau and soon found herself in Madame Adélaïde's private parlor, where the king's aunt awaited her seated on a fauteuil that might as well have been a throne.

"Madame," Adélaïde said, and curtsied as low as her knees would permit, praying she wouldn't topple over.

"I am pleased to welcome you as our *premier peintre*. Please, rise."

Adélaïde gave her brief speech of thanks, saying what an honor it was that Mesdames had placed their trust in her and how she was looking forward to painting their portraits. "When may I be given that honor?" *Please let it be soon*, Adélaïde thought.

"My sister and I would prefer to wait until we are better acquainted with your work. I understand you are a pastellist? We would prefer our portraits to be on canvas."

Oh no, Adélaïde thought. "Madame, although I am more well known for my pastels, I have executed several oil portraits—including a self-portrait with two of my students that received high accolades in the salon last August." This was not what Adélaïde had hoped for. She'd assumed it had been those oil portraits that had, at least in part, inspired Mesdames to offer her the position.

"I see." Madame Adélaïde paused for a while, her face blank. Adélaïde was afraid she was supposed to say something, but she didn't know what. Just as she was about to open her mouth to compliment the king's aunt on her beautiful gardens, the princess spoke again. "I should like to see that portrait before agreeing to my first sitting. We shall be in Paris in September. I will have my equerry arrange a viewing."

September! Adélaïde thought. Her position didn't come with a stipend. It was considered a lucrative honor in itself. But to reap those benefits, Adélaïde needed a portrait of one of them to prove her mettle. If they wanted to wait until September, she would see no payment for any portrait until the end of the year, because payment was only rendered on completion. She might be destitute by then or at least on the brink of defaulting on her rent. The Louvre accommodations suddenly became not only desirable, but essential. "Madame, if I may be so bold, I have a request to make that the Comtesse d'Angiviller assures me would be well received by you and that would help me a great deal as I pursue my art."

Madame Adélaïde raised one eyebrow and pursed her lips. "You may speak."

In as few words as possible, and with great attention to the manner of her request, Adélaïde explained how being afforded accommodations in the Louvre would both ease her financial situation as well as place her in a position of greater respect.

"And you say, this is the custom for most academicians?"

Adélaïde was surprised that the princess was unaware of the arrangement, but then, she had to remind herself, artists were generally beneath the notice of royalty. "Yes, it appears so, Madame."

"Tell me, has any other lady ever had such an honor bestowed upon her?"

"No, Madame." And, Adélaïde thought, how dare she ask to be the first. In such a tradition-bound setting as Bellevue, Adélaïde thought for certain that single fact would put an end to the possibility and prepared herself for disappointment.

"Very well. I shall put it to my nephew that he must grant you accommodations in the Louvre."

Adélaïde could hardly believe it. "I'm deeply grateful, Madame," she said, sweeping down in a curtsy once again. Was it really so easy? Surely the king would listen to his favorite aunt. It wasn't such an enormous favor to ask and involved very little expense on the part of the treasury.

On the way back to Paris, Adélaïde's hopes soon faded. There had been no mention of when Madame would speak to the king. Adélaïde's visit to Bellevue might turn out to have been an expense she could ill afford to no immediate purpose whatsoever. How did Madame Le Brun manage to be so affluent? She even possessed her own carriage and horses—an elegant calèche Adélaïde had seen her in one evening as she walked back to her apartment on the Rue de Richelieu from the Louvre. Adélaïde tried not to be envious. What was the point? In any case, ever since the affair of the fan at the 1783 salon, her rival had not been in the same place she was for even the briefest moment. She did not move in the same circles, even with Madame d'Angiviller's gentle encouragement to enter into society more. Adélaïde had no desire to spend money on the clothes she would need for such a life. And she hated the idea of the time it would all take, as well. Her days were fully occupied with painting and teaching. Everything she made from teaching and from commissions went to paying her apartment and studio rents, buying food, and purchasing canvas, pigments, oils, and brushes. She was an artist, first, foremost, and always.

But so was Madame Le Brun. How on earth did she manage to keep up a style of life that must cost her a fortune? The family's money didn't come from her husband, Adélaïde had heard. It was whispered that, were it not for his wife's endeavors, Pierre Le Brun's expensive tastes meant that his business would make no money at all and that Madame Le Brun supported the entire household. Of course, her highly successful portraits of the queen encouraged many noble-women and aristocrats to commission portraits of their own. Still, producing so many works would be exhausting—it must have been exhausting for Madame Le Brun. Adélaïde suspected that even if she were able to gain as many commissions, it would take her longer to complete them because of her teaching schedule and the simple fact that her style of painting was not as easy and effortless as Madame Le Brun's, who had had more opportunity to practice painting in oils and apparently no students to otherwise occupy her time.

Stop it! Adélaïde thought. What was the point of becoming obsessed with her rival's success? She could not complain, not with a royal appointment, the respect of some of the finest artists of the age, and a studio full of eager, accomplished students. And soon, perhaps, she would have the added honor—and money-saving convenience— of free accommodations in the Louvre.

With that, Adélaïde thought, she could give herself more time to paint and more time to do the necessary socializing to put herself in front of potential subjects. She sent a quick prayer up to whoever in heaven was listening and made the sign of the cross on her breast, just in case it would make any difference.

cℯↄ

Unfortunately, it was not to be. Madame Adélaïde turned out to be true to her word and apparently asked the king to award her portraitist accommodations in the Louvre the week after Adélaïde's visit. But as it happened, even Mesdames did not possess enough influence to overcome the Comte d'Angiviller's prejudice against women. Apparently, he persuaded the king that allowing not just Adélaïde but her female students to mingle with the men in the Louvre would be morally indefensible. The one consolation was that in lieu of the accommodations, the court granted her a pension of one thousand livres per annum. One thousand livres was less than a quarter of what Madame Le Brun commanded for a single portrait. It would make very little difference in Adélaïde's ability to pay her bills.

Nonetheless, she would have to write and thank Angiviller for the stipend. She supposed it was better than nothing. André would tell her it didn't matter. But in her heart, Adélaïde knew that her fortunes could reverse in a moment. Nicolas could return and extort more money from her. Another anonymous pamphlet could accuse her of immorality and unwomanly behavior and provoke an exodus from her studio. More rumors that André—and not she—had painted her best portraits could inhibit portrait commissions or lose her the prestige of her court appointment. Or André could tire of her and cast her aside, and she would lose both a lover and all her best friends with a single blow. She needed a cushion; she needed enough money to survive for a year at least with no other income and no one to surreptitiously supply her with pigments or give up his studio space so she could work. Her independence was illusory, Adélaïde knew. No matter how far she'd come, she had only the power over her own life that men were willing to give her.

That, and the talent she knew she possessed, even if not everyone who mattered was aware of it yet.

Eighteen

Paris, November 1786

The disappointment over not getting apartments in the Louvre was bad enough. Adélaïde scraped by for several months, pinching every centime she could and trying to put a little away in the jar hidden under the floorboards in her bedroom. She thought she could manage, until one early November day, when she entered her studio to teach, there were three empty easels.

Adélaïde took Gabrielle over to a corner and spoke to her quietly. "What happened? Where are Louise, Hortense, and Brigitte?"

"They sent word that they would no longer be coming for lessons," Gabrielle said, and then leaned and whispered into Adélaïde's ear, "Apparently they have been accepted into Madame Le Brun's studio."

"Since when does Madame Le Brun have a studio?" She said it a little too loudly, and the remaining students glanced up from their easels. It was well known that her rival had no desire to take students because of her busy schedule of portrait commissions.

Gabrielle cast a quick glance over her shoulder to make sure the others had resumed their work and said, "That is true enough. But her husband pressured her because they need the money. And apparently, rather than advertise in any way, she found out the names of your students and invited them to join her."

Madame Le Brun needs money? "How do you know this?" Adélaïde asked.

Gabrielle reached into her pocket and withdrew a folded note on elegant paper. "She invited me, too."

So, Adélaïde thought. Was this punishment for the affair of the fan three years ago? Why not sooner, then? Or, perhaps she really did need the money. Her extravagant lifestyle would be difficult to maintain. "Well, they were the least talented among you. There's that, at any rate."

"More students will come to replace them," Gabrielle said. "You're so well known now."

Yes, more students would come. But how soon? And would they pay in advance for the lessons, or would she have to wait for a few months? Adélaïde shook off her annoyance and commenced the lesson for the day with her remaining students, mentally trying to envision what Madame Le Brun's studio would be like. It would no doubt be more richly furnished than hers. But Adélaïde doubted the light could be any better.

⌒⌒

As she lay in bed that night, André twitching in some dream that came to him moments after he fell asleep, Adélaïde went over and over her financial situation. It was untenable. She had been barely managing even with a full complement of students. And now?

Like it or not, she only knew of one way to bridge the financial gap until such time as Mesdames gave her commissions that would bring her to the attention of those willing to pay much more. What she was thinking of doing had worked before, but she had placed herself at risk last time by involving an intermediary—an intermediary she thought she could trust but who very likely had informed Nicolas of what she was doing. This time, absolutely no one could find out that she was reentering the tenebrous world of erotica—not a single person outside of herself. She would work by candlelight, alone. She would use her own body as model—her own body, and her imagination. For this group of pictures, she had an idea: put a shadowy suggestion of a man in each one in order to make it easier for the viewer to imagine himself touching the model.

Touching. It sickened her to think that the body that would inspire such naked lust would be hers, that the eyes of men she might possibly detest would become intimately acquainted with her contours. But she was two months behind on the rent for her apartment, and she hadn't yet paid for all the pigments she'd had to use to paint her grand self-portrait. The merchant who supplied all the artists in Paris sent her bills nearly every day.

As Adélaïde made her plans, it crossed her mind that her father would be only too glad to give her more money. But he'd already done enough for her. He was old and ready to retire. He needed whatever he'd saved to support himself and Jacqueline in comfort. *It should be his daughter who supports him at this point*, Adélaïde thought. A daughter with a wealthy husband was probably what he had envisioned at one time. But her obstinacy had made that impossible. And here she was. Still, even though she couldn't imagine being able to give money to anyone other than her creditors, she wasn't sorry for the decisions she had made. Difficult as things were, she was happy to be with André, to have her students, to have her independence.

So, erotic pastels it would be. Yet how was it that she, who—aside from her liaison with André—had led as stainless a life as one could in that city, was driven to such extremes? And if such a circumstance had come to pass for her, with friends and a loving father, it was not hard to imagine what women with far fewer resources and talent might be pushed to do to ensure a dry place to sleep and food to fill an aching stomach. With nothing else, why not use one's only possession of value, one's body?

Although only in drawings, she was doing exactly the same thing. She was no different from those women who lingered in doorways outside the Louvre, hidden until the sun set and they could emerge in the half-light that masked the imperfections of their bodies or the sores on their faces, trading on the heedless desire of men with angry, dissatisfied wives to return to—or men who simply craved variety and didn't care who they hurt. She had no doubt Nicolas had availed himself of such pleasures and hoped he'd caught some pestilential disease to make him suffer for a long time. Perhaps he was unfaithful to his wealthy widow. The lady was older than he was, after all.

At least, Adélaïde thought with a chuckle, she could not become ill by selling pictures of her body.

All this passed through her mind on a chilly day a few weeks later as she taught her remaining students. Even Marguerite came less frequently, her weak condition worsening day by day. And no new students had yet come to take the place of the defectors.

"Madame, are you well?"

It was Victoire d'Avril, a student who had joined the studio a year ago and showed immense promise.

"Yes, I am quite well. Just preoccupied by thoughts of what I must do before the next salon."

And so they all continued. When they left, after everyone except Gabrielle had gone home, Adélaïde took a roll of blue paper and about twenty pastel crayons, put them in her satchel, and tucked a mahlstick under her arm.

"What will you do with those?" Gabrielle asked as she finished cleaning the brushes she'd been using for her latest oil painting, a grouping of students laughing and talking.

"I have a fancy to make a pastel of André while he is working. I don't know if it will amount to anything," she lied and wondered if Gabrielle noticed.

Of course, André was a problem. Most nights he spent in her apartment. She'd have to tell him that her courses had come early, and she wished to sleep alone—an excuse she resorted to when her head ached or she felt too oppressed to be loving. He never questioned her, even when the bleeding started as expected only a week or two later. Men were generally content to remain ignorant of such things. That bought her about five nights to herself, at least.

Oddly, Adélaïde's apartment, for all the financial burden it placed on her, had become her refuge. Much as she adored André, the solitude of her own space settled a calm over her heart she could find nowhere else. She often wondered why it was that she sought out solitude when her own childhood had been so lonely, watching her brothers and sisters die off one by one. Perhaps she was simply accustomed to seeking the comfort of solitude. In any case, she needed to be entirely alone with her mind and her body in order to cross the threshold of exposing herself to lascivious, unschooled eyes. Even though they were only pictures, she felt the violation as if a crowd of men stood there watching her as she worked.

The night she began her project, Adélaïde laid out the pastels, sliced the right sized piece of paper from the roll, fixed it to backing, and tacked it to the easel. Once everything was prepared and the mirror placed just right, she stripped off all her clothes. One unexpected benefit of using her own body as a model was that she didn't have to worry about making someone else, some young girl who might not understand all that it implied, pose in a way that would cause her embarrassment. It also meant that she had to do most of the pastels looking face on, although one—it took her a long time because she had to position the paper in an awkward place in order to manage it—she was able to draw facing away, leaning on her elbows with her breasts dangling down, legs splayed over the bed with the covers disheveled, so that the viewer would be gazing into the dark suggestion of what lay below the curve of her buttocks and between her legs.

And then, when five nights had passed and she'd completed five of the six pastels, all safely hidden in a drawer until such time as she found a buyer, she thought, *Why not? If men were so easily titillated, why not show them what a truly aroused woman looked like?*

Adélaïde sat on a chair facing the mirror, knees apart, with her fingers reaching down between her legs. She began to touch herself with her left hand, drawing on the paper with her right hand. She just needed to get the sense of it like this, imprint the look on her mind, and then she could complete the details later. Her hips tensed and her nipples hardened as she stroked herself, imagining André's fingers, his tongue, playing with her and driving her mad with desire. She watched and touched and drew, bringing herself slowly to climax, reaching the moment at which her eyes glazed over with ecstasy and her lips parted, her fingers massaging and driving waves of pleasure through her body so that she gripped the crayon in her other hand and cried out into her empty apartment. It was hard to stop, to return to the business of recording it all—her expression, her tension, the lightly glistening wetness between her legs. It took a full evening of climaxing again and again to capture what she wanted. By the end, when she had the image she wanted, she found that even touching the soft pastels and blending them on the picture sent a shiver into those same places, as if she had transferred her soul to that roughened blue paper.

This, too, was a masterpiece. Adélaïde knew it when she saw the finished drawing—a masterpiece very few eyes would ever gaze upon and that would never see the light of day. If circumstances were different, she would have given the pastel to André. It was really only suitable for his eyes. But she had to let go of that thought and accept that other eyes would enjoy the picture instead—at a price. Five thousand livres. She would not take less for the set. To make such a huge risk worthwhile, the sale would solve all her financial worries or it would have been for nothing.

Now all that remained was to find a buyer without letting anyone know the identity of the artist—or the model.

⟳

To avoid using Gallimard or any other intermediary, Adélaïde placed a small, cryptically worded advertisement in the *Mercure de France*, indicating that an answer by the same method would suffice to arrange a transaction and encoding the amount of money the purchaser would be expected to pay, saying the knowledge gained would be commensurate to reading five thousand books—*cinq-mille livres*. She had no idea if anyone reading the advertisement would understand the message, but it was all she could think of to do.

To her surprise, a week after the advertisement appeared, a cryptic answer in the same paper indicated to Adélaïde that she had found a buyer. The exchange was to take place late at night, halfway to Versailles. Adélaïde hired a carriage and wore a heavy veil to hide her face and covered all of her body with dark clothes. She had no desire to see the person who purchased the drawings from her.

At the appointed rendezvous location, the driver of her carriage pulled up his horses, and they waited. No one was about. The silence was broken only by the occasional snort and stamp of the two horses harnessed to the carriage, eager to return to a stable on this cold night. So when Adélaïde heard the approach of another carriage from the opposite direction, she knew instantly that it must be her buyer. She'd taken the precaution of hiring a particularly burly driver who might act as a defender if need be, but she hoped the transaction would take place so quickly there would be no time for mischief.

The drivers navigated the carriages abreast so that the pastels and the money could be handed across quickly without either of their occupants having to descend. Adélaïde was too curious not to peek out of the curtains that covered the windows of her hired vehicle, and spotted a crest she didn't recognize on the door. A minor noble, perhaps. It would have to be someone wealthy.

The window opposite hers in the other carriage lowered. "May I see the merchandise?" The voice was cultivated, businesslike.

Adélaïde didn't dare speak. She had no intention of revealing her

sex to the purchaser. But here was a circumstance she hadn't anticipated. She didn't want to let her work out of her sight until the money
was secure. She extended a gloved hand, palm open, hoping the man
would understand.

"How can I know I am getting the full value without seeing what I
purchase?"

This was going worse than she hoped. It would take very little for
her identity to be discovered, and then all would be lost. Heart racing,
she knocked on the roof of the hired carriage. Better to leave and find
another buyer. She would have wasted the money on the carriage, but
it wasn't worth the risk to do anything else.

As the driver clucked his horse to a walk, the voice from inside the
other carriage called out, "Wait!"

Adélaïde knocked again, and her driver pulled his horse up. By
now her heart was pounding into her ears, drowning out and at the
same time magnifying all the night sounds—the wind, the distant cry
of a night bird. She felt certain this man who was willing to come out
after midnight to purchase pornographic images could hear it all the
way in his own carriage.

"Let me look at one of them."

She heard coins jangling, and a hand held out a small leather
pouch. She took it quickly, and reached in to feel the weight and size
of the coins. *Louis d'Or.* Of course. How else to carry so much money
but in large increments? This was only a small portion of the payment
she expected, but the man took a risk by giving even that much to her
without the drawings in his possession.

Taking great care not to spoil the other pastels, Adélaïde teased one
out of the portfolio, glancing at it on the way, seeing herself exposed
and wishing, all at once, that she could just leave. But she'd gone too
far for that.

The gentleman took it carefully, as though he understood how to
handle delicate pastels. *A connoisseur,* she thought. At least there was

that. He angled it toward the window to catch the moonlight. She heard him breathe, "*Magnifique.*"

The pastel disappeared inside the coach, and a moment later, someone descended from the opposite door and walked around to the other side of Adélaïde's carriage, the side that cast a moon shadow and would have hidden anything from her view. *Another man.* It wasn't until then that Adélaïde realized how vulnerable she was. If there were two men and a driver in the other vehicle, she could be overpowered, robbed, or worse. She quickly latched both her carriage doors shut so they could not be opened from the outside, not knowing if that would prevent anything, and waited, listening to the soft crunch of shoes on packed, gravelly dirt passing behind her and to her left. She caught a glimpse of someone in opulent livery, wigged, carrying a valise. The valise was too large to fit through the window opening. She would have to open the door.

Adélaïde coiled herself from her middle like a spring that would jump into action at the press of a lever. She grasped the portfolio with the pastels in her right hand, put her left hand on the door latch, pulling it toward her in case the man on the outside opened it as he approached. Her hands were sweating inside her gloves. She swung the door open quickly, handed the portfolio to the footman and grabbed the handle of the valise, pulled it inside and slammed the carriage door shut so fast she nearly slid off the seat, then rapped on the roof and kept rapping until the driver whipped his horses to a canter. As she left, she heard a voice behind her say, "*C'était une dame, Monsieur le Comte.*"

Adélaïde wished she could have seen the crest on the carriage well enough to figure out whose it was. But it was too late now. *Well,* she thought, settling herself in the seat of her hired carriage and trying to still the rapid beating of her heart, *that's one way to break into high society.* And then she started to laugh and was still laughing when she surprised the coachman when they returned to her apartment by pressing a Louis d'Or into his outstretched hand.

Nineteen

It seemed odd to Adélaïde that on this day, like every other, the world was still waking up. Outside, as she walked from her apartment to the studio, the letter from Marguerite's sister clutched in her pocket, everything felt louder, harsher, more insistent. She wanted to tell the crows not to caw and the merchants with their barrows not to call out so insistently. Didn't they know? Of course not. And now she would have to tell Gabrielle, who had left the apartment just after dawn to open the studio for what she thought would be a normal day of instruction and painting.

Never had the stairs up to her bright new work space, the larger studio with its skylights and northern exposure she had rented on the Rue Ménars, felt so long and difficult to climb. And yet, she didn't want to reach the top. Because then, once Gabrielle knew, it would be real, an unavoidable fact.

As soon as Adélaïde entered, Gabrielle looked up from where she had been laying out the materials for the morning of teaching, everything in order with a dozen easels set up for all the students, a question in her eyes. What was it about her steps, her expression, that gave it away?

"Leave that, Gabrielle. I've sent word to the others not to come today. I don't think I have the heart to teach."

Gabrielle put the crayons she'd been carrying down quietly on one of the supply shelves. "What is it?"

It would be hardest for Gabrielle, of course. She and Marguerite were friends. Adélaïde took the letter she'd received that morning out of her pocket and unfolded it. Gabrielle came and threaded her hand through Adélaïde's arm and leaned her head on her shoulder as she read aloud.

Dear Madame Guiard,
I am sorry to tell you that my sister, Marguerite de Rosemonde, will no longer be coming for lessons. As you know, she has been ill for some time, and the doctors fear she is in her final days now. I know how much her hours in your studio meant to Marguerite, how they made her life fuller and sweeter, and I'm grateful, even if Maman cannot see it.

Silence stretched its arms into the studio along with the strengthening sunlight. Adélaïde handed the note to Gabrielle, who read it over and over. "How do they know it's just days? She was ill before, and she recovered."

It was hard to figure what had drawn Gabrielle and Marguerite together. From such different worlds, they nonetheless found common ground, perhaps in art, perhaps simply in being young women with more than fashion and fripperies in their heads. Whatever it was, Adélaïde knew that Gabrielle wouldn't be quite the same without her friend.

"I'm so glad you didn't sell it," Gabrielle said.

At first, Adélaïde didn't know what her student was talking about, and then she saw that Gabrielle had turned and was facing the self-portrait she had painted for the salon in 1785—the one with Gabrielle and Marguerite standing behind her chair. Thanks to the ample space in her new studio, Adélaïde could display it along with other paintings she used for teaching and so justified not accepting one of the many offers of purchase she'd had after the salon—one of them from Madame Adélaïde herself, in the end. She could never part with it, not now. It captured the three of them perfectly, as they were and had come to be: a family. Marguerite's eyes gazed directly out of the painting and met hers, as if she were standing in the room with them right at that moment. *The doctors might be wrong*, Adélaïde thought. And no sooner did she think it than she knew it wasn't true.

"I'll go home now," Adélaïde said. "You'll be back in time for supper?"

Gabrielle nodded. Although she still spent most of her days in the studio either painting or teaching the less advanced students, Adélaïde's new apartment on the Rue de Richelieu included a bedroom for Gabrielle so she no longer occupied a cot in the corner of the studio. It was the logical next step for both of them. In the past seven years, Gabrielle had become essential to Adélaïde. Not only was she a student and friend, but she also acted as her assistant, coming with her to sittings and helping her prepare the necessary materials, seeing to the expenses and making sure students paid their fees. It gave Adélaïde added cachet to have such a factotum. And Gabrielle was happy to have the experience.

As she walked through the streets toward home, Adélaïde thought how ironic it was that of all her pictures, the self-portrait was the only one that remained in her possession. Madame Adélaïde had offered her ten thousand livres for it at Christmas time in 1785, a sum that would have solved all her financial difficulties with ease. And she would have had to take Madame's offer if she had not already secured five thousand from the pastels. Also, her refusal to sell had possibly hastened Madame Adélaïde's commission of the monumental portrait Adélaïde exhibited in the 1787 salon—her first as Premier Peintre de Mesdames. That portrait was even grander than the self-portrait, and Mesdames paid Adélaïde fifteen thousand livres for it. At long last, Adélaïde thought, she had begun to command the kind of fees that gained her not only security, but a certain freedom—the kind of freedom that allowed her to ignore the small advertisement in the *Journal de France*, placed a year after she'd sold those last pastels, which she was certain was meant for her eyes alone. She had no need to "renew the profitable acquaintance that had given so much pleasure," as the advertisement said. She'd given enough of that kind of pleasure, thank you, and could now put that part of her life behind her.

When Marguerite died a few days later, Adélaïde and Gabrielle— not invited to the private funeral—followed the cortège to Père Lachaise cemetery and stood apart to watch her interment in the family crypt. The gunmetal sky loomed like a dismal threat, as if the weather itself partook of their sadness at the loss of such a beautiful young woman.

They turned their steps back toward the center of Paris, silence between them. About halfway home, Adélaïde said, "I won't come to the studio. But you may go there, of course." However heartbroken her student was, Adélaïde knew that once Gabrielle had a brush in her hand, she would be distracted a little and find it easier to put her grief aside, at least for that day.

☙

They parted at the Rue Ménars. Adélaïde simply wandered for a while with no particular destination in mind, until she found herself standing in front of the door to the studios at the Louvre. She reached for the handle, then hesitated. How did she get there? She had no recollection of taking the turns that would bring her to that exact point. Yet it seemed fitting that she should be. Open the door, walk to his studio, and see André's face, feel the warmth of his arms, hear his voice murmuring words of comfort. That's all she had to do—all she wanted to do. Wasn't it? She'd grown used to him filling up the empty places in her life. But the space where Marguerite had been he could not occupy. No one could.

Adélaïde shivered. The threatened sleet had begun to fall, and her cloak was soaking through. She pushed the door open. The scent of oils mixed with dust and mildew greeted her as she walked into the familiar corridor. It was dark, but she didn't need light to conduct her to the door behind which André both lived and worked. She stood outside it for a moment and listened.

Adélaïde expected to hear nothing other than the distant sound of footsteps and doors opening and closing elsewhere in the vast palace or the wind whistling around the building and the needles of sleet driving against window panes. But that evening, she heard voices. At first she thought they must be coming from someone else's studio, perhaps Vien's just across the hall. But when she stepped closer to André's door, she heard the voices more distinctly. He had said nothing about receiving guests that evening. She pressed her ear to the door and could just make out a few words.

"We should all have a say . . . just officers . . . younger would be better."

"It shouldn't be the royal . . . that's all going away."

"How do we do it?"

Should she knock or just go in and pretend she hadn't been listening? She could make out three voices—André's and Roslin's, but she couldn't identify the third.

At a pause in the conversation, Adélaïde pushed open the door and strode through it as if she'd just walked in from outdoors.

The three men froze in a tableau she wished she could sketch— André, Roslin, and Jacques-Louis David, who was newly returned from Rome. They were all seated at the table in their shirtsleeves drinking cups of wine, the remnants of a supper on plates and a platter full of chicken bones picked nearly clean.

"I'm sorry," she said. "I didn't realize . . ."

André scraped his chair back and stood, coming to greet her. "We were just discussing something some of the younger members have been talking about. I didn't expect you this evening. I thought you'd want to be on your own."

"So did I. But then I found I didn't."

By then Roslin and David had risen from their seats and gathered up their coats and hats. Only Roslin would have to brave the chill to return to his apartment on the Rue Neuve des Petits Champs. He kissed Adélaïde and smiled, and David gave her a curt nod, quickly turning his deformed cheek away from her. Adélaïde didn't mind this imperfection. She was in awe of the man's extraordinary gifts and couldn't help being drawn to him despite his looks.

After André's guests had left, Adélaïde helped him clear the table, putting the plates in the soapstone tub where a servant would come and get them to wash in the morning. They didn't speak for a while. She wondered if André would voluntarily tell her what they'd been talking about. When he didn't, she asked, "Why were they here?"

"It's nothing to concern yourself about. Académie business."

Adélaïde stopped what she was doing and glared at André. "I believe I'm still a member of that august assemblage."

André's cheeks flamed. "I mean, I didn't mean—it's just that some of the younger members among us along with the *agréés* are growing tired of having a small group of old men make all the decisions. They have a very narrow view of who's worthy of being admitted to the Académie and who isn't, and the view is as old-fashioned as they are. You of all people should understand that. This body should represent the vibrant life of the arts in France, not ossified tradition. Things are changing."

He'd started pacing back and forth in front of her, his hands alternately clasped behind his back and gesticulating to make some point. ". . . strictly merit based . . ." he said. And, ". . . no limit on the number of women."

"Hah! You'll not find any agreement about that!" Adélaïde said. Even though the crusty Monsieur Pierre, director of the Académie, had died, his successor was no more open to change than Angiviller was. "It would take a revolution to bring such alterations about in this place." Adélaïde wondered why, if that were a change the young men desired, they hadn't thought to include a woman in their discussions.

André stopped pacing and cocked his head on the side. "How aware are you of what's going on in the government? The deficit? The coming Estates General?"

Adélaïde read the pamphlets and broadsheets avidly and, in the privacy of her studio, among women, often discussed them. "A great deal more than you probably assume."

"I didn't mean to imply—"

His face softened, and Adélaïde realized she'd snapped at him. Such matters weren't in their vocabulary, at least not before. When they were together they only spoke of art and love, technique and ideals and other small things. No wonder he thought she was ignorant.

"Forgive me," she said. "Of course you wouldn't know my thoughts on those matters. Let's not talk about this anymore. My head aches."

André approached her and wrapped his arms around her. "Poor Marguerite. Poor you. I should have asked you before."

Adélaïde sagged into him and laid her head on his shoulder as he took the pins out of her hair and let it fall, dragging his fingers through its length all the way down her back, sending a sweet tremor through her body.

I'm still alive. I still feel.

Twenty

Paris and Versailles, November-December 1788

Life was forced to return to its normal pattern very soon after Marguerite's funeral. A pall of sadness lay over Adélaïde's studio for a while, and she spent time every morning gazing at the portrait and remembering everything she could about her talented student. But there was no time to retreat into the private world of mourning. The next Académie salon was less than a year away, and Adélaïde had a great deal to do before then. It was better to be busy, she thought, both for herself and for Gabrielle.

And change was in the air, not just in politics, but also in the rarefied world of the Académie. When David had returned from Rome the previous year, he brought with him a sharpened, dramatic style of neoclassicism that had forced the critics and artists to rethink the purpose and scope of history painting—and students to flock to his atelier. His return to Paris had not been without scandal, though. It was during the competition for the Prix de Rome the previous year. The officers of the Académie discovered that one of the artists favored to win had been preparing his drawings in David's studio, not in the loges, as required. The most unkind among them accused David of touching up his students' paintings to give them an unfair advantage in the competition.

Adélaïde didn't know whether to believe such accusations. David's naked ambition and fierce protectiveness of his own clique of devoted artists disinclined her to like him as a person. But as an artist? One thing she could not help but admire was his ability to make the male human form appear so real, so nuanced, that she expected the figures to stand up and walk right out of his paintings. The effect was enhanced by the way he posed them in extreme attitudes of action, muscles tensed, frozen at a moment when something was about to happen. The men in his paintings, at any rate. The women—Adélaïde knew he was perfectly capable of painting beautiful portraits of ladies, as he had of the chemist Lavoisier's wife in his portrait of the couple. Yet the women in his history paintings were not women, but emblems, cast into a symbolic role that enhanced the importance of the drama being enacted by the men. This irritated her.

David's neoclassical revolution in style might have set the Académie's history painters alight with the prospect of new subjects to conquer in new ways, but for portraitists like Adélaïde and Madame Le Brun, little changed. Perhaps their backgrounds might acquire some classical reference in a bust or the suggestion of a painting or a lady would be reading a book by one of the *philosophes*, but generally, people wanted to be commemorated on canvas in much the same ways they always had, as far as Adélaïde could see.

It was a delightful surprise, therefore, when she discovered that Mesdames were keen to do something unique with the portraits she would paint to be exhibited in the Académie salon in August 1789. Adélaïde had come to know the king's aunts a little in the years since she'd been appointed their first painter. Far from empty-headed princesses, they were both accomplished and learned women. Madame Victoire had a genuine interest in botany and horticulture, and her gardens reflected both her knowledge and her taste. Madame Adélaïde studied philosophy and languages and was as well read as anyone Adélaïde had ever met—and had a sharply witty tongue. But the two older ladies were united in one pursuit: that of taking every opportunity they could to criticize the queen. Adélaïde didn't know the particulars of why they hated her so much, but their enmity had driven them out of their lavish apartments at Versailles to their palace at Bellevue, except when their attendance was required at state occasions.

To her shame, Adélaïde sometimes found it useful to appeal to their vanity and spite against Marie Antoinette. The more she assured them that their grand portraits would be nothing like those that the queen's pet portraitist, Madame Le Brun, produced, the more they were inclined to allow her the freedom to experiment, to do something that would set her work apart when compared with the predictable prettiness of her rival's work.

Adélaïde's tactics had the desired result and succeeded in ingratiating her to her patronesses. But she didn't much like herself when she employed these tactics. It was beneath her to stoop so low. Still, even though she felt that Madame Le Brun had deliberately lured her most affluent students away from her, her rival's studio had not grown, Adélaïde heard, because apparently it was true that she had no interest in teaching.

The desperate measure that Madame Le Brun's spiteful gesture had forced Adélaïde to take, however, meant that she felt less and less charitable toward her rival. Madame Le Brun had the ear of the queen, but Adélaïde had the ear of the king's favorite aunts. And Mesdames were eager to hear anything ill of the queen or her portraitist. To gratify them, Adélaïde occasionally broke one of her personal rules and passed on gossip she had no way of verifying. She knew for a fact, for instance, that Monsieur Le Brun had sold the Hôtel du Loubert where the couple had been living and had built a magnificent new house—the Hôtel Le Brun—so that he could enlarge the gallery where he sold his paintings and sculptures and vastly increase the size of his wife's studio. It was only a rumor, though, that they had gone deep into debt in order to finance this endeavor and were dodging creditors.

"Just like the queen!" Madame Victoire had said when she heard this from Adélaïde. "Spending money she does not have. I suppose the lady is accustomed to giving lavish entertainments."

As far as Adélaïde knew, Madame Le Brun hadn't given any entertainments there yet. The building wasn't quite finished. She knew this because Madame Le Brun's few students were being taught by David while her studio was being built. Apparently, she had no interest in getting them back. Of course, three of them had previously been students of Adélaïde. It didn't surprise her that Madame Le Brun sent them to David instead of back to her. She supposed they could have chosen to return to her studio, but perhaps they were embarrassed or Madame Le Brun had said unkind things about her. She would never know. But she was nonetheless annoyed at David for taking them and giving his tacit blessing to her rival's art—and tactics.

Adélaïde had no choice but to move on. Especially since she persuaded Madame Victoire to allow her the freedom to paint her portrait posed in her beloved English-style gardens at Bellevue, not in an interior setting like all Adélaïde's other portraits. The more time Adélaïde spent at Bellevue the more the splendid gardens enchanted her. She had begun work on the background of the portrait when it was still high summer, the trees fully leafed out and flowers in riotous bloom. To capture the fluidity of the vegetation, she modified her style by employing looser brush strokes, less precise lines, and colors that evoked sunlight rather than candlelight. It was a departure, but she reveled in this new challenge. Now, in the drear of late November, it was time to put the elderly princess in the picture, standing and gesturing toward the statue of Friendship. That had been Madame Victoire's idea, as had been clutching a spray of periwinkles in her other hand—flowers beloved of Rousseau himself.

Adélaïde was very pleased with the results. She could have painted a more conventional portrait, something more in keeping with her earlier portrait of Madame Adélaïde, and it would have been a success, she was certain. But if she were to teach and nurture other artists, she had to continue learning and growing herself. Always being safe, doing the expected, did not lead to growth. And besides, she felt obligated to live up to her expanding reputation as a bit of a renegade and not exactly what one would expect of a woman portraitist.

The resulting portrait delighted Madame Victoire. Adélaïde had delivered it to Mesdames for their approval—and payment—only a week earlier and was preparing her posthumous portrait of Mesdames' younger sister Elisabeth, Duchess of Parma, for delivery the next day when a messenger arrived at her studio in the late afternoon, after the sun and her students were gone.

She opened and read the note. "It's from the Comte d'Angiviller," she said to Gabrielle, who stopped painting her self-portrait and turned her attention to Adélaïde.

"What does it say?"

"It says I am to go to Versailles tomorrow in order to receive a commission for a painting." Adélaïde looked up, perplexed. The message hadn't said who wished to engage her for a portrait. She knew it couldn't have been the queen—she was the exclusive purview of Madame Le Brun. Who else could it be? Whoever it was, a carriage would be sent for her the next morning to convey her to the chateau.

"Would you like me to come with you?" Gabrielle asked.

"I would, but until I know what to expect, I should probably go alone. The invitation was for me only. And you can supervise the students while I'm gone."

⌒🟢⌒

Gabrielle waited with Adélaïde in the vestibule of the house on the Rue de Richelieu the next morning. Who could blame her? In her place, Adélaïde would have been curious too.

"*Mon Dieu!*" Gabrielle had just rushed in from stepping outside to look up and down the street for a carriage that might be the one sent for Adélaïde. "Could this be your carriage? It's magnificent!"

Adélaïde resisted the urge to look for herself, instead waiting for the footman to knock on the door. When he did, Gabrielle pretended to be a servant and opened it for Adélaïde. As soon as she saw the carriage, she understood Gabrielle's exclamation. On the street stood a large, crested carriage drawn by six horses and sporting a postilion, a driver, and two footmen in opulent livery. Whoever was commissioning the portrait must be of very high rank to have sent such a vehicle, but Adélaïde didn't dare ask any questions. The carriage quite dominated her street, making the urchins gawk and the merchants, whom she saw casually stepping out of their shops and stalls to have a look, pretend not to be impressed. The footman who had knocked on the door helped her climb into the carriage, saying, "Monsieur le Comte de Provence awaits you."

So, that's who it was. The king's next younger brother. What had made him request her for a portrait commission? Many thoughts raced through her mind as they rolled along at a brisk clip on the well-kept road to Versailles.

When the same footman helped her descend from the carriage after the hour's journey, it was all she could do not to stare open-mouthed at the sheer scale of the palace she had only seen once as a child. She knew the Louvre was almost as large, rambling along the Seine, gobbling up land in the heart of Paris, but much of it blended with the surroundings, as it was made of the same color stone and had similar architecture as the townhouses and other buildings nearby. Only the arched entrance leading into the courtyard distinguished it from other *hôtels particulier.* The Louvre's state of disrepair contributed to the diminishment of its grandeur, and it was also difficult to get a view of the entire palace from far away because of the crush of buildings, so its size was not immediately apparent to a casual observer. Versailles, on the other hand, sat on a slight rise and could be seen from a long way off—a gilded, shimmering eminence, reaching out and commanding the landscape in a deliberate attempt to impress.

It succeeded, especially at that time of year, when the countryside surrounding it was brown and barren. Bellevue was like a jewel box compared to Versailles.

The interiors of the palace were much more ornate than those of Bellevue. Ladies with powdered wigs and too much vermilion on their cheeks clustered in groups in every chamber and whispered, casting catty glances at Adélaïde. Courtiers strode by as if they actually had important business to attend to. And everywhere, liveried servants stood at attention and armed guards took up their posts by the doors to apartments where visitors could pass only if they had an invitation.

Adélaïde had an invitation. She had presented it to the footman who greeted her at the top of the stairs that led to the grand entrance, and she followed him through what seemed like miles of rooms and corridors. At long last, he stopped at a guarded door and knocked before entering. Adélaïde didn't know whether she'd actually have to sketch anything that day or not, so she'd dressed simply and carried a satchel with paper and crayons in it. She looked more like the servants she caught occasional glimpses of than someone who had an appointment with royalty—a sparrow in a peacock's nest. The image brought a smile to her face as she walked forward to curtsy in front of the seated Comte de Provence.

"I see what she meant," the comte said, after indicating that she could stand. He placed a half-eaten pastry on the tray that had a few uneaten ones remaining, then brushed his hands off and dabbed his mouth with a lacy handkerchief. The comte would have been quite handsome if he weren't so bloated. "You are an unprepossessing creature. My sister the queen wanted me to give this project to her favorite painter, Madame Le Brun. But my aunts persuaded me you were the better choice because of the realism in your figures. And because you have been accustomed to working on very large canvases."

He motioned to a footman Adélaïde hadn't noticed to bring him a roll of paper. The comte spread the paper open on a table and beckoned

Adélaïde forward. It was a pencil sketch, very crude, of a scene in what looked like a throne room, with many figures dotted about.

"We require a monumental painting, commemorating a great beneficence from my brother to the order of Hospitalers. He has gifted them the buildings of the École Militaire. As minister of the order I shall be seated and receiving the first new member. I shall be surrounded by at least a dozen chevaliers, and their faces must be recognizable. You shall inspect the chamber yourself where the picture will eventually hang, and my secretary will give you the names of the men you are to include in the tableau."

Adélaïde's mind reeled. This would be a massive undertaking. "Monsieur, how large do you envision this painting to be?"

"At least twice the size of the portrait of my aunt, Madame Adélaïde. It must be clearly visible on the wall of the extremely large and undecorated hall."

Twice as large! "That will require a great deal of time and many costly materials," Adélaïde said, not certain how to broach the subject of payment.

"The *bâtiments du Roi* has suggested a fee of thirty thousand livres, which, I understand from my aunts, would likely be agreeable to you."

Adélaïde curtsied, as much to hide her expression of astonishment as to acknowledge the immensity of the fee. "Of course. I should like to begin by sketching your likeness."

"My equerry will arrange everything."

Adélaïde's heart raced as she followed the footman back through the endless halls of Versailles. There was so much to arrange: canvas to order from the Low Countries so it could be stitched together to make it the right size, pigments and grounds and oils to buy. And working on such a large piece—ladders, scaffolding. She wasn't sure what small thing it was that broke through her preoccupied mind—a creak of a door, someone coughing perhaps—but she turned at one moment and caught sight through the open door of a smaller chamber where a woman sat in front of an easel, painting what looked like a portrait of children. The woman must have heard the same small noise, because she looked up, and her eyes met Adélaïde's briefly before someone on the other side of it closed the door. *Madame Le Brun*, she thought. She hadn't seen her so close since the 1787 salon.

ᨁᨑᨒ

For whatever reason, the carriage that conveyed Adélaïde back to Paris was much smaller than the vehicle that had transported her to Versailles in great state, and it was drawn by only two horses, making the journey last a bit longer. Adélaïde didn't mind as it gave her time to go over everything, to try to solve some of the problems that such a large project created. Thank heavens she could call upon Gabrielle's assistance. It gave her a pang, though, to think how lovely it would have been to have Marguerite's help as well. She stifled the impulse to be sad, putting it away for the moments before sleep when she often recalled her late student's sweetness, her joy and sincerity. Her place had soon been taken in the studio, but there would be no replacement for her in Adélaïde's heart.

She shook her head and returned to the practical matters at hand. Her studio would be too small to work on the full-size canvas, although she could do the initial oil sketches there. She wondered if André's studio at the Louvre would accommodate it. It would depend, she thought, on how big the paintings he was working on would be. In any case, she needed to talk to him about it, so she requested that the driver take her to the Louvre rather than the Rue Ménars.

Her heart still fluttering and her mind still reeling from the enormity of the commission she'd just been granted, she flew to André's rooms and entered without knocking. The model who posed on the dais in a position that looked as if it would be exhausting to hold shot her a grateful glance. André was seated on a high stool, working on a head that was six feet off the ground.

"Take a break, Maurice," André said. He had his concentrating look, the indentations above his eyebrows remaining even when he turned to smile at Adélaïde and climb down from his perch. "*Bonsoir, ma chérie,*" he said before heading to the workbench to clean his brush and hands. "Well? What was it? *Who* was it?"

Adélaïde had told André about the summons to Versailles the night before. What would he think, though? "I—I can hardly believe it! The Comte de Provence has asked me to paint an enormous group portrait with him at its center that's to hang in the new hall of the Order of Hospitalers."

André didn't respond right away. Perhaps he thought she wasn't capable of such a thing. But no, Adélaïde thought. He might well be the only one who saw her potential for grandeur. "Felicitations! But how enormous?" he asked, swishing his brush in the glass of turpentine and then wiping it with a rag he pulled out of the pocket of his smock.

"Nineteen by fourteen feet."

André whirled around to face her, mouth open. "How on earth will you manage such a thing?"

"For thirty thousand livres, I'll think of a way."

He didn't speak for a moment. *He's stunned*, she thought. Adélaïde imagined he'd never been paid that kind of money for one of his history paintings. But a moment later he smiled and approached her. "You deserve it. Your studio isn't large enough, though."

"I'll rent something bigger. And I'll need scaffolding, of course. But I have to do the sketches first, so I won't worry about it right away. I have enough of my own money saved to get started, and with the commission coming from Provence, I'll be able to get credit easily for the materials." She was babbling, she knew, talking herself out of facing the major difficulty that no payment would be forthcoming until she delivered the picture and such a large project would take a year or more. It was the usual way of things. Mesdames had made up for it with small gestures, sending her a pupil they paid her twelve hundred a year to teach, for instance, and recommending her to others for smaller pictures she could complete quickly.

André wrapped his arms around her and lifted her off the floor in a tight squeeze. "This calls for a celebration! Let's go to the café and make everyone there jealous and force them to toast your health anyway!" André nodded to the model indicating that they were finished for the day.

Adélaïde laughed.

"But first, a toast with just the two of us." André fetched the carafe of wine and two glasses and poured them out.

Once she'd taken a sip, Adélaïde said, "I don't understand, still, why he chose me. I would think someone like David would have been the more obvious artist for such an important commission."

"And won't he be annoyed that not only did the Comte de Provence choose someone else, but he chose a woman!"

A mere woman, Adélaïde thought, although she knew the slight on André's part was unintentional. She said, "Perhaps the power of Mesdames' antipathy to the queen could not be resisted."

"Yes, of course. They must prove that their lady portraitist is superior in every way by showing that she is capable of painting something even a man would find challenging."

Would she ever be more than a *lady* portraitist? Adélaïde sighed and threaded her arm through André's. "Gabrielle will be so pleased," she said, thinking that she would more pleased than anyone other than herself, including André.

Twenty-One

Paris, March 1789

O nce they heard about the great honor their official portraitist had been granted, Mesdames made it possible for Adélaïde to move to a much larger studio, in the Bibliothèque du Roi down the road from her apartment on the Rue de Richelieu, within the compound of the Hôtel Mazarin. The location was convenient, but it still required a lot of moving to get all the necessary materials and equipment into the space—which was on the second floor in a long and drafty gallery. The space was illuminated by floor-to-ceiling north-facing mullioned windows, which gave wonderful light but proved no protection at all from either extreme heat or extreme cold. Fortunately, the worst of the winter was behind her. When Adélaïde felt the chill and shivered, she looked up at the ceiling and its magnificent frescoes by Italian masters, gritted her teeth, and got back to work.

Adélaïde's expenses mounted quickly as her work on the project progressed. She had to buy yards of fine Dutch cloth and have it stitched together to make a support, hire the artisans to build the frame and stretch the canvas over it, purchase the enormous quantity of gesso it would require to prepare the canvas, and order more pigments than she'd ever imagined she could use on a single painting. Without putting a drop of color on the canvas, she'd already spent over three thousand livres of her own money.

While all these preparations were being made, Adélaïde returned to Versailles several times to draw the oil and pastel sketches of the

Comte de Provence and the dozen other Hospitalers whose faces and figures must be recognizable. All that was well within Adélaïde's abilities and experience. The difficulty began as she started to plan the work, a composition with Provence seated on a dais and a group of men approaching him. She tried many different arrangements of the figures, but all her designs fell flat. They had a static quality that made the individuals look more like objects than people.

"What is wrong with it?" she asked Gabrielle, after she'd reworked the disposition of the figures for the fourth time.

Gabrielle stood back and examined the small oil sketch on the easel next to the massive, gessoed canvas, blank and intimidating. "I don't know. But I think you're not using the space well. I'm not sure how to solve that problem, but what you have here looks like a small painting."

Gabrielle, in her usual perceptive fashion, had identified the heart of the problem. A group portrait like that was something entirely new to Adélaïde. No other woman artist had ever completed such a project that she knew of. Mostly, their lack of access to training and models limited them to individual or small family portraits. Intimate spaces were easily filled with the characters of the sitters, the details of expression and attitude that revealed their personalities. Even her large self-portrait was in essence an intimate portrait of a family of three.

"You know, you could ask Monsieur Vincent about it." Gabrielle persisted in referring to André that way, although he'd asked her many times to call him by his Christian name.

"Yes. I was hoping to avoid that."

"Why?"

Sometimes Gabrielle said or did something that revealed her essential innocence. Was she really ignorant of Adélaïde's reasons for avoiding any perception of influence by her lover? Adélaïde smiled at her. "Because you know that if I so much as walk by his studio with a sketch of it, the critics will say it was his hand that held the brush in the end."

⌒℮⌒

Despite the risk, Adélaïde decided the next day that she must swallow her pride and confess her difficulties to André. She brought him to the studio in the Bibliothèque du Roi so that he could see for himself the magnitude of the project and why she struggled to find the exact disposition of figures in the architectural space. "I am not anxious about getting the faces and personalities right. I know I can do that. It's the composition I fear."

"So you should. That's always a hazard when dealing with such a large image. You can't simply make everything bigger to fill the space." He walked the length of the canvas several times, looking at it from different distances.

"I just need a hint, a suggestion of how to approach it. Your *Chaumont de la Galaizière*, for instance. It was nearly as big, and it appeared effortless," Adélaïde said.

"Well, it wasn't quite as large. About half the size of this. Nonetheless, you've chosen a good example."

"Why? What is it about your painting that would help me figure out mine?"

"There's a trick. Something Vien taught me. Think of it as a drama, only it's all unfolding at the same time in front of the viewer. You have the main plot, the one that concerns the central characters and theme. But there are also subplots, in which minor characters take a turn upon the stage and enact their own, smaller stories. And there's the matter of time. You have what is transpiring at the exact moment you have chosen to illustrate as well as the suggestion of what happened before and what is yet to come."

Yes, Adélaïde thought, and a clear idea came to her, of how to draw the eye through a story that ultimately led to the presentation of the order by the Comte de Provence. In that one utterance, André put his finger on precisely what was wrong with her approach. *That, she thought, is what makes him such an excellent teacher.* She must remember his words and use them as she instructed her own students. "The question is how to decide what this subplot should be, and how to manipulate time."

"Talk to your sitters. See if a thread emerges. I have no doubt that the composition will fall into place."

By then it was dinnertime, so they went to André's studio from there, buying a baguette and a wheel of cheese on the way. Those were the kind of evenings Adélaïde liked best, when it was just the two of them, and they had the simplest fare with a bottle of wine to wash it down. In such an atmosphere, she felt she could ask André anything.

The table strewn with crumbs and her fingers sticky with melted cheese, Adélaïde asked, "What is it like knowing that your talent will have a path to acceptance if you just follow what custom has dictated?"

"How do you mean?"

"I mean, given that you have the desire, you have a father who is a respected artist, you were admitted to study with Vien without hesitation, you then won the Prix de Rome, studied there, and came back to be an *agréé* in the most prestigious academy in the world, then a full member, and were awarded free accommodations in a community of the finest artists in Paris. None of those things were true of me, and most of them are not even possible—except being a member of the Académie, and that was far from likely until it actually happened. I work all the hours I'm given and still struggle to pay my bills because I am not eligible for accommodations in the Louvre, and I have no doubt I will be vilified for having received a commission that many will deem more suitable for a man. You, for instance, or David." She had not meant to go on like that, her indignation growing with every word. It wasn't André's fault, after all, that he had those advantages. "And what bothers me the most is that many will assume that it was you, in fact, who painted the picture when it is finished. Merely asking for your advice has no doubt already exposed me to some gossip of that sort. I ask you, why are men never accused of having a woman paint their works?"

André kept his eyes to the floor during her entire screed. When he looked up, his gaze was full of compassion tinged with shame. She knew he agreed with all she said. If only there were more like him.

"All you say is true—and just. You have to trust me when I tell you that there are several in the Académie who would like to see such circumstances changed, who believe that we limit our artistic horizons by not according women the same rights and privileges with regard to training and professional status. But the time for that has not yet come. I believe it will be part of bigger changes, which, if they can be undertaken in a civil and peaceful manner, will be to the benefit not just of artists, but of the entire country."

"You're talking about the Estates General and the reforms, I assume."

"Yes. And possibly more."

Adélaïde smacked her palms on the table, rattling the glasses and sending a knife tumbling to the floor. "You see! That is exactly what I mean! We women are excluded from all that is important in the world. I want to know what you know. I want to go to your political meetings and hear what men say of matters that also affect us women."

"Doing so could put you at risk."

"At risk of what? Becoming more educated? More equal to a man in knowledge and the ability to act? You should know by now that I am no delicate flower. I have had to do things . . ." Her voice trailed off. She had never told André about the erotic pastels and had no intention of doing so, ever.

"I do know. And once again, you're right. Women should be included in such discussions. We're meeting tomorrow evening at the café. Come."

⌒ℰ⌒

The café on the Rue Neuve des Petits Champs was the regular meeting place of the young artists who either lived or studied at the Louvre. Adélaïde knew it well from her days of scrambling under the feet of the men and listening, drawing amusing sketches that caught the attention of one or two who gave her pastel crayons and paper. She couldn't have been more than eight or nine years old then and had little understanding of what it meant to be an artist, only knowing in her heart that she must capture the moment and fix it to paper or whatever else she had at hand.

Raucous laughter spilled out of the café into the early spring evening as Adélaïde approached, bolstering her courage by reminding herself she was there by invitation and André would be with her. She drew herself up and entered, asking the proprietor to show her to the artists' table.

The man peered at her for a long moment. "Eh, I didn't know they let women into their seditious gatherings."

Seditious? As far as Adélaïde knew, the only subject under discussion that evening would be the management of the Académie Royale. There was nothing seditious about that, unless you were Angiviller.

She looked for André as she approached the table, but he wasn't there. *Courage*, she thought, and smiled as she took one of the empty seats. All conversation stopped. Adélaïde looked around at faces she recognized, nodded politely, and smiled. No one smiled back at her. The ones she knew personally kept their eyes averted. Several of the others started whispering to each other. *Where is André?* Adélaïde thought, willing herself not to blush or display her discomfort in any way. She folded her hands and placed them on the table in front of her. An artist she didn't know—likely an *agréé*—stood at the opposite end of the table and cleared his throat, staring straight at her. Just as he was about to say something, André rushed in, his face flushed.

"I'm terribly sorry I'm late!" He sat next to Adélaïde. "Shall we start? I think we are all at least acquainted with one another. Perhaps we should review the recommendations we will make to the officers."

The artist who had stood a moment before lowered himself slowly into his seat. All eyes still glared at Adélaïde, except André's. He seemed intent on ignoring the obvious disruption of her presence. Adélaïde decided to take his lead and simply be there, a fixture, as if she had every right. Which she did. She doubted any of them had as grand a commission as she had at that moment. Keeping the image of that enormous canvas in her mind gave her courage and confidence. Soon, as tongues loosened with wine and the men warmed to the subject of reform, Adélaïde began to speak up concerning the matters that most affected her: allowing women to both teach at and enroll in the art school at the Louvre and doing away with the arbitrary limit of women members.

When Adélaïde pointed out how unjust it was to deny women the right to take the all-important classes at the Louvre, Augustin Pajou said, "But Madame Guiard, I see no hordes of aspiring women painters and pastellists pounding on the Académie's doors to be let in."

"Monsieur Pajou, I don't believe you have ever visited my studio. You are welcome anytime, it's on the Rue Ménars. There you would find at least three who have both the talent and the desire to study in the Louvre, where so many more opportunities abound for instruction by the greatest masters of the day. You know I must be sincere because if such an eventuality came to pass, I'd probably lose my three best students! Unless, of course, I were one of those professors both men and women sought out to learn the technique of pastels or painting in the Louvre."

Several in the group laughed. A few others frowned. André inched closer to her.

Adélaïde had no idea if any of their suggested reforms would ever be enacted in so tradition-bound an institution as the Académie Royale. But being able to sit among her fellow artists and raise her voice, express ideas and hopes, gave her a feeling of exhilaration almost equal to the act of painting itself.

Twenty-Two

O ne balmy morning a couple of months after the first artists' meeting Adélaïde attended, as she was about to give her students a lecture on backgrounds, Gabrielle burst into the studio waving a hastily printed pamphlet.

"Riots! They've called in the French Guard!"

Everyone clustered around Gabrielle, all talking at once.

"Let me see, please," Adélaïde said and took the paper from Gabrielle.

It seemed that a Monsieur Réveillon, who owned a wallpaper factory in the Saint-Antoine district, had let it be known that he intended to reduce his workers' wages so the prices of his wallpaper could be lowered. Although Adélaïde spent almost all her time painting or teaching, she was well enough aware that the price of bread had risen to close to ninety percent of a laborer's daily wage—already a volatile situation. To threaten to reduce their incomes at a time like this was not only cruel, it was foolhardy. Word had spread, and workers in several places—the Faubourg Saint-Marcel, the Marais, and Saint-Antoine—had been marching in protest. That much Adélaïde already knew. The marches had started peacefully a few days before. The news had disquieted her but did not disrupt her daily life. But that morning, apparently the marchers had grown violent, smashing windows, looting shops.

"It says that people have been killed," Adélaïde whispered.

A few gasps, and then silence in the studio.

Gabrielle snatched the pamphlet back from Adélaïde. "I want to go and help nurse the wounded. I am just like they are, a laborer, from laborers' stock." Her origins were not quite so lowly, but Gabrielle had always looked with a critical eye on the lavish lives of the aristocrats and royals who paid Adélaïde handsomely for a portrait sitting.

"It's not safe. You must stay here." Adélaïde encompassed all nine of her students in her gaze and said, "All of you must remain here until I deem that it is safe for you to return home."

Something's happening, Adélaïde thought. Despite her preoccupation with her commissions and her students, Adélaïde couldn't help but be aware of the turbulent forces that buffeted the Paris streets. Whenever she was outside, she could hear the grumbling and dissatisfaction oozing from every café and market stall she passed. The stirrings of dissatisfaction in the Académie did not arise in a vacuum. Each day saw the publication of another pamphlet with the most outrageous libels against the royal family—particularly the queen. Mesdames did not think much of Marie Antoinette, but she herself had never heard anything worse than that she was ignorant and ineffectual. The queen most certainly did not participate in orgies on the street or declare she would be glad to bathe in the blood of the commoners, as the pamphlets suggested.

Gabrielle stood in the middle of the studio for a moment, then, not having removed her jacket, dashed out the door as quickly as she'd come in. Before her rapid steps had reached the ground floor, Adélaïde tossed her brush in a jar of turpentine, tore off her smock, and grabbed her own hat and cloak.

"I'll be back. Work on your projects on your own," she called to the other students as she raced to catch up with Gabrielle.

cℯↄ

Adélaïde looked up and down the street, hoping for a glimpse of Gabrielle's green jacket, but she had vanished. Pulling her cloak

around her, more to hide the clothes that marked her out as a pros-
perous artist than for warmth, Adélaïde half walked, half ran to the
Rue Saint-Honoré, then on to the Rue Saint-Antoine. By the time she
reached the Hôtel de Ville, men, women, and children, some in rags,
some dressed in the simple garb of workers, were streaming past in
the opposite direction, running and shouting. She swore she could
smell the fear and desperation in the air.

Adélaïde's heart raced. Where was Gabrielle? She stepped into a
doorway to get out of the way of an even bigger surge of frightened
people coming from the east. As they ran past, they cast terrified
glances over their shoulders. At a brief break in the crush, Adélaïde
peeked out and saw exactly why. Over the heads of the panicked,
running crowd she saw the glint of steel bayonets rising and falling
in the rhythm of a steady march, carefully choreographed to instill
terror in the hearts of those in front of them. The panic grew, and
people fell and were trampled. Screams erupted all around her. She
covered her ears and closed her eyes and shrank as far back as she
could into the protection of the doorway. The grinding squeak and
crunch of boots on cobbles crescendoed until they drowned out the
screams. Adélaïde opened her eyes. The guards were now directly in
front of her, their faces set in dispassionate masks, the spring sunlight
glancing off the blades of their bayonets and their silver buttons. Who
trained them to be so blank, so unseeing? They were perfectly turned
out, only the very bottoms of their boots showing so much as a speck
of dirt, an absurd contrast to the squalor of the crowd that fled before
them. How much time, Adélaïde thought, had they spent polishing
their buttons before marching that morning?

Adélaïde closed her eyes again and pressed her back against the
wooden door. She couldn't bear to look a moment longer at those
hollow men, those empty shells devoid of life but willing to take
someone else's if the order were given.

Once the sounds of marching faded and the screams died away,

Adélaïde forced herself to open her eyes. The crowds were gone, leaving broken glass and rubble strewn across the street. Several unmoving lumps covered in clothing lay on the ground, as if laundry had been dumped out in heaps here and there. These were the senseless casualties of antiquated laws and failed policies. Adélaïde knew she should try to return to the studio, perhaps take a different route back, but she couldn't look away from what she saw. Instead, she walked slowly through the devastation as injured laborers crawled toward the gutters and others like her picked their way through those that remained, perhaps looking for someone, perhaps simply wanting to help.

As Adélaïde passed one of the smaller lumps of dirty clothing, a moan escaped, and a bare leg extended a little way out and twitched. A child's leg. Adélaïde crouched down. "Let me see," she said.

Uncovering the child revealed a long gash slicing from his shoulder down to his stomach. Blood flowed in a steady stream into a red puddle that blossomed out around him. The child's eyes gazed up at hers, round and confused.

"Is your *maman* here? Your *papa*?"

He did not respond.

Adélaïde looked up. "Help! Help me here! He's just a child!"

Two nuns and a priest walked slowly toward her, looking down as they went, crouching to help people or to cover the faces of one or two who were dead. By the time Adélaïde looked back at the child, his eyes held not a spark of life.

She stood, her knees stiff from bearing her weight on the hard ground. Her cloak and skirt were soaked with blood. A gentle touch on her arm made her turn.

It was Gabrielle, her eyes red and angry. "You see? They're already close to starving. Now this."

The street soon swarmed with people rushing to do whatever they could. Some of those Adélaïde had thought must be dead got up and walked away. Others lay where they were, never to move again. The air that had recently echoed with the screams of fleeing workers now rang with the sobs of anguish.

"Let's go home," Adélaïde said. "There's nothing more we can do here."

cℰↄ

That night, as she lay in André's arms in bed, the boy's face loomed before her eyes. All their concerns, about representation in the Académie, are petty and small-minded compared to what's happening in the rest of Paris, likely France. Is there nothing they can do that will have greater effects? Do more good? Her work for Mesdames and the Comte de Provence, work that brought her enough money to lead a comfortable—if not luxurious—life, felt tarnished and dirty. Yet it was what she had been fighting for as long as she could remember. It was what her students wanted from her, the ability to gain portrait commissions that would enable them to live through their art. Could art itself not perform a higher function than simply recording the faces and figures of the wealthy for posterity? Gabrielle had started a pastel as soon as they returned to the studio, a picture of a poor man, shoeless, clothing torn, arms outstretched begging for money to buy the barest essentials to keep him alive. No one would purchase such a work. But Adélaïde understood her need to create it.

In the morning when Adélaïde awoke, she would work as always. Only, after what she had witnessed that day, she vowed that as much as she could spare once she received payment for her commissions would be donated to relieve the suffering of the poor. She had to do more than just toss a few sous to beggars on the street.

Yet she knew that anything she could do would be nothing even so. The price of grain had to be controlled. The Assembly of Delegates had failed, the finance minister Calonne had failed, and his successor was even worse. The papers were full of the election of deputies to the Estates General, an event that had not taken place for a hundred and seventy-five years. It was an extreme step for the king to take, and everyone hoped that the body of clergy, nobles, and commoners would be able to enact reforms that would solve the deficit and alleviate conditions for all. But what if they failed too? Adélaïde prayed—something she rarely did unless she was at Mass—for all to be resolved before conditions deteriorated further and brought disaster in their wake.

Twenty-Three

Paris, June 1789

The artists presented their proposal for reforms to the officers and were ignored. The Estates General convened with double the number of members of the Third Estate, the commoners, so that their votes would have equal weight to the other two estates. But they spent all their time arguing about how the voting would work, which groups would meet independently, or if all of them would be permitted to meet in a single body.

Neither institution had enacted any reforms, not by early June of 1789.

No more riots disturbed the peace of Paris, although the conditions that had provoked them in the first place did not abate. The normal pace of life resumed, and Adélaïde's days once again followed their usual predictable pattern. She had finished most of her initial sketches for the painting that would hang in the building that used to be the École Militaire, the one the king had given to the order of Hospitalers. Now pleased with the composition, she'd started figuring out which faces would go where in the different groups.

"I must go to Versailles to finish the pastel sketch of the Comte de Provence," Adélaïde said, packing up the half-completed picture and the crayons and mahlstick. "I expect to return late in the afternoon." Her students were all deeply engrossed in their work and would have no trouble keeping busy in her absence. They spent half their time working on their own as it was, with Adélaïde spending hours at the studio in the Bibliothèque. Gabrielle usually stayed and supervised while she worked on her series of pastels of the poor and working-class Parisians, saying she intended to show them at the next Exposition de la Jeunesse. Victoire—who had progressed by leaps since joining Adélaïde's studio a year ago—was close to finishing a creditable oil portrait of the Comtesse d'Angiviller. The others had projects large and small to occupy them.

The day blazed with early heat. Adélaïde decided to hire an open carriage to take her to Versailles so she could feel the caress of a breeze on her face. Much had happened during the months since Monsieur had given her that huge commission. The deputies to the Estates General would continue their as-yet unfruitful meetings that same day in the Hall of the Menus Plaisirs in the town of Versailles. Ever since the Reveillon riots, Adélaïde had devoured the pamphlets and the papers every day in hopes that this collection of worthy men from all three estates would be able to agree on reforms that would set the nation to rights. So far, little resulted other than bringing a few rising political stars to public notice, especially Mirabeau, who, despite his noble lineage, had been elected to the Third Estate, the commoners.

As her carriage passed mansion after mansion along the road to Versailles, Adélaïde couldn't help thinking of the contrast between these magnificent residences with their well-tended gardens and the Saint-Antoine district, with families living in one or two rooms and barely able to afford their daily bread. She had kept to her vow after the riots and made as many charitable donations as she could, but it would never be enough.

Her contemplation came to an abrupt end, however, when they reached the village of Versailles. What was normally an uneventful route through a sleepy town had erupted in turmoil. Carriages and pedestrians clogged the streets, impeding her progress beyond the middle of a wide avenue where they had stopped, unable to proceed or turn for the crush of people and vehicles. She called out to a man with papers rolled under his arm, thinking he looked official and might know what was going on. "What's happening? Where is every-one going?"

"To the tennis court," he said, nodded to her, and hurried away.

The tennis court? She could do nothing but sit and wait until the crowd cleared enough for the driver to continue to the palace. Why the tennis court? No doubt the papers would have something to say about all this the next day, but she wished she could know right then. Something told her she had witnessed an important development.

A footman conducted her through the chateau past courtiers and servants who—unlike the last time Adélaïde was there—wore expressions of studied blankness. Of course, the death of the sickly dauphin had put the court in deep mourning, transforming what had previously been a feast of vibrant colors and luxurious textures into a monochromatic shadow of its former self, as if a massive painting had been halted at the dead layer.

That untimely death highlighted the growing rupture between the Bourbon king and the head of the cadet branch of the royal family, the Duc d'Orléans. The court had had to greatly dimin-ish the usual ceremonies of a state funeral, but one tradition that should have been upheld was for the Duc d'Orléans to conduct the dauphin's heart to be buried at Saint-Denis. But the duke—who had become more and more radical in his politics—claimed to be too busy with affairs of state and sent his son instead. It was a mark of the greatest disrespect, and must have rubbed salt into the king and queen's wounds of grief.

That grief, itself, had only exacerbated the chaos of the govern-ment. The king spent days in his palace at Marly hunting rather than governing, and those he left in charge were doing little to solve any of the seemingly insurmountable problems.

But the expressions on the faces of the courtiers inside the palace were not just sad. Adélaïde swore she detected a glint of fear in many eyes as they followed her on her way to the apartments of the Comte de Provence.

She entered the comte's chamber as usual and curtsied deeply, expecting a courteous greeting in return. Instead, the king's brother hastily shuffled away some papers he'd been looking at and spoke without turning toward her. "I have little time for you today, Madame Guiard. I must return to Marly to be with the king in his period of mourning. Be quick about your business."

Adélaïde stood and got directly to work. This was not at all the jovial prince she'd encountered ever since the first time she met him. Although she could detect no fear in his demeanor and very little sadness, a furrow of vexation was etched between his eyebrows. Adélaïde worked as fast as she could, careful not to translate that furrow to the more sanguine face with its air of faint amusement that looked out at her from her half-finished picture.

It took her less than an hour to get what she needed, and she didn't think she'd have to return to bother him anymore. As she rose from her parting curtsy and headed to the door of the comte's private chamber, eager only to be on her way, she caught a glimpse of something that brought her up short, something she hadn't seen before, either because it wasn't there before that day, or because the open door had always blocked it. A pastel, hanging on the wall in such a position that it would always be hidden from view by anyone entering and once the door was fully open upon exiting. She only saw it briefly before the door hid it again, but she knew instantly what it was, and her blood ran cold. It was she herself. Her naked body, drawn by her own hand, stretched out in an erotic pose in a pastel that had been glazed and framed and hung in full view on a wall at Versailles. In all her imaginings about what her illicit trade might lead to, she never thought it would come to this. She hurried out of the chamber, barely able to breathe and hoping Monsieur did not notice her involuntary gasp and flaming cheeks.

What could she do? The man who'd purchased her pastels had clearly either sold one of them to the Comte de Provence or given it to him. Or perhaps . . . *No, it couldn't have been.* The carriage that greeted her the night she sold the drawings belonged to a comte of something, but not a royal one, from what she remembered of the crest.

No. An heir to the throne of France—however distant—would never have undertaken such a task himself. Or would he? Adélaïde's heart thumped as she hurried through the corridors of the palace. It hadn't been the most salacious image, thank heavens, but its intent to arouse was clear enough. Even if he hadn't been the original purchaser, she wondered if Monsieur would ever make the connection between her and that picture, if he would be observant enough to note the similarity of technique between his erotic pastel and the pastel portrait sketch of him she'd just finished. But he needn't see her finished sketch. All he cared about was the final painting. She had no idea how such grand commissions were managed, but she hoped she could simply deliver her painting to the École Militaire, collect her fee from Angiviller, and be done with it.

Her mouth felt as dry as the dusty courtyard by the time she climbed back into her hired carriage. It wasn't until then that Adélaïde thought back to the crush in the village and could shake herself out of her own distress enough to try to discover what had happened that day. She called out to a passing servant, "You there, what is the news from the Estates General?"

The girl looked all around her to make sure no one was listening and approached Adélaïde's carriage. "You mean, the National Assembly."

So, something had changed. A name was a powerful token. "Why did everyone go to the tennis court?"

"The Menus Plaisirs was locked by order of the king because things weren't going as he wanted." She lowered her voice to a whisper. "They say the commune—the Third Estate, as it was—has taken control and is writing their own constitution. Mirabeau and the Comte de Lafayette talk of revolution."

Adélaïde reached into her pocket for a livre coin and gave it to the girl. "Thank you."

The driver said, "*Va!*" and his horses trotted on, as Adélaïde felt both a growing lump of dread in the pit of her stomach and a glimmer of hope in her heart.

⌒⥀⌒

Paris, July 12, 1789
Adélaïde was a Catholic by rote rather than conviction. Her religion counted her separation from her husband a terrible sin and her taking up with another man even worse. Nonetheless, she went with Gabrielle and Victoire to Mass at Saint Eustache most Sundays now, and continued to meet her father and Jacqueline there, more to bask in the massive, Gothic interior with its Rubens paintings and stained-glass windows than from any true sense of piety.

That Sunday, July 12, they'd walked through the quiet streets to the church along with other neighbors and taken their places in the vast nave close to the altar. About halfway through the Latin service, as the priest intoned the Agnus Dei, the great west doors beneath the pipe organ opened and a woman ran in, right up to the altar rail, genuflected and crossed herself, then turned to the stunned worshipers.

"Necker! The king has dismissed Necker!"

Necker was the finance minister who had introduced reforms that were very popular with the people. Without another word the woman ran back out. In the interval when the door was open, sounds of crowds on the street rushed in, and the congregation of a few hundred erupted in murmurs that grew to loud voices.

"Please, remain calm, for the sake of the blessed sacrament," the priest said, but no one listened to him. A flurry of genuflections led to the hurried exodus of the entire congregation, Adélaïde and her students among them.

When they spilled out onto the Impasse Saint-Eustache, ahead of them on the Rue Montmartre thousands of people streamed from the direction of Les Halles—men, women, children—most of them workers and artisans. Shouts of "Necker!" and "*Vive le Duc d'Orléans!*" echoed off the buildings. Adélaïde turned around to see if her father had followed them out, but he and Jacqueline were nowhere to be seen.

"Let's go with them," Gabrielle said, already running to join the crowd.

Adélaïde and Victoire ran after her and caught up as she marched next to someone who held a bust of Orléans, a man everyone believed to be the advocate of the people against the excesses of the royal court. A transformation that had begun seemingly just weeks ago had solidified into a movement that was being called Orléanist. The crowd was too noisy for Adélaïde to ask any questions and hope to have them answered. She'd been reading the pamphlets every day and had some idea. The reforms proposed by the Commune, led by Mirabeau and Lafayette, had met with resistance from the king and the conservative nobility. And now, it seemed that instead of continuing to negotiate, the king had sent Necker, the man who wanted to end the nobility's exemption from taxation and stabilize the price of grain, away in disgrace.

No wonder the common Parisians were incensed. And it wasn't just Paris. Gabrielle had received a letter from her mother in Lyon that told of riots against the price of bread in which all the city's toll gates had been destroyed.

By the time they reached the Palais Royale, seat of the Orléans family, the crowd must have numbered nearly ten thousand. Adélaïde grasped Gabrielle's and Victoire's hands. "Don't let go of me. We'll be all right if we stay together."

Adélaïde had every sympathy with the crowd, but the back of her neck prickled with anxiety over what a mob of angry people could pose to women like them, dressed more elegantly and clearly more affluent than those who had come from Les Halles and beyond. Gabrielle, heedless of the risk, dragged them forward to where they could see three men who appeared to be the ringleaders. One of them climbed up on a chair hauled out from a café in the garden of the Palais Royale. To Adélaïde's horror, they were armed.

The man, eyes wild and spit spewing from his mouth as he spoke, said, "Citizens, there is no time to lose; the dismissal of Necker is the knell of a Saint Bartholomew for patriots! This very night the Swiss and German battalions will leave the Champ de Mars to massacre us all; one resource is left—to take arms!"

All around them people screamed and raised hands that held hammers, knives, spoons—anything that might serve as a weapon. The mob began to move away, as if it were a single organism with one unified thought. People shouted, "To Saint Lazare! There are arms and grain!"

Adélaïde's knuckles were white from gripping Gabrielle's and Victoire's hands, but she refused to let go, even though Gabrielle struggled against her. Resisting the flow of the crowd was almost impossible, but Adélaïde dragged her students sideways, letting those intent on pillaging squeeze past, not caring when she felt a hand reach into her pocket and take the few sous she had brought to church to light candles for her dead mother and siblings.

When at last they broke free of the tidal wave of angry people, Adélaïde said, "To the Louvre! We'll be safe there."

But as they approached the Rue des Orties and the entrance to the studios, crowds were running toward them from the direction of the Tuileries gardens, shouting, "The soldiers! They're murdering us!" A few ran by with blood streaming from wounds on their heads and holding arms that looked as though they had been broken.

The three of them clung to each other and pressed on. Madness, all of it. Whatever had happened in the Tuileries, Adélaïde didn't want to remain on the street to find out.

It wasn't until they were safely within the corridors of the Louvre that Adélaïde realized her dress had been torn, and all three of them had smudges of dirt on their faces and disheveled hair. Their sudden entrance drew artists out of their studios to stare at them. Adélaïde ignored them all and raced up the stairs to André's lodgings, hoping he was there and not caught up in the riots that were springing up all around the Louvre.

"Adélaïde! What happened?" André put down the paper he'd been reading, and Adélaïde rushed into his arms.

"It's starting. I think the crisis has been reached, and the citizens are rising up to take control." Her breath came in gasps and sweat soaked through her bodice.

"I can hear the shouts. Why did you go out? Sit down. Rest. Tell me." They all sat at the table, and André poured them wine. Adélaïde's hand shook as she lifted her glass to her lips. Gabrielle simply stared at hers, and Victoire sipped, her eyes round and frightened. Adélaïde forced herself to calm down and described what they'd seen to André.

"What next?" she said. "They mentioned German mercenaries. Will there be fighting?"

"According to the *Mercure*, the foreign soldiers are mostly staying at Versailles to protect the king and queen."

"I don't think that's true," Gabrielle said, standing and scraping her chair back, then pacing up and down. "The people fleeing the Tuileries said something about German soldiers."

This silenced them all, and from outside, Adélaïde could hear the continued shouting and screams. "It's all because he fired Necker," she said.

"Where are the French Guards in all of this?" Victoire asked, looking back and forth from Adélaïde to André for answers. "Aren't they supposed to keep the peace?"

"It seems the French Guards are in sympathy with the people and have been largely abandoned by their officers. Lafayette may come to Paris to command them." André held up the newspaper he'd been reading and pointed to the article.

An army of French soldiers not loyal to the king? Adélaïde's heart started to pound again. "It's unthinkable that it's come to this. The reforms made so much sense. It only needed a unity of purpose to bring everything about peacefully. Why could they not see it?"

"I'm afraid we are well beyond that," said André. "Those who are starving don't care to wait for wealthy politicians and nobles to decide their fates."

Adélaïde stared at André's half-finished canvas, a scene of battle and carnage. He hadn't started painting in the blood from the wounds, which gave the scene an oddly sterile quality, as if one could pierce the heart of a human being and have no ill effects result. She shuddered.

The sounds of chaos from outside had subsided. "I should return to my studio," Adélaïde said, "and take some measures to protect my work and ensure the safety of my students—if they come at all tomorrow. Come with me, Gabrielle, Victoire. We must do what we can while we can."

⌒⌒

Late that evening, from the windows in her apartment, Adélaïde could see the eerie light of a sky that should have been dark but was lit up by what must have been fires all around the city.

"Judging by their locations," Gabrielle said, having gone from window to window, "They're attacking the toll gates and the customs houses. Just like in Lyon."

"You must try to get some sleep, both of you," Adélaïde said. Victoire would share Gabrielle's bed, since she could not go home in safety that night.

"How can I sleep, when so much is happening?" Gabrielle's eyes shone.

Yes, Adélaïde thought. Gabrielle might well think that this is the beginning of something great. But all Adélaïde could see in her own mind was destruction. What would such mobs do with the royal palaces? Wouldn't the opulence of places like Bellevue and Marly inflame their anger? And, of course, Versailles. Could the Swiss Guard keep the king and queen safe? Did she really want them to? And all that magnificent art. Would it survive the wrath of people whose only concern was having enough bread to stay alive? What could possibly be the place of artists in a world turned upside down?

Adélaïde retired to her own bedroom. Sleep would not come or, if it did, she merely dozed, awakening with a jolt whenever her dreams took her to scenes of carnage.

Twenty-Four

Paris, July 14, 1789

The morning dawned to a fitful rain. Adélaïde hoped it would continue long enough to at least cool down the air and perhaps inhibit the tightly wound populace from starting any further riots. A citizen militia had quickly been formed the day before—after a mob stormed Saint-Lazare convent and stole more than fifty wagons of grain and whatever armaments they could find, then desecrated the relics and set upon the monks. Reports of it in the pamphlets were terrifying. And yet, the prospect of dramatic change, of ending the mindless adherence to a system that benefited only royalty and nobility, had the peculiar effect of lifting Adélaïde's spirits. If change were in the air on such a grand scale, could it mean that the iron-clad rules of the Académie would at last be demolished? Of course, there was also a side of her that said, *I'm all for change, but please let me be paid for the Hospitalers commission first.*

Gabrielle and Victoire had left the apartment before Adélaïde awoke. She imagined they'd been no more successful at sleeping well than she had. There was a note from Victoire saying she intended to go home to her family in Meudon. She would look in at the studio to do a little work, then collect some things so she could paint at home. It would be good for both of them to go to the studio, Adélaïde thought, to immerse themselves in work and try to recover from the disturbance of the day before.

Work was Gabrielle's religion. She had been with Adélaïde for seven years and in that time had proven to be the hardest-working student she had ever known. Indeed, she was hardly a student anymore. But it wasn't just that fact that endeared her to Adélaïde. Aside from her abilities with a brush, she'd been a support, a confidant, a member of Adélaïde's family, a younger sister. Adélaïde looked out for her. They sometimes had disagreements, but Gabrielle had painted herself into Adélaïde's life and, as far as Adélaïde was concerned, she need never leave it. And now, by virtue of circumstances, Victoire was apparently part of this motley family. *So be it*, Adélaïde thought.

As soon as she was dressed, Adélaïde walked to the Louvre to visit André in his studio. Even before the riots of the past two days, they had spent fewer nights together recently for the simple reason that André was anxious that the Louvre could be a site the mob might attack, as it represented the epitome of royal privilege and decadence. Adélaïde agreed with him. As long ago as the salon of 1787, the large portrait of the queen with her children that the king had commissioned from Madame Le Brun had been taken down just before the salon began. It was ostensibly because of the death of the infant princess Sophie, but the word around the Louvre was that exhibiting the queen and the children of France in such sumptuous clothing and surroundings would inflame anti-royal sentiment. By the time the officers had arrived at the expedient of not exhibiting the painting, it was too late to remove the large, ornate frame that had marked out its intended position on the gallery wall. On opening day, someone at the salon had written in the ostentatiously empty space, "*Voilà le déficit.*"

The streets that morning were calm but watchful. Only a few people were preparing for their work day, picking up the stones that had been thrown the night before and scooping up soggy pamphlets that lay curled up in the gutter and stuck to shutters and cobbles. The sky had started to clear by the time Adélaïde arrived at the artists' entrance to the Louvre, and inside, she could hear sounds as of a normal day of painting and teaching. From behind the door of Vien's studio, the master's voice instructed students in a monotone about the correct way to draw the eye around a picture in which several characters were grouped. Adélaïde chuckled to herself. Perhaps if she'd been able to take his classes, she wouldn't have had such trouble settling on the composition of the Hospitalers portrait.

In André's studio, a group of the younger academicians and *agréés* had already gathered and, rather than treating that day as if it were just like any other, were poring over the papers and pamphlets they'd likely picked up near the Palais Royale. David was not among them.

"Are those from today? And where is David?" Adélaïde asked. He'd been one of the most vocal regarding reforming the Académie, due more to his perceptions of his own injuries at the hands of the officers than any sense of general injustice. He had not been at the recent meeting Adélaïde had attended, but his name was invoked many times as a champion of reform. She would have expected him to be there.

"Some. Others are from yesterday. I suppose you've heard about it already. David has gone to join the militia under Lafayette." André said.

"The militia—and the fires, yes, I could see them from my windows." Adélaïde greeted André with a kiss on both cheeks. She shook her head. "Does David know what he's doing? Waging battle is a far cry from making pictures."

"I expect it's more a gesture than anything that will come to pass in reality," said Simon-Charles Miger, an engraver who was one of the most outspoken about reforming the Académie.

"What example is the man trying to set? Reform is all well and good, but armed revolt? Surely it needn't come to that." It was Augustin Pajou, whose pastel portrait Adélaïde had shown in her first Académie salon. He had returned the favor by sculpting the handsome portrait bust of her father that she'd placed in the background of her self-portrait with Gabrielle and Marguerite.

Her father. His establishment was precisely the sort that could be targeted by dissatisfied poor people, with its rich silks and velvets and laces catering to the highest echelons of Paris society. On Sunday, the shop would have been boarded up and locked and its wares hidden behind closed shutters. Today was Tuesday, a day when normally he would open for business at noon. After yesterday . . .

"I must go," Adélaïde said.

"You've only just arrived!" André reached out and took her hand.

"I'm sorry, I must go and see my father. I beg everyone's pardon."

She rushed off and headed for the Rue Neuve des Petits Champs, uncertain what she would find after the events of the day before. The troubles had mostly been in other parts of the city, but with the citizen militia on the streets and after the attack in the Tuileries by the Swiss Guards, she shuddered to think what might have happened.

The rain had now completely stopped and revealed a sky littered with scraps of clouds in different shades of gray. A breeze kicked up off the Seine, bringing with it the unavoidable stench of raw sewage. Adélaïde put her hand over her nose and continued up the street. The shops and ateliers that lined it hadn't yet opened, and the normally bustling thoroughfare looked naked and forlorn. It felt like a foreign country, not like the place she'd known as long as she could remember. People should already be out sharing news, buying bread, catching up with each other in the normal way of things, but the blank faces of the buildings and lack of pedestrians gave her old stomping ground a dead, deserted aspect. A few beggars had taken up the most coveted positions in sheltered alleyways, careful to keep mostly out of sight until they spotted someone who might give them some money— although with matters as they were, Adélaïde doubted they'd see much business that day. Only the cabinetmaker was out, sweeping debris off the cobbles in front of his atelier, his brow drawn into a crease in the middle as he glanced up and down the street from time to time, as if he expected something to happen and wanted to be ready for it. It was only ten, but the baker had already put out a sign saying, *"Pas de pain."*

Adélaïde quickened her pace toward her father's shop. As she drew closer, she saw that À La Toilette, still closed, showed signs that it had not come through the past few days unscathed. Splinters and chipped paint marred the previously pristine shutters, and the painted wooden sign with the needle and thread hung by one of its two chains and swiveled in the breeze. She knocked on the door. "Papa! It's me!"

A moment later someone opened the peephole, looked out, and, seeing who she was, slid the heavy bolt and opened the door just enough so she could squeeze inside, then slammed it shut again and shot the bolt home. It was Jacqueline, who greeted her with a kiss.

"How is Papa? Is everything all right?"

"You'd better come and see."

She conducted Adélaïde through the darkened shop to the door that led to the apartment above. Adélaïde followed her up the stairs.

"Is that you Adéla?" Her father's voice sounded weak and shaky.

It took a moment for Adélaïde's eyes to adjust to the dimly lit sitting room. When they did, she saw her father lying on a settee, his head wrapped in a white bandage and what looked like dried blood staining a spot above one of his eyes. She ran to him and knelt by his side. Only then did she notice that glass littered the floor below one of the shuttered windows. "What happened?"

"I told him not to do it. We'd closed the shutters, and it was hot. We could hear the disturbance outside, people yelling and running." Jacqueline approached her father and took one of his hands. "The fool had to see what was going on."

"This is my livelihood! I wanted to protect it if I could." Tears stood in his eyes. "It's nothing. I will recover. I just don't know if Paris will."

"Someone saw him and noticed his velvet coat and lace jabot, and before I could pull him away from the window, a rock was thrown. It broke the glass and hit his forehead, driving a sliver of glass in deep."

"Have you summoned an apothecary?"

"No shops opened yesterday, not after what happened."

Yes, so much more than her father's blood had been shed then. Adélaïde put her hand on her father's cheek. "What did you do? Who bandaged you up so carefully?"

Jacqueline answered "I was able to get the glass out, cleaned it up, and stitched it closed. He will no doubt have a scar."

Adélaïde nodded her thanks to Jacqueline, but she was angry. Not just because of her father's injury, but because she understood the deep dissatisfaction that made the people turn on anyone they saw as contributing to their misery. They could not—or did not—distinguish between those responsible for it and those whose lives and circumstances insulated them from woes like theirs. "The militias should keep the mob under better control. I hope the streets will be safe again soon."

"Do you think this will pass quickly?" Jacqueline asked.

"It will pass quickly only if the king and his advisors come to understand that they must make changes that many will resist. The world is not the same as it was ten years ago. The time of absolute monarchy is ending."

Claude Labille lifted his head a little. "You sympathize with the revolutionaries?"

"With their ideals, yes. I'm less enamored of their methods." Adélaïde took her father's hand. "I presume you have no plans to open the shop today. I would keep it shut until order is fully restored. You'll be safe here, with everything locked as it is. Have you food? Water to drink?" Adélaïde directed her questions at Jacqueline.

"We have enough for a week. The serving girl ran off, so we are alone."

A pang of guilt clutched Adélaïde's heart. She should have checked on them sooner. But what would that have accomplished? She couldn't have stayed with them. Her father understood that. It didn't change the fact that he was now getting to be an old man and vulnerable in times like these. "I must go back to André and see what is to be done.

The artists have their own revolution brewing, insignificant as it is compared to the larger events." She bent down and kissed her father on the cheek. "If I can I'll return with provisions, bread if I can find any."

Jacqueline stood by her father and watched Adélaïde leave. "You take care as well, Adélaïde," she said.

$$\backsim$$

By then it was midday. Before returning to the Louvre, Adélaïde ran to her studio; if anyone had come for lessons, she would send them home immediately. But she found only Victoire there. "I expected you'd be gone to Meudon by now," Adélaïde said. "It would be smart to stay away from Paris until the unrest dies down." Adélaïde glanced over her shoulder at Victoire as she closed the shutters over the windows and fastened them all shut.

"I tried to hire a carriage, but no one would take me."

"Why not?" Adélaïde asked, stopping what she was doing.

"They say that the French Royal Guard has surrounded the city, and no one is permitted to enter or leave."

Has it come to that? Half a year ago, no one would have dreamed such a thing was possible. "Where is Gabrielle? Has she gone out to get some bread?"

"I don't know. She left over an hour ago and didn't say."

Over an hour? Where could she have gone? What had she done? Adélaïde took hold of Victoire by the shoulders. "Did she say anything to you, anything at all that would reveal where she might be?" After her actions at the Réveillon riots, Adélaïde feared that Gabrielle would do more, would involve herself in a struggle she saw as that of her own class, her own people, no matter the danger to herself. The idea of losing Gabrielle made her heart clench. So much talent. Such a soul. Adélaïde loved her more than she could imagine loving a sister or a child. She could no more do without Gabrielle than without André.

"N-no. Do you think she's in danger?" Victoire's voice rose to a near squeak.

"Everyone who is not safely at home behind locked doors is in danger today, from what I've heard. Especially if what you say is true, that the royal troops have surrounded Paris."

Victoire's lower lip quivered. "I swear, if I'd known she might be in peril I would have stopped her!"

Adélaïde drew Victoire into an embrace and squeezed her tight. "I'm so sorry. It's not your fault, not at all. I'm just worried, for you as well. Perhaps she has just gone out to . . . to . . ." Try as she might, Adélaïde could not think of a single thing that would explain Gabrielle's actions other than a desire to join the revolutionaries, to repeat the same actions as she did during the Reveillon riots in April.

But what would she be able to do? Gabrielle had no experience or skill with firearms. Or had she? Adélaïde didn't know everything about her student from Lyon. Living in the countryside, perhaps she had had an education in hunting as well as serving at table. But that was absurd. Adélaïde's mind sped along any route she could find no matter the sense. She released Victoire and held her at arm's length again. "I shall go and look for her. You—just stay here. Work if you can. Try not to fret, but do not, on any account, leave this studio. If anyone comes to the door, do not let them in."

Now Victoire's enormous brown eyes filled with tears. "Oh, Madame!"

"It's all right. All will be well. I'll return soon, I promise."

Adélaïde left her student in charge of the studio and locked the door behind her.

ᴄᴇᴐ

Not seeing Gabrielle on the Rue Ménars, Adélaïde headed for the Louvre. On the way, she encountered a gathering of common servants, artisans' wives, and market women milling on the streets as if waiting for some signal telling them what they should do next. Anticipation electrified the air. The latent power Adélaïde sensed all around her could achieve anything, she thought: great works of creative genius or great works of destruction. The people were not exactly a mob at that moment. They had coalesced, though, into a body that held within it the force of nature. Adélaïde continually scanned the crowds for Gabrielle but had seen no sign of her by the time she reached the Louvre.

As she entered the gates and started on the path to the door of the artists' residences and studios, she heard a sound coming from the direction of the Pont Royal, the bridge that connected the Quai near the Louvre to the University district on the other side of the Seine. The sound grew and soon Adélaïde realized it was the noise of many people walking. No, marching. In boots. *The citizens' militia!* She dashed the last hundred yards to the palace, grabbed hold of the door handle, and pulled.

It wouldn't budge. Not the tiniest bit. This door, as far as she knew, was open night and day. It was up to the artists who lived and worked there to secure their own lodgings and studios, although a guard was posted outside at night. Adélaïde knocked on the door, suppressing her rising fear. She knocked louder. The knuckles of one hand started to bleed, so she knocked with the other. The last thing she wanted to do was call attention to herself, but now she could see men carrying weapons, some of them more than one, flooding along the street that led from the bridge. Suddenly more aware than she'd ever been of her diminutive body, she commenced pounding against the unyielding wood with the sides of both fists. "Let me in!" she screamed. But by now the crowds who'd been waiting for a purpose took up a chant and drowned her out completely.

"*À la Bastille!*"

To the Bastille? But why? The ancient fortress was virtually empty, as far as Adélaïde knew. It was not used to house prisoners anymore, except for a few whose crimes were more political than otherwise, those who would not be suitable as inmates among the petty thieves, brigands, and murderers who populated the Conciergerie.

She could not fathom the reason until someone in the mob yelled out, "The gunpowder! The ammunition! They moved it to the Bastille!"

The crowd must have come from Les Invalides, the garrison of old soldiers where armaments were stored. Hence the multitude of weapons.

Realizing no one had any interest in her but were intent on other mischief, Adélaïde gave up trying to raise someone in the Louvre and left the compound to hover on the edge of the crowd, an edge mostly occupied by older women. She recognized one of them, the baker's wife. "Madame Boulanger!" She called it out three times before the woman turned and saw Adélaïde's wave.

Madame Boulanger elbowed her way through to stand in front of Adélaïde. "What are you doing here, Madame Guiard? You'd best go home and leave the lowly citizens to their business."

"I am one of those lowly citizens, Madame. You mistake me if you think otherwise."

"I've seen the royal carriage coming to fetch you and bringing you back."

Adélaïde thought quickly. "Ah, you see, I am little more than a servant. It's just that my royal clients prize the service I provide and wish to protect their investment." She did not mention that their value of her service extended to a recent commission worth thirty thousand livres, more money than the bakery had probably ever seen in all its years of existence.

Still skeptical, Madame Boulanger nonetheless listened to Adélaïde's questions.

"Who controls the militia? Are there women among them? What will they do at the Bastille?"

"There are a few women, but it is mostly men who joined the militia.

Lafayette leads them. But this is not the militia. At least, not all of them. These are ordinary citizens who simply want bread and who want their champions returned to the National Assembly."

"What will you do?" Adélaïde asked.

"I intend to follow them. *Je m'excuse.*" She nodded and rushed off, melting into the stream of people who now came from every direction to be absorbed by the mob heading to the Bastille.

Adélaïde glanced back at the Louvre. No one would let her in. And she knew in her heart that the one place Gabrielle was likely to be was in the thick of it all. She had no choice but to join the crowds too.

⤬

The squat towers of the Bastille, peering over the other buildings nearby, came in view within an hour. Shortly after that, the crowd stopped moving. People were pressed so close together that Adélaïde could not go forward or backward. They stayed like that for hours, as the sun climbed higher in the sky and Adélaïde felt the sweat stream down her back and under her arms. An eerie quiet descended, as if the many thousands of people gathered there all strained to hear what was happening at the front, where the armed ragtag militia stood.

At about five o'clock, Adélaïde began to feel as if she might faint. She turned away to see if she could get out of the mob and return to her studio. It appeared little would happen now, and there was no hope of finding Gabrielle if she were in the middle of the crowd. But just as she took a step, everyone surged forward, and she was borne along with the press of bodies. In a ripple coming from the direction of the Bastille, the silence erupted into shouts of, "*Ils sont prisonniers! Nous devons les libérer!*" What prisoners? Adélaïde thought.

Soon after that, gunshots rang out, and from the top of the great towers the boom of cannon shook the air and plumes of black smoke rose into the sky. It was like a clarion to the masses, who rushed forward to see what was happening. With as much strength as she could muster, Adélaïde stood her ground and let the crowd jostle past her. She could not imagine—did not want to imagine—what drew these people with their gaunt, angry faces forward. Despite the heat, she shivered, and she prayed that Gabrielle would remain safe wherever she was. Pushing with all her might, Adélaïde gradually eased herself to the side, out of the main current of the human river. On the way she was buffeted by elbows and in one case she thought a fist. But she kept her head down and fixed her eyes on the entrance to an alley. She reached it, gasping for breath, and waited until the crush had passed her by and the bodies around her thinned. Then she turned and ran back along the Rue Saint-Antoine, weak with hunger and thirst, hardly feeling her legs move but racing as fast as she could.

By the time she reached the Hôtel de Ville, Adélaïde's legs simply refused to move. She was only halfway home. She would have to rest, there was no denying that fact. Her heart pounded painfully in her chest, and bright dots gathered at the periphery of her vision. *Not now,* she thought. *I can't faint now.* She closed her eyes and tried to slow her breathing, all the time aware of the growing roar of a crowd now approaching from the east. What had happened? What made them all turn around? Her only desire was to run home, but her body refused to cooperate. She was still leaning against the corner of a building when the mass of angry people reached the Place de l'Hôtel de Ville. Several men—a couple in uniform, at least one in the ordinary clothes of a gentleman—were being dragged along, their hands tied with ropes. Soon they had been shoved to the center of the square and completely surrounded by people so that Adélaïde could no longer see them. But she knew where they were by the intent focus of all the others.

Adélaïde remembered long afterwards the smell that emanated from so many furious and wild men and women. It wasn't just a smell—it was a charge of energy, like the air before a lightning strike. Someone yelled something unintelligible, and the entire crowd roared.

Those near the very center, where the captives had been led, began moving in a menacing way. Adélaïde saw fists fly and the guttural cry of blood lust. A blade flashed. And then, within very little time, three severed heads rose above the crowd, and everyone began to move again, this time in the direction of the Palais Royale.

Adélaïde's stomach roiled and churned until she had to double over and vomit into the gutter. She heard rather than saw the crowd move on to their next destination, wherever that was, and when the cries and shouts faded, she gathered her strength and ran all the way back to the Rue Ménars and her studio.

Adélaïde had no recollection of the route she took or how much time elapsed before she arrived. Her hands shook so violently she could barely fit the key into the lock on her studio door. "Victoire! Victoire!" she called, but, just as in a nightmare, she could hardly make herself heard.

The door opened before she succeeded in inserting the key, and Adélaïde fell into Gabrielle's arms.

⌒ᖯ⌒

Once she had drunk the tisane Gabrielle prepared and eaten the morsel of bread her student had miraculously been able to procure, Adélaïde felt strong enough to talk. "I can't begin . . . it was horrible. Where were you?"

"I wanted to see what was happening and also get some bread for breakfast. I stayed out longer than I meant to, talking to people, watching the crowd." Gabrielle gestured toward a just-begun pastel, where she had sketched in the outlines of women and men wearing tattered clothing. "When I saw the armed men coming from Les Invalides, I knew I had no place among them, that whatever would happen I had to trust would work out for the best. I came back here. Victoire told me you'd gone to look for me."

Victoire peered out from behind Gabrielle and said, "I assumed you'd be back quickly, Gabrielle, from what you said. And when you weren't, I didn't know what to think."

Adélaïde looked back and forth between her two students. "I thought I'd lost you," she said, taking Gabrielle's hand. "I would have done anything to find you and bring you back. Thank heaven you did not witness all that I did."

Gabrielle said, "I knew you would come after me. Which is why— tempted as I was—I didn't follow the soldiers. I'm so sorry I wasn't here when you arrived this afternoon."

Rested now and her strength somewhat restored, Adélaïde stood, looking Gabrielle straight in her eyes. "It seems more than one of us is capable of being unwise."

They all embraced, and Adélaïde's heart swelled with gratitude— that she had this to come home to, these young women to help her and keep her safe.

"Now it's my turn," Gabrielle said. "I must make you promise never to do something so foolhardy again—at least, not without me."

Twenty-Five

Paris, August 1789

The fall of the Bastille ricocheted throughout Paris and beyond. The event itself proved to be symbolic rather than substantive, since few prisoners had been released and the fortress itself was merely a relic from a bygone age. Nonetheless, nothing was the same afterwards. Something about the violence of the gesture seemed to impress upon those at the heart of government that the situation as it was could not simply be ignored or papered over with meaningless pseudo reforms. Every day, pamphlets cried out with news of changes that would have been unthinkable a few months ago. Nobles and aristocrats no longer had immunity from taxation. And government posts were to be filled by those who merited them, not those who paid money to the right officials.

In the midst of so much change, Adélaïde, André, and the other artists and students had no choice but to continue on their same daily rounds—teaching, learning, fulfilling commissions, and preparing for the imminent biennial salon. But the world outside the corridors of the Louvre managed to filter through in insidious ways. For Adélaïde, everything she did felt harder, took longer, and seemed less significant. What did getting the right shade of red for the shadows in the folds of a scarlet uniform matter compared to reimagining the way a nation would be governed? And the prevailing uncertainty made her question every action, every decision, and weigh it for importance and relevance. Would it be better for her to concentrate on her own work or to involve herself in the Académie reforms? If she did not raise her voice, would women be forever left out of the mainstream? Or would doing so only justify the criticism of many, that women were not capable of the sustained effort required to produce great art?

Some of the artists at the Louvre appeared to hardly notice the disruption around them. Others threw themselves into it, abandoning their work unless it directly related to larger events. David, for instance. On the day that Adélaïde had been on her way to Versailles to continue work on the biggest, most important, most prestigious commission of her life, he had been at the tennis court witnessing the oaths, watching as a new order was born—something he made sure everyone around him knew as he began work on a canvas that would dwarf the one Adélaïde was painting for the Hospitalers, using sketches of events he had seen as they happened. Adélaïde had thought David would envy her the commission from Provence. Once she knew what he was up to, she imagined he more likely thought of it with disdain. What did such a painting matter now? To Adélaïde, it mattered a great deal, of course. In fact, she had thirty thousand reasons to finish it with all haste.

Adélaïde was caught between the structure of patronage that supported her career and her desire to embrace radical change. She felt her impossible position most keenly when she left the safety of her apartment or studio. From morning until late at night, the streets vibrated with suppressed fury. Adélaïde's students arrived for their lessons distracted, some with a glimmer of fear in their eyes, others with barely suppressed excitement. At least half an hour at the beginning of every lesson was occupied with chatter about the latest political developments—a change from the art-world gossip that had previously been her students' obsession.

And Adélaïde was very glad that, despite pressure from André to do so, she hadn't given up her smaller studio on the Rue Ménars when Mesdames secured the larger space in the Bibliothèque du Roi for her. It was bad enough that she herself had to go there every day to work on the canvas that she was now painting in earnest, having finished all the sketches in June. But because the building belonged to the crown, there were always clusters of men and women glaring at everyone who entered or left the premises. Adélaïde took care to nod to them in a friendly way and made an effort to appear as if she were no more than a lowly servant, dressing in serviceable work clothes with paint stains, wearing only a turban on her head. But no one ever smiled back.

Once inside the massive studio, she continued to translate what she'd laid out on a small scale to the huge canvas—which was perhaps an even greater challenge than everything that had come before in this project. As she worked all the hours of daylight she could spare, the suspicion that the Comte de Provence was by now occupied with more pressing matters than a painting to decorate a grand hall niggled at the back of Adélaïde's mind. How many thousands of livres had she spent on the painting already? Would she ever see any of that money again? Yet she could not fail to complete it. So long as there was a chance everything would settle into a constitutional monarchy, she must uphold her commitments. All the other academicians she knew were working as if nothing were likely to change. What else could they do? Even those fortunate enough to have grace-and-favor accommodations in the Louvre had to eat and purchase art supplies.

Adélaïde had already completed the paintings she would show in the Académie salon, which was due to open in a matter of days. Her three previous showings had been enthusiastically received. But this year, she was exhibiting the portrait of Madame Victoire and the posthumous portrait of Mesdames' sister, Elisabeth of Parma. These portraits represented such a departure for her that she dreaded what the critics would say. Would they find her use of color too bold? Her composition too derivative? It was true that she'd patterned the portrait of Elisabeth on the style of northern masters like Van Dyke. As such, she had turned her back on the growing Italianate neoclassicism that André, as a history painter, was forced to adopt.

And then, Lafayette wrote and the Assembly adopted the Declaration of the Rights of Man, two days before the Académie salon opened. The document mimicked the American Declaration of Independence and was full of the language of equality and fraternity. It had been circulating as a pamphlet, and Adélaïde had read it with joy at first. It gave her hope that things would change for the better. However, it didn't take long for her to see that the rights it outlined were all for men. No mention was made of how they applied to women. She could only hope that the enthusiasm for equality would spill over to the needs of her own sex.

The world was changing so fast that everything hanging on the walls of the Salon Carré that August looked stuffy and out of date, remnants of a time when a different order prevailed. Hardly surprising that the salon was not well attended and few critics wrote about it. The ones who did were scathing about Adélaïde's portraits, going back to the old criticisms that a male artist must have executed her work or at least had painted the backgrounds for her because they were not in lock-step with her usual style. She was disappointed but not surprised.

༄༅

A few days after the salon opened, Adélaïde sat staring at a blank canvas in her small studio. She intended to start a portrait of her father, something manageable to break the strain of working on the Hospitalers canvas, but couldn't seem to get beyond laying the ground. Gabrielle was also there, but she, too, could not settle to her work. The rest of the students were not due to arrive until later so the studio was uncharacteristically quiet.

Finally, Gabrielle said, "There's a meeting at the Louvre in an hour."

"Oh? What about? I haven't heard anything of it." Normally André would keep her informed of such meetings when the younger academicians and *agréés* would try to reach an agreement concerning the reforms they wanted to propose to the officers, and he had said nothing.

"All the wives and daughters are meeting to discuss a delegation to the National Assembly."

The wives and daughters? "How did you find out about this? Should I come?" She was no artist's wife or daughter, but neither was she entirely woven into the predominantly male fabric of the Académie.

"They invited me and Victoire. I suppose we count as your daughters!" She smiled. "I'll tell you everything and see if it's something you should take part in as well."

Gabrielle left and took the vestiges of liveliness out of the studio with her. She'd been in a heightened state ever since the riots last April. Far from being frightened or upset about the massive changes in the air, Gabrielle had come into her own. She took part in anything she could, from sewing cockades with the market women to joining a club of young men and women formed to explore how to help the government out of its disastrous financial situation. It was as if the real Gabrielle had been asleep within the artist, only venturing out in tentative steps, until the fabric of society tore enough for her to step through and announce herself to the world.

Adélaïde hoped all these activities wouldn't distract Gabrielle completely from painting, but she understood her student's need to be active. She herself yearned for something constructive to do. There would be a time when painting would be important again, but right now everything was too undefined. The idea of fixing an image inside the boundaries of a square of canvas felt impossible. What could be fixed, after all, in a time of such fluidity? Painting a portrait or a historical scene was a lengthy process, and the sentiments that existed at the beginning could not be counted upon to survive by the end. This was especially true for Adélaïde's commission from the Comte de Provence. She did her best not to be distracted from day to day by some new reversal or by the prospect that everything she thought would be the state of affairs when she started would be nothing but a distant memory by the time she finished this gigantic canvas.

No wonder André had barely picked up a brush in months. As to Madame Le Brun, she had left the chaos of Paris to stay in Louveciennes with Madame du Barry—the late king's mistress, who had managed to maintain a luxurious lifestyle thanks to her affairs with other nobles. Adélaïde couldn't entirely blame her rival for leaving Paris at such a time. Madame Le Brun's connections to the court were deeper and more entrenched than Adélaïde's and, thanks to the debacle of the portrait that left a blank space on the wall in the 1787 salon, the commoners of Paris knew of her too. A short step from her notoriety as a society portraitist was common knowledge concerning her love affairs. The rumor that she had been bedding Monsieur de Calonne—the finance minister who had been dismissed in disgrace two years earlier—refused to die. The more unkind whispers suggested that Calonne had diverted funds from the treasury to underwrite the construction of the Hôtel Le Brun. Adélaïde doubted that was true. Nonetheless, Madame Le Brun sent only one entry to the 1789 salon: a conventional portrait of a Polish prince in an allegorical role.

Adélaïde did wonder, though, how Madame Le Brun justified leaving her daughter behind when she visited Madame du Barry. The little girl must have been nearly ten years old by then and possibly confused and frightened by the uproar in Paris without her mother to protect her. She knew she could never have done the same, if she'd had a child. Then again, she would be unlikely to have found herself in the same position. It would be much harder for someone like Madame Le Brun to adjust to a radically altered artistic milieu than it would be for Adélaïde, who, despite her appointment with Mesdames and commission from Provence, had always remained on the periphery of the system of royal patronage.

Two hours passed while Adélaïde continued to think about what all the changes could be for women artists at all stages of their careers. During that time, she'd painted in the outline of a hand and then painted it out and moved it slightly, not concentrating at all on what she was doing.

At last, she heard Gabrielle's and Victoire's excited voices as they ran up the steps to the studio and burst through the door.

"Well? What was the meeting about?"

"You know about patriotic donations, yes?" Gabrielle didn't give Adélaïde time to answer. "Well, we've thought of a way to encourage more people to make them, to help fund the government during this crisis."

Victoire spoke up. "You see, it really is absurd that people—women especially—go around wearing costly jewels that could be turned to much better use. My gold bracelet, for instance." She circled her fingers around her wrist where the bracelet had been.

"We're taking up a collection of all the jewelry and precious objects that could be sold or melted down that are owned by the women of the Académie—well, the wives and daughters, anyway—and we shall present it, in person, to the National Assembly. It may not amount to enough to make much of a difference, but the object is to be very public about it to encourage women all over Paris and France to do the same. Isn't it a marvelous idea?"

It seemed rather small and futile to Adélaïde. But she didn't want to dampen the spirits of her two favorites. "You know I don't wear any jewelry. Any extra resources I have go into my paintings, especially the one at the Bibliothèque. But I will gladly donate some money."

"We don't want money, not yet. It's the symbolism that's important." Victoire continued to rub her wrist. Adélaïde felt a little sorry for her. The simple gold bracelet had been a gift from her mother.

Astonishingly, in a matter of days the artists' families came up with objects worth close to five thousand livres. Adélaïde went with Gabrielle and Victoire to the Louvre to help the delegation prepare. Those who would accompany the gift to the assembly dressed like Roman women in flowing white gowns, and Guillaume Moitte's wife had agreed to give a speech to the assembly. Adélaïde was still a little skeptical that the gesture would achieve anything, but she helped pin cockades and dress hair with everyone else and waved enthusiastically when they set off for Versailles in hired carriages.

To everyone's surprise, it worked. Once word got out about the dramatic gift by the wives and daughters of the academicians, groups formed all over Paris to take up similar collections.

These activities kept Adélaïde and her students busy, but the money they raised all went to help the government pay its debts. Thousands of the common people were still on the verge of starvation. The beggars on the streets near the Louvre and the Palais Royal were more gaunt, more hollow-eyed than ever. The Revolution hadn't reached them yet. Adélaïde feared that the power of an angry mob lurked just below the surface, barely under control of the Paris Guard.

Twenty-Six

Paris, October 5, 1789

"Ssh!" Gabrielle said as Adélaïde and her students worked intently on their paintings and drawings during morning teaching hours in her studio—which she'd resumed when the unrest had settled down a little.

"No one's speaking," Victoire said. "How can we be quieter?"

But Gabrielle held up her hand and put her finger to her lips. Adélaïde lifted her brush from the surface of her father's portrait and nodded to all the others to do the same, so the swish of paint on canvas and scratch of pastel on paper also ceased. After a moment, they all heard it. A drumbeat, approaching from the east.

Adélaïde shivered, the memory of the violent crowd surging from the Bastille still raw inside of her. She knew of no public event scheduled for that day. None of the pamphleteers had shouted from street corners for people to assemble for any reason. Soon the drumbeat became louder until it was clear it wasn't a single drum but many. As they listened in taut silence, the sound of booted feet marching in time to the beat came into focus. Marching, yes, but not in a crisp, trained, military way. This wasn't a detachment of guards, Adélaïde thought. If not soldiers, then who?

"I need to see what's happening." Gabrielle's voice made everyone jump. Before an instant had passed, she'd cleaned her brush and untied her smock.

"No!" Adélaïde said. She wasn't going to lose sight of her again. She couldn't bear to go through the same fear and panic she had last time.

Gabrielle approached her and took both her hands, holding them with a firm and steady grip. "I promise I am just going to look. I have to find out what this is. I will be no more than half an hour, I promise."

Victoire tossed her brush into the glass of water hooked onto the easel where her watercolor drawing was propped. "I'll go too. It's safer with two of us."

Adélaïde pushed her fear down as deep as she could and nodded. She couldn't force them to stay anyway. "Half an hour. No longer."

After the two friends closed the door behind them and hurtled down the stairs to the street, Adélaïde looked back at her other students, all wide eyed, none of them working on their pictures. "I don't know what's happening," she said, "but I think you should all return home. Do not go near the Hôtel de Ville, whatever you do. Better to go far out of your way than risk being caught up in something of which we know nothing."

The students hurriedly cleaned their implements and tore off their smocks. In less than five minutes, Adélaïde found herself alone. She desperately wanted to run over to the Louvre to find André, but it was hard to tell how quickly the crowd was moving. The Rue Ménars wasn't on the way to anywhere important, and, in any case, it was too narrow a street to accommodate hordes of marchers. But to get to the Louvre, she'd have to cross the Rue Saint-Antoine, the main route from anywhere east in Paris to anywhere west.

Adélaïde paced around the studio, stopping now and then to look out the windows—a futile exercise since she could not see beyond the buildings on the other side of the street. Soon the drumbeats and footsteps were accompanied by the dull roar of a chant, words too indistinct to discern.

A moment later, the street-level door of the building opened, and the excited chatter of Gabrielle and Victoire crescendoed up the stairs. Within moments, they burst through the door of the studio.

"It's all women! The fishwives and market-stall owners. They're marching to Versailles." Victoire was breathless.

Adélaïde fetched two cups of water and handed them to each of them. "Why now? Why today?" Adélaïde asked.

"Because," Gabrielle said, pausing to wipe her mouth on her sleeve, "they couldn't buy any bread."

The shortage of bread was nothing new. Nonetheless, to go to Versailles, where the royal family—including Mesdames, now—was protected only by elite guards neither numerous nor well-armed enough to keep determined attackers at bay was an escalation. These were not the assemblymen or the politicians. These were angry women—mothers, wives. This changed everything.

"Which way were they going?" Adélaïde asked.

"Past the Louvre, over the Pont Royale," Victoire said, and Gabrielle added, "They should be on the other bank very soon."

"Let's let them pass by. Then we'll go out." Adélaïde didn't want to risk any more than necessary.

When they could no longer distinctly hear the chants and the drums and the marching feet, Adélaïde, Gabrielle, and Victoire put on their hats and coats and went down to the street. Just before they stepped out the door, Gabrielle pulled six tricolor cockades and six pins out of her pocket. "We should wear these," she said.

Adélaïde pinned her two to her hat and her breast. The constitution, a document meant to inspire unity, instead forced everyone to choose sides: the royalists on one side, and the Jacobins on the other. The poor sided with the Jacobins, whose token was the tricolor, which meant that now, in Paris, failure to wear the cockade made one likely to face jeers and ridicule. The fishwives that day had pushed matters a notch further. There was no telling whether the taunts Adélaïde sometimes faced on her way out of her large studio in the Bibliothèque Royale would transform into actions. Gabrielle was right about wearing the badges. At a time like this, they must not be mistaken for royalists.

As the three of them walked toward the Palais Royale, watchful, waiting crowds gathered. "What happens next?" Adélaïde whispered.

"They will know at the Palais Royale," Gabrielle said.

Since last spring, the residence of the Duc d'Orléans had become a center of Jacobin activities. If there was printed information to be had, it would likely be churned off the presses in the arcade by the gardens. It didn't surprise Adélaïde that they hadn't even reached the northern gate of the palace when a man strode past them and thrust a broadsheet into their hands. The three of them clustered around to read it.

Fishwives go to Versailles to demand the king and his family come to Paris. Procession to arrive at Versailles at midday to convey the king and queen to the Tuileries, the sheet said.

A knot of dread formed in Adélaïde's stomach. Not since the days of Louis Quatorze and the Fronde had the Bourbons resided in the city, preferring the more easily defended palace of Versailles.

"Should we go home?" Victoire asked, her voice shaking.

"No." Somewhere deep inside her, Adélaïde understood that this moment was a turning point, a threshold beyond which nothing would ever be the same. "I think we need to be here, to bear witness. Besides, everyone knows Gabrielle. We'll be fine."

How odd that Gabrielle's low birth should serve as a talisman— against what, Adélaïde couldn't say.

More and more people streamed out of apartments and shops. Adélaïde and her students followed the general movement and took up places along the Quai du Louvre among a crowd of men and women, all, like them, wearing their tricolor cockades as prominently as possible, waiting for the procession to return from Versailles. For, according to another broadsheet handed out about an hour later, by the time the fishwives had reached Versailles, their numbers had swelled into the thousands and comprised both men and women.

And on the nine-mile march back to Paris, the entire court would be traveling with them as well. Even with carriages and horses, they would be unable to move faster than those who surrounded them on foot.

Hours passed, and everyone remained locked in anticipation. No one wanted to relinquish a spot with a clear view of the arrival in Paris of King Louis XVI and Queen Marie Antoinette, their children, the officers of the court, their aunts, and siblings. This time, they were not just on an outing to the opera or the theater. This time, they would remain in the capital, taking up residence in the dilapidated palace of the Tuileries.

By the time night fell, torches blazed all along the route the caravan would have to traverse—across the Pont Royal, along the Quai du Louvre, and onto the Cours du Caroussel. Feet shuffled and a restless murmur of conversation rose and fell, but still, no one moved.

At about nine o'clock, just as Adélaïde was sure her legs would decline to hold her upright any longer, shouts arose from the vicinity of the bridge and washed toward them like a wave. "They're here!" All those who'd been stretched out along the perpendicular streets pressed as close as they could to the route from the bridge. So many bodies squeezed into the space that the air warmed and it could almost have been a late-summer night.

When the procession came into view, the crowd grew denser still, and in the confusion, Adélaïde lost sight of Gabrielle and Victoire. They'd doubtless been swept forward with everyone else, eager to catch a glimpse of the no-longer invincible monarchs.

The king and queen's gilded carriage was first to appear. It towered above the heads of the people and rocked from side to side as it was jostled, rolling near enough to where Adélaïde stood that she caught a glimpse of the queen within. The lines drawn from the corners of her mouth to her chin and the deep circles under her eyes made her look much older than she was. She stared out at the chaos, unseeing, as if she were already somewhere else. Just before she passed beyond view, Adélaïde thought she saw the queen's lips form the words, *Dieu nous protège*, but she couldn't be certain.

Adélaïde fought the buffeting around her to stay rooted where she was as a dozen more carriages, not quite as ornate, rolled past her. They carried courtiers and cousins, ladies-in-waiting and valets, the bloated hangers-on who littered the halls of Versailles. Adélaïde wondered how many had managed to flee before this day, if they had any idea what was ahead. She doubted it. The world within the vast palace had been in its own enchanted bubble until very recently.

After a time, the crowd thinned a little. It seemed most people had surged on to follow the queen's carriage, to catch a glimpse of the woman who had been the object of so much hatred and scorn for so long.

But Adélaïde didn't move with them. Mesdames' carriage had not been among those that had already gone by. Perhaps they hadn't been at Versailles after all, Adélaïde thought, relieved for reasons too complicated to grasp in that moment.

But her relief was short lived. Close behind a crowd of women— many of them chattering and laughing, waving to the crowd and calling out, "We did it! We showed them!"—the coach that had occasionally come to collect Adélaïde from Paris to attend a sitting at Bellevue rocked slowly along, the jaunty feathers at its corners waving incongruously above the bedraggled women that surrounded it. Would the elderly ladies be looking out? Would they see her and recognize her? Perhaps, for the sake of their dignity, she should turn away. Or perhaps it would comfort them to spy a familiar face in this hostile crowd.

In any case, Adélaïde found she was incapable of looking away. The driver on the box stared straight ahead, above the crowd. His livery coat was misbuttoned, as if he hadn't had time to dress properly and likely didn't dare put it to rights once he was in public view. There was no sign of the usual postilions or footmen. Perhaps they had all fled at the first inkling of trouble. The lack made the carriage appear vulnerable. It would take little effort for the accompanying crowd to topple it and spill out its fragile occupants. Adélaïde put her hand over her heart as the four glossy black horses clopped up, flanks sweating and nostrils flaring in suppressed panic. Without even thinking of it, her feet arranged themselves to curtsy, one behind the other balanced on its toe. She bowed her head and started to dip, but a hand gripped her elbow and held her up. She looked to the side. It was the baker's wife, who didn't give any sign of noticing what Adélaïde had just done. Adélaïde's initial annoyance turned to gratitude when she realized the woman had prevented her from betraying her connection to, her sympathy for, Mesdames. By the time she looked again, the carriage had almost passed by, but it was near enough for her to see that the curtains had been drawn across the windows. Perhaps that was for the best.

A moment later, Adélaïde understood that the king's elderly aunts had an even more pressing reason than those who went before them for closing their eyes to what lay outside their carriage. Only a few yards behind it, three men held long pikes that lifted the severed heads of three of the palace guards aloft for all the world to see, their tongues lolling out of their mouths, blood caked to the poles themselves. Adélaïde covered her mouth and looked down at her shoes, toes dusty from the dirt kicked up from between the cobbles, fighting the wave of nausea that threatened to overcome her. *Please no*, she prayed. *If there is a God, stop this madness before it has a chance to spread.*

⧼ↄ

Later that night, after the ogling crowd had watched the carriages enter the gates that led to the Tuileries palace and everyone went home, Adélaïde laid out some bread and cheese and a bottle of wine for the three of them back at her apartment. But none of them had any appetite, and the food lay untouched on the table.

"Must there always be someone killed?" Victoire asked. Her hands still shook as she brought her glass to her lips. She'd seen the heads as well.

Gabrielle must have had a clear sight of them too, but altogether tougher fiber held her together. "What will it be like, trying to get into the Louvre now? Guards will no doubt impede our entrance," she said.

The Tuileries was right next door to the Louvre. It was inevitable that the surrounding streets would be disrupted, making it difficult for anyone who needed access to the studios. Oddly, Adélaïde hadn't thought about André all day. Had he been out on the street among his friends too? Or had the artists mostly stayed out of sight? She had no doubt, though, that however André had spent this momentous day, David must have been in the thick of things. The arrogant artist was becoming insufferable, especially since he'd lost his battle to have his late student's works exhibited in the Louvre. While enjoying all the privileges of being an academician, he spread dissension among anyone who would listen to him. Was he a harbinger of things to come? Were there men in the assembly who harbored the same destructive impulses?

Icy dread gripped Adélaïde's heart. But for the sake of her students, she had to pretend not to feel it. "Whatever the difficulty, we must all go to the Louvre tomorrow and look in on our friends. Life must go on as usual. We all have work to do."

Twenty-Seven

Paris, September 1790

The streets all around the Tuileries, the Palais Royal, and the Louvre bore little resemblance to the neighborhood Adélaïde had known and loved all her life. Not only was it saturated with uniformed guards and frequently disrupted by one or another Jacobin standing on a table outside the Palais Royal to spout political rhetoric, it positively crackled at all times with the tension created by the juxtaposition of untold, unthinking wealth and privilege with abject poverty and starvation. All it would take, Adélaïde thought, would be for a guard to accidentally fire a rifle, and the entire heavily armed and densely populated vicinity would erupt into chaos. And yet, day after day, it did not happen.

Nonetheless, a current of indefinable threat flowed through the gutters like sewage. People looked over their shoulders whenever they came to a street corner, glanced down alleyways they'd never noticed before as they passed, and kept their eyes focused a few feet in front of them as they hurried to their destinations instead of raised with open confidence to greet friends and neighbors. Adélaïde thought with longing of the days when no one noticed her as she passed from her apartment to the Louvre and back again or, just a few months ago, when she made the short walk from her apartment to the Bibliothèque du Roi to work on the commission from the Comte de Provence. Now, she felt eyes on her everywhere. Where before she assumed no one cared that she had secured a court appointment, albeit only with the king's aging aunts, now it seemed it was everyone's business and her biggest liability.

As a result, she didn't dare leave her apartment without wearing the tricolor cockade so prominently that anyone could see it at a casual glance.

"Madame Le Brun is making quite a name for herself in Rome, apparently," Gabrielle said over breakfast in Adélaïde's studio one morning. "Why does it not surprise me that she should flee at the first sign of peril?"

"That's not entirely fair, Gabrielle. You know it would have been dangerous for her to stay here," Adélaïde said.

"And whose fault is that? If she will go flaunting her wealth and socializing with the disreputable elite, she couldn't expect otherwise."

Adélaïde decided there was no point in arguing with Gabrielle. She had always stayed true to her roots, even as she accompanied Adélaïde to sittings with her royal patrons. Gabrielle suffered no sense of divided loyalty.

Still, it had never occurred to Adélaïde to leave Paris, let alone France. She could no more leave France than carve her own heart out of her breast. The dirty streets, the cries of the market women—even the foul air—were the shading that had filled in the outline of who she was from infancy to the age of forty-two years. Yet Madame Le Brun's close ties to the queen and several members of the court—ties that the celebrated portrait painter had done everything she could to publicize—put her in much graver danger than Adélaïde would ever be in. Adélaïde had heard that she'd been attacked on the street outside the Hôtel Le Brun. No one deserved that. No wonder she fled soon after, taking her young daughter with her. But she'd left her husband behind. That was something Adélaïde could not understand.

The conversation soon passed to the proposed Académie reforms. Opinions had solidified into different factions, all refusing to budge from their positions. Only one group, the one to which Adélaïde and

André belonged, cared about making changes that would improve the status of women artists.

"I don't understand why David isn't with us, why he's not taking the part of women," Gabrielle said before taking the last bite of her breakfast and washing it down with what was left in her bowl of coffee.

"It's not just David. I don't know why you single him out," Adélaïde said. "There are many others who don't believe we have a right to teach in the Académie, or to be elected based on true ability rather than set aside because we are women. Director Vien, for instance."

"Yes, but David is younger. And he is against Vien. And then there is his work. His paintings. They're so modern, so forward looking. Not to mention that he has taught many female students."

"Female students bring money. Besides, look closely at the women he portrays. I think that will tell you all you need to know. They are not women, but cyphers," Adélaïde said. In fact, David had done very little painting or teaching for the past year. All the time he didn't spend lobbying for his vision of the Académie went toward organizing elaborate fêtes and commemorations of important events, with choreographed tributes, patriotic banners, and symbolic gestures. The first anniversary of the fall of the Bastille had been his own magnificent concoction. *What did he hope to achieve by that?* Adélaïde wondered.

As her mind traveled those well-worn paths, Adélaïde slipped her arms into the sleeves of her smock so she could work. It did no good to ponder the incomprehensible David when she had a painting to finish. Whatever was going on in the wider world, her life must continue. The irony of her current position, poised at the apex of her career as an artist, was that in order to exist in this new Paris, she had to divide herself in two. One side cleaved to the old order. That was the side that continued to slave away at the nearly finished painting for the Hospitalers. The other faced resolutely forward, hopeful for the best, but wary. That was the side that went to committee meetings and gave generously to republican causes. The truth was, she needed the money from the way things used to be in order to survive. She feared, though, her loyalties would hang around her neck like a noose if matters went too far.

☙

The following evening, Adélaïde had to adopt her reformist personality and help André prepare to go to the Salon Carré for the meeting of the officers. "You promise you will propose everything we discussed the other day?" she said as she brushed a drift of wig powder off his shoulder.

"Of course. Did you think I wouldn't?" He took her hand and kissed it.

"All the same, I know how these things can go."

This meeting was the one at which each of the three factions would present their proposals for restructuring the Académie. With modifications, the proposals would then go to the National Assembly to be judged on their merits and decided upon—decided upon by men only, and men who had no vested interest in art and were no doubt ignorant of its many facets. It seemed ludicrous to Adélaïde that the matter had ever gone beyond the walls of the Académie. But like so much else that was happening in her world, common sense had little to do with it. The Académie was a symbol and must be appropriated to whatever cause won the day.

Adélaïde feared that the internecine squabbles might end in having the Académie disbanded entirely. But would that necessarily be bad? If it didn't exist, women could not be excluded from its privileges. The virulence with which Vien and the officers on one side and David and his Jacobin Commune des Arts on another had insisted that women had no place in the Académie of the future cut deeply.

The cruelest betrayal, though, was indeed David's, as Gabrielle had said. He'd blazed into the Académie from his sojourn in Rome setting traditions alight and advocating for the training of women artists.

Now, it seemed, he'd changed his mind. Like a storm cloud, he did not care who was beneath him when he rained down his thoughtless polemic, upending hard-won privileges with the stroke of a pen. Adélaïde told herself she should have expected it, though. He'd proven himself a creature of politics in his behavior over the directorship of the Académie de France à Rome. Not getting that post soured him to everything touching upon the Académie Royale. If he was miserable and disappointed, so should be everyone else.

And so, the privileged male artist who gladly took the money of women students had turned his back on all of them. Adélaïde had seen David's report. It singled her out cruelly, accusing her of using her feminine influence on the men of the Académie, bringing her modesty into question, and begrudging her the insufficient pension granted by the Bâtiments du Roi. It would be the most ironic outcome of all if—after struggling so hard for so many years—her tiny foothold in the established art world would crumble, not because of misguided artistic judgments but because of petty-minded men who did not want to relinquish their dominance in all spheres of life. Her triumphs, her proofs that she could measure up to any of the members of the Académie as both a portraitist and a teacher, were of no consequence. Now she knew for certain that the insinuations were still there, the prejudices, ready to leap out at the slightest provocation. This, then, was the legacy of that revolting pamphlet. Even Vien, who at least normally treated her with respect, had said in all seriousness that one's judgment of a woman's art was always at risk of being swayed by seduction. Seduction! At her age, most women would have long been considered well beyond the capacity to seduce.

Now it remained to be seen how the National Assembly would deal with this unruly bunch of artists who couldn't agree among themselves about anything.

༄

A peculiar, prolonged, carnival atmosphere prevailed in the neighborhood around the Louvre and the Tuileries for the remainder of the year and the beginning of 1791. Adélaïde did her best to remain out of the way, quiet, not calling attention to herself or to her activities as an artist yet still providing what support she could for the new government.

But no matter how hard she tried to be unremarkable, her name repeatedly arose whenever the question of the future of the Académie was dragged out before the assembly—and not in a good way. Somehow, she had come to represent everything that was wrong with women as artists. Before long, she was almost as familiar a figure on the streets as the queen herself.

Worse, she could not cease her interactions with Mesdames for one very important reason: they owed her money. She'd tried writing letters to them so that she wouldn't have to present herself at the Tuileries but never received answers. Clearly, there was only one way to settle her accounts with them. She would have to meet with Madame Adélaïde at least, if the guards would admit her to the palace. And that meant dressing in attire that would call attention to herself even more. A silk gown, a velvet coat, and a hat trimmed with ribbons and feathers.

"If you allowed me to go with you, I could vouch for you on the street," Gabrielle said as she helped pin Adélaïde into her *robe* à *l'anglaise*. "And then, once we reached the palace, I would wait outside as if I were your servant, which should give you some added credibility with the guards."

The idea was ludicrous. How had Gabrielle become her protector? The world was rapidly turning upside down. "No, I shall manage. I can't do much more to sully my reputation. But I—we—need that money."

It was an icy day, with a raw wind kicking up from the east. Adélaïde wore her serviceable boots, drawing the line at satin slippers—Mesdames' preferred footwear. They would have to understand.

"Ooh! She looks like someone's going to get a beating!"

The comment was followed by laughter and a bit of rotten cabbage that sailed past Adélaïde's head. She realized that, in her concentration and worry over the coming interview, she was probably marching along with a scowl on her face. When passing by the women in the now-ubiquitous market stalls on the Rue Saint-Honoré, it was important to look neither friendly nor unfriendly, but to maintain the most neutral expression possible. Adélaïde had learned her lesson the hard way once, when a woman and her friends handled her roughly because they thought she was being smug due to the suggestion of a smile on her face. Now, she'd risked the opposite.

She quickly adjusted her expression and continued. The cold weather worked in her favor. Fewer women were out that day, and those who were huddled close to the little fires that dotted the roadside.

However, the vicinity of the heavily guarded entrance to the Tuileries palace was not so sparsely populated. She could barely make herself heard above the jeers that followed her as she passed through the gates and into the palace itself.

Adélaïde wasn't certain exactly what she expected to find in this disused royal residence. Still fresh in her mind was the opulence of Versailles and Bellevue. But seeing the wallpaper hanging in strips, the moldy walls underneath, the bare rooms—she felt as if she'd entered an orphanage or a hospital, not the home of the monarchs of France.

The footman ushered her to a stairway, and they ascended to the floor above. Here, efforts had been made to repair things and to furnish the apartments comfortably, at least.

Madame Adélaïde was dressed as usual in sumptuous silks and velvets and seated in a fauteuil next to a blazing fire that warmed the room. "We are pleased—but somewhat surprised—to see you here. As you know, we are hardly commissioning portraits at this time."

When she rose from her curtsy, Adélaïde said, "I do not come seeking additional work. Rather, I was hoping Mesdames would see fit to compensate me for the paintings I have already completed. As you know, it is harder and harder for artists to earn a living now, with students abandoning our studios and no one with money to spare for portraits."

The expression on Madame Adélaïde's face did not change when she said, "Of course. I have instructed my household to see that you are paid. I cannot imagine why they have not yet done so. There is nothing more I can do, I'm afraid." She rang a little bell on the table by her side.

Adélaïde curtsied and followed the footman back out through the palace.

After that, she kept hoping for payment, wishing for the funds to be delivered to her apartment, until one cold day in February. On her way to the Bibliothèque du Roi, a single voice cut through the noise announcing that Mesdames had fled the country. Adélaïde scanned the crowd around her until she saw a pamphleteer waving his latest scribblings above his head. She elbowed her way through the crowd and grabbed one out of his hands in exchange for a sou. She read with increasing anger that the king's aunts and their retinue were risking the journey over the Alps to Rome, where they could escape persecution.

Their departure may have enabled them to live in comparative peace, but it had the opposite effect on Adélaïde. How did people find out about her previous appointment? How had it suddenly become so generally known that as she walked down the street, strangers hurled insults at her, accusing her of having aided and abetted the elderly ladies in their flight. *If they only knew*, Adélaïde thought. With them went all hope of ever being paid the tens of thousands of livres she was owed. And with them went the rest of her students, except Gabrielle and Victoire, who were more family than students. If that were not the case, between the general scarcity of money and the risk of being associated with someone supposedly sympathetic to the Bourbon monarchy, the two of them would also have had reason enough to leave.

No one really knew how to be during those days. Things changed moment by moment. Adélaïde rarely went anywhere but to her own studio and the Louvre and sent Gabrielle out to buy groceries and provisions. She hadn't dared cross the threshold of the Bibliothèque du Roi for weeks. For all she knew, her painting—completed but for the final varnish—could have been destroyed.

It crossed her mind that she could, once again, solve her financial predicament in the way she had done before. But no sooner did she have the thought than she dismissed it. The kind of men who would purchase erotic drawings at an absurd price had either already fled the country—like the Comte de Vaudreuil—or were cash strapped as well.

"I can't continue to live like this," she said to André one day in his studio as he put the finishing touches on a rare portrait commission. Funny how many of the artists' lives went on as usual, unaffected by the momentous changes occurring right next door to them in the Tuileries and the Salle de Manège where the assembly met. "I have to do something. I have to prove once and for all that I'm not a spy for the monarchy or an enemy to the republic."

She paced up and down, tidying the jars of pigment and straightening brushes, her mind whirring. And then, she stood still behind André, watching him daub in a shadow in the indistinct background, and suddenly it all fell into place. She should use her talents to make a point, to prove her value to the republic. "I shall paint my way out of disfavor," she said.

André looked over his shoulder at her and said, "How will you do that?"

"I must go back to my apartment and write letters to the deputies to

the National Assembly offering to paint their portraits in commemo-
ration of the momentous work they are undertaking."

André lowered his brush and turned away from the canvas. "You
are remarkable. Of course, that is the very thing. I wonder how many
will agree to it."

That was the trouble. She didn't know. Perhaps her ties to Mesdames
would make them hesitant to agree. "It's difficult to say. But it's the
only thing I can think of to try."

◦◦◦

As Adélaïde hoped, vanity won out over politics. A dozen deputies
consented to sit for her over the coming months, including the Duc
d'Orléans himself, as well as Talleyrand, Alexandre de Lameth, and
Barnave—the three most important deputies among those who advo-
cated reasonable, gradual reform. The portraits would be simple, but
perfect. They would be ready in time to show in the 1791 salon, which,
despite everything, was scheduled to take place as usual.

She had almost given up thinking that any more deputies would
answer her letters, when one arrived a month later care of the Académie,
after she had already had several sittings. She was in André's studio
when she received the florid note and read it aloud to him.

"I apologize for my tardy reply. They tell me that the graces want
to paint my portrait. At what day and hour may I present both myself
and the homage I owe to you?"

The note was signed Maximilien Robespierre.

◦◦◦

When the king and queen and royal family attempted to leave
France in June 1791, Adélaïde breathed a sigh of relief. They drew
the focus away from Mesdames. Everyone knew she had never benefited from their particular patronage, so her neighbors had other
people to revile than herself. And now, thanks to the portraits she'd

painted, the deputies thought of her as an artist loyal to the republican cause.

The furor, Adélaïde thought, had calmed down, and it seemed as if cool heads would prevail when, on July 15, the delegates had agreed on a constitutional monarchy. The king would retain his position as head of the government but with changes that gave others much more power. However, she, like many, underestimated the popular sentiment against such a thing. Once again, it was Gabrielle who brought the news into the studio in the Bibliothèque du Roi.

"I knew it," she said. "It was what I kept hearing on the street. The people are sick of royalty, sick of being thought of as little more than animals." She reached up to where Adélaïde sat on a ladder and thrust a tattered copy of *Les Révolutions de Paris* in between Adélaïde and the canvas.

A familiar feeling of dread worked its way from Adélaïde's stomach, up to her head and down her arms. The paper rattled as she held it in her shaking hands. There had been a massacre by troops led by the Marquis de Lafayette of citizens gathered in protest on the Champs de Mars.

The field of the federation is a vast plain, at the center of which the altar of the fatherland is located, and where the slopes surrounding the plain are cut at intervals to facilitate entry and exit. One section of the troops entered at the far side of the military school, another came through the entrance somewhat lower down, and a third by the gate that opens on to the Grande Rue de Chaillot, where the red flag was placed. The people at the altar, more than fifteen thousand strong, had hardly noticed the flag when shots were heard. "Do not move, they are firing blanks. They must come here to post the law." The troops advanced a second time. The composure of the faces of those who surrounded the altar did not change. But when a

third volley mowed many of them down, the crowd fled, leav-
ing only a group of a hundred people at the altar itself. Alas,
they paid dearly for their courage and blind trust in the law.
Men, women, even a child, were massacred there, massacred
on the altar of the fatherland.

"Even a child," Gabrielle repeated and buried her face in her hands.

Adélaïde couldn't help thinking back to the Réveillon riots, the events that precipitated everything. But no, seeds had been sown before then: in the price of bread, the failed grain harvest, and centuries of subjugation. Yet here she was, glorifying the system that had led step-by-step to all the bloodshed and disruption that was happening now. She had no choice. Art demanded it of her. Portraits of the deputies—that was all she could do to counterbalance her dependence upon royal favor, not just for her livelihood, but for the fulfillment of a calling that had directed every decision she had made throughout her life, good and bad.

Lafayette restored peace, and life went on. Less than a month later, two events occurred within days of each other that directly affected Adélaïde and her students. One was the drafting of the new French constitution, a document that had taken years to compose and amend and that the Champs de Mars massacre had finally pushed to conclusion.

At almost the same time, a few days before the salon of 1791 would open, the Assembly finally addressed the fate of the Académie Royale. Their decision caught Adélaïde off guard. In fact, it caught everyone off guard. They not only chose not to adopt any of the proposed reorganizations, they made a decision about the Académie that changed everything. None of the members or officers were pleased with it.

"I suppose this is all part of leveling society, so that fewer people have advantages because of royal favor." André did not sound happy.

But unlike André, Adélaïde secretly rejoiced at the deputies' decision. She couldn't wait to go back to her studio and tell Gabrielle and Victoire about it.

⌒℮つ

The biennial salons were always chaotic. That year was no exception. The massive Salon Carré was stuffed to the bursting point with paintings and sculptures. The pictures covered every inch of the walls, from floor to very high ceiling, and lined the staircase that led up to the exhibition room. Crowds often came to a standstill on the stairs as they tried to squeeze into the salon, which was already so crowded that the sculptures on the long tables in the center of the hall were in danger of being toppled by the enthusiastic masses. Although the mix of high and low social strata had always been a feature of the salons, this year, more of the poorest Parisians came, willing to wait for hours to get inside. Anyone could come and look as much as he wanted for as long as he pleased. It was no mystery to Adélaïde why so many chose to do so. Inside the Salon Carré, beauty smiled from every surface, the most skilled and talented artists fixed moments of intensity to canvas or portrayed individuals as their essential beings or gave glimpses into magnificent landscapes. Those whom the common people would never meet could be stared at, their features taken in, details of dress scrutinized, expressions analyzed. And places they would never see could be absorbed and enjoyed for free.

The exhibition was particularly crowded that year because the National Assembly had decreed that exhibiting in the salon must be open to any artists in France, male or female, academician or not. With the flourish of a pen, they erased close to a century of tradition.

When the word had come through, Adélaïde had raced back to her studio. She had already submitted all her deputy portraits and the portrait of the Prince de Bauffremont, but the opportunity for her two talented students to submit pieces was too good to let slip. Who knew if the deputies might change their minds before the next salon? Or if there even would be any more salons?

"You should submit your self-portrait," she advised Gabrielle, "And why not a few of your pastels of commoners? They would reflect well on the ambitions of the Académie to become more democratic."

The committee accepted all Gabrielle's work and one pastel by Victoire as well. In fact, that year, twenty-one women artists saw the products of their hard work hanging in the Salon Carré next to paintings by the legendary artists of the day. It seemed like the beginning of a new era, one where—despite Vien and David—women could at last take their place alongside men as worthy of being considered artists of the highest level.

Perhaps, Adélaïde thought, the Revolution would soon be over and everyone would be able to get to work finding where they fit in a society much altered for the better. And at first, when the long-awaited constitution was finally ratified and agreed upon by the king himself in September, such a state of affairs seemed within reach.

She, André, Gabrielle, and Victoire were to join the younger artists in the Académie for a celebration that included a reading of the constitution the day after it was signed. They were, that is, before Adélaïde bought a copy of the document on the street and brought it back to the apartment to read in peace before changing out of her painting clothes and into something more festive. When Gabrielle and Victoire arrived, they found her pacing back and forth in front of the long windows that faced the Rue Saint-Honoré, her jaw set in fury and the constitution crushed in her hands.

"What is it?" Gabrielle dashed over to Adélaïde and grabbed her hand, prying the pamphlet from her fingers that were rigid with rage.

"Read it. Read it. Nothing has changed. If anything, we're worse off."

"But the constitution is said to have established a much more just system of government, where power is distributed among all men." Victoire said.

"Ah, there you have it. Among all *men.*"

By then, Gabrielle had finished her swift perusal of the document and handed it to Victoire. "How could they have betrayed us so?" she asked, hurt written on her features.

Gabrielle, Adélaïde thought, had put the most store by the political changes, had been the most involved in committees and discussions. But the discussions she was a part of took place among women, and there were no women assisting at the constitution's drafting. "We are now not citizens. Only men who pay the poll tax are citizens with any rights of voting or governing. We are classed among the lowest, the weakest, the most subjugated. We are like the children, domestic servants, slaves, Jews, and hangmen who have no political rights at all. And actors too! Poor Ducis. At least Brizard is not alive to face this insult." The two actors whose portraits she had painted had not only been kind to her, but Adélaïde would always remember Ducis's actions concerning the slanderous pamphlet after her first Académie salon.

"I, for one, will stay home this evening rather than attend a celebration for this travesty of a constitution," Victoire said.

"Or," Gabrielle said, a mischievous smile lighting up her features, "We could take our turn to read this." She reached into the pocket under her petticoats and withdrew a different pamphlet. "I got a copy at the meeting of the Amis de la Vérité."

Gabrielle had been attending these public meetings and often came home from them bubbling over with enthusiasm. This was the first time she'd brought a pamphlet, however. It was written by the actress and playwright, Olympe de Gouges. It answered, point by point, the Declaration of the Rights of Man, and was titled "*Déclaration des droits de la femme et de la citoyenne.*"

"I just haven't the heart to start the arguments that reading this aloud to a room full of male artists—even those who would be sympathetic to it—would undoubtedly provoke. Let us, instead, be quiet at home. Perhaps we will have another chance to put our case at some later point," Adélaïde said. She didn't believe it, though. She had spent too much time battling the entrenched forces of men who clung to their modicum of power and were afraid to allow women the least bit of their share.

ꙮ

In late September, after the salon had closed and they'd subjugated their disappointment over the terms of the constitution, a knock on the studio door interrupted Adélaïde as she was sketching a new portrait of Gabrielle.

"Victoire, would you kindly?"

Victoire laid her own brush aside and answered the door. A male voice Adélaïde did not recognize said, "I am here with a message from the deputies for Madame Guiard."

Adélaïde stood, her heart racing. A visit with a message from the deputies could spell danger. "I am Madame Guiard." Had she done something wrong? She'd heard of people being arrested for not demonstrating enough patriotism. She slipped off her smock so the cockade pinned to her breast would be visible.

"Here is a commission from the deputies." The messenger held up a large folded and sealed letter.

Adélaïde walked forward and took it from him.

"I am to await your response."

She cracked the seal to open it, forcing her hands not to tremble, taking unhurried breaths, as if she was quite accustomed to receiving messages directly from the deputies to the National Assembly. She scanned the formally worded text, and her whole body released the tension that had built in those few moments. "Tell them I accept," she said.

The messenger bowed and left.

Gabrielle and Victoire ran to her, each of them reaching for the paper, which Adélaïde now held over her head out of their reach. She smiled. It was good news, of a sort.

"Don't torture us! What is it?"

"I should tell André first," she said, already fetching her straw hat and stuffing her arms as quickly as she could into her short jacket.

"Then we're coming with you!"

All three of them ran through the crowded streets from Adélaïde's studio to the Louvre, waving to the guard who made a feeble attempt to stop them. They burst in without knocking, a trio of windblown, rosy-faced women. Adélaïde was on the point of running to André and embracing him when she saw that he wasn't alone. David was with him.

"Madame Guiard," David said, with a polite, unsmiling bow. "I was just on my way out. I merely wanted to share the information that I have been asked by the deputies to paint a portrait of the king accepting the new constitution."

Adélaïde felt as though he'd kicked her just below her ribs. "How extraordinary." She didn't want to proclaim her news in front of him, but she felt she had no choice. "I, too, have been commissioned to paint a similar portrait. I received the message less than half an hour ago." She brandished the letter. She had greeted the news with mixed feelings but couldn't help being flattered at the deputies' choice of her, a woman, to commemorate the occasion. Now it seemed they had hedged their bets.

"So, your portraits of the deputies had the desired result, I assume. Very well executed. I assume you've made gifts of them all to the sitters?" David said.

"What an honor for both of you!" André placed himself between the two of them, a nervous smile on his face. "And I am delighted to have heard the news from its sources." He put his hand out to shake David's, who ignored it and strode through the door, not closing it behind him.

"What did I do to make such an enemy of that man! And I so wanted to tell you and let us all celebrate in our own way," Adélaïde said, as soon as David's footsteps had faded away down the corridor.

"It's just David. It's how he behaves. He'd have been the same with any other painter, you know that."

Perhaps André was right. But added to his dismissal of women in the Académie, she could not say so with the same confidence. This could give the art world the opportunity it had long sought, to be able to compare her work directly with a man's of the same subject and find it lacking.

But Adélaïde knew hers would not lack anything that the eyes of the critics did not invent.

Twenty-Eight

Paris and Pontault, 1792

Adélaïde's first thought when she heard that the monarchy had been abolished and the royal family imprisoned was that now she knew for certain she would never paint that portrait, the one of the king accepting the constitution. She and David had only gotten as far as preliminary sketches when it became clear that the constitutional monarchy had collapsed in the face of the belligerent radical faction of the Jacobins.

Then she felt ashamed for thinking only of the effect this alarming turn of events had on her life, her career. And it wasn't just those connected with the monarchy who found themselves imperiled. The moderate deputies, the ones Adélaïde hoped would ensure that common sense prevailed, had either bowed out of the government or gone to prison as well.

It was all because of Robespierre and his Montagnards. Robespierre, that vain, obsequious man whose portrait she had painted a couple of years ago, had somehow worked his way into a position of power based in fear. Orléans was no longer the people's champion, and Robespierre set about stirring up the beleaguered, confused population in a way that terrified Adélaïde. It was all so pointless. The Jacobins, the Girondists, the Montagnards—they'd all been part of the same spirit of reform to begin with. And now, the world had gone mad. That horrible device, the guillotine, was being used to separate heads from shoulders in the most gruesome way. Gabrielle had seen an execution. She had thought it might be a swifter end for those who faced it. But that was not always the case. Her face was gray as ash when she returned to the studio.

Perhaps foolishly, Adélaïde still held out a morsel of hope that one day, when everything had settled into whatever would pass for normal again, she would be paid for the portrait of the Comte de Provence. He was not in prison, at least. He had fled France with his family months before to stay with the dukes of Courland on the Baltic Sea, out of reach of Robespierre and his mob.

Keeping up with all the rapid changes in politics and ideas had been exhausting and disorienting. She'd amended her actions and her ways so many times over the past year, done her best to prove her loyalty to whatever form the new order appeared likely to take, and accepted that the time for women to be treated as equal had not yet come, but it was no use. This Paris, this place where people eyed each other with suspicion and were quick to judge everyone whose views differed from theirs, was not the city she knew and loved. Yes, previously society had been rigid and unequal. The lower classes suffered much because of the heedless aristocrats. But basic decency had prevailed, at least superficially. She could walk down the street without being jeered at or accosted. Something as insignificant as her tidy appearance provoked the insults now. And if anyone on the street knew who she was, the cries against Mesdames and accusations of being a royalist followed her to her destination, wherever it was.

It seemed that no one could simply be an artist anymore. Instead of being thought of as skilled artisans who trained to work for and be paid by people far above them in station, to bring beauty to the world in whatever way they could, they were suddenly in league with their former employers to defraud the republic. She had tried everything and run out of options. Most of the other artists had already gone, seeking a measure of fragile peace in the provinces or abroad.

All except David. He stood at Robespierre's side and joined the chorus of voices that wanted to destroy everything and start anew. Total destruction would be a loss Adélaïde could not bear. There was too much loveliness in her imperfect Paris, too many memories, to wish it all annihilated. She had postponed the decision long enough. She would have to leave.

Leave Paris. Never in her life did she think it would come to that. Her father and Jacqueline had gone a year ago. André had remained in his studios at the Louvre, but only because he was waiting for her to reach that same precipice and understand that her only choice was to leap to uncertain safety. She'd come to that point just the day before. So here she was with Gabrielle and Victoire, at the Bibliothèque du Roi, making difficult decisions about what to take away and what to leave, what could be of use and what would be a liability.

"Gabrielle, you must help. We have to get out while we can."

While Victoire dutifully rolled brushes up in linen and put pots of pigment into a wooden crate, Gabrielle paced back and forth across the studio in the opulent gallery, twitching the covers off the easels that Adélaïde had just draped them over. "How can we leave when everything is only half finished? There is more to do. We artists must be part of creating the new order. Our voices may still be heard."

Adélaïde grabbed hold of Gabrielle's hand as she passed by. "Listen to me! Look around you! Do you see anything here that would not put us in danger of being accused of having monarchist sympathies?" The painting of the Comte de Provence dispensing regal honors to men who had pleased the crown with their service loomed over everything in the high-ceilinged space, an insult to the republic. "We must find a way to get this monstrosity off the stretchers. I may have to cut the canvases apart to roll them."

"Surely no one would bother with us!" Gabrielle replied. "Besides, you've proven where your sympathies lie, we all have."

"Painting portraits of deputies who are now in prison or in exile proves something but not what the Montagnards want it to prove."

She pulled Gabrielle to her, wrapping her in a fierce embrace. "We cannot be an army of two or three. We did all we could. It's time to protect ourselves."

Adélaïde could feel the quivering tension in her student's body, and then all at once, Gabrielle wilted under the pressure of reason. It was a shame to have to dim her bright white enthusiasm, so honest and pure. But she would not allow Gabrielle to plunge forward into disaster. Somehow, Gabrielle had become her responsibility, as much as her own child would have been, even though she was only a dozen years younger. She and Victoire—whose family had moved away to the coast fearing the unrest would reach to the suburbs of Paris— were under her protection now. Who knew how long it would be necessary or even possible? "Now, let's finish, and then we'll have some supper."

An hour later, after nearly toppling the enormous canvas face down on the floor, they gave up. The painting was too big for the three of them to manage alone.

"We'll have to get help," Adélaïde said. "I'll fetch André."

"Does he, too, think we should leave Paris?" Gabrielle said, a querulous edge to her voice.

Gabrielle had come to adore André as a daughter would an indulgent father, one who took her side in every argument and gave her treats behind her mother's back. She had always liked him, but her affection had grown after she received word of her real father's death of a stroke the previous year.

Adélaïde touched Gabrielle's face and smiled. "It was he who suggested it. At first I thought he was overreacting, but now I know we must do as he says." She could barely stand to meet Gabrielle's doleful eyes. "Now, you two finish gathering up all the supplies, and I'll fetch André."

Adélaïde had taken to wearing a cockade pinned to her bodice and two others pinned to each side of her turban cap to make certain no one would mistake her for a royalist. In fact, the walk from the studio to the Louvre—once so familiar and joyful to her—for months had acquired a palpable sense of danger. She was sure one of Robespierre's men would leap out from an alley and drag her away to be imprisoned. It had happened to many, so the pamphlets said, and with her ties to the court—slender as they were—there would be excuse enough to detain her. She hurried without running, not wanting to appear frightened, and had to remind herself to breathe as she went.

To her relief, she arrived without attracting any notice. All she wanted was to enter the reverent quiet of the nearly empty old palace and talk to André about their plans to depart. She pulled open the heavy door, ready to release the tension in her shoulders and pause to still her pounding heart. But to her dismay, the normally silent corridors were filled with guards running here and there carrying unframed paintings and stacking them in piles that might have had some sort of organization but appeared haphazard at first glance. When Adélaïde heard David's voice shouting instructions to the guards, her heart twisted. Whatever he was doing, she had no doubt he acted on the instructions of Robespierre. A moment later a wave of nausea washed over her when she recognized one of André's smaller pictures passing by, carelessly tucked under the arm of a burly fellow who seemed to have no idea of the value of the object he carried.

She ran forward against the stream of guards, weaving among them and stepping around portrait busts abandoned in the middle of the floor. The scene on the upper floor was less chaotic, but still frantic, and she found the door to André's lodgings ajar. André stood in the middle of the space that was his studio, watching, hollow-eyed, as strangers gradually denuded it of all of his works in progress and one or two completed paintings that he had decided to keep for his private collection.

"What is happening here?" Adélaïde's voice came out strangled and shrill.

"It's all right. They're removing everything for safe keeping. All paintings will be returned as soon as order is restored."

Adélaïde could tell by the tone of his voice that André didn't really believe it.

"I'm to work on approved subjects in the meantime, help paint murals to display republican ideals. It's a fitting use of my talents." It was clear that he spoke for the benefit of the men taking the final painting away. They struggled under the bulk of his *Belisarius Begging*, cursing under their breath.

Once they had the studio to themselves and André had closed the door to shut out the disruption in the corridors, he sank onto a stool and put his head in his hands.

Adélaïde took his shoulders and pulled him to her, bending over as though to kiss him, but instead murmuring into his ear, "Before dawn, before any of the neighbors have awakened. That's when we have to leave. My father writes that the house is ready for us. We just have to get there." Adélaïde had written to her father weeks ago to ask if he knew anyone who could provide them with accommodations outside of Paris, and he replied with news of a distant relative with a vacant house in Pontault, about twenty miles east of the city. Although not far enough away for complete safety, it was a sleepy enough suburb to be out of the notice of anyone important. This relative had agreed to let the house to them for a minuscule rent. Adélaïde wondered how much her father had had to pay for the favor, but she could hardly quibble about that now.

"Bring only the materials you absolutely need," André said, "or you risk being labeled a thief."

"Do you think we'll be far enough away to be safe?"

He pulled her into his arms, still seated, nestling his head against her stomach. "It will have to do. We'll be all right. Will Gabrielle and Victoire be ready?"

⤳

In the dark the next morning, Adélaïde, André, Gabrielle, and Victoire climbed into the cart André had hired, André driving with Adélaïde next to him and Gabrielle and Victoire sitting on the bench behind them. They each held a single bag with clothing and other personal items. Stacked in the back were three rolls of blank canvas, half a dozen rolled-up paintings, crates of paint and brushes, and wood to build easels—all covered with heavy cloths. Adélaïde had made the decision to leave the Hospitalers portrait behind. Even if she cut it in pieces, it would be too bulky. She would have to hope that no one would discover it, that they had hidden it well enough by, with André's help, rolling it up against a far wall of her studio in the Bibliothèque du Roi. For the rest, nothing they'd brought with them revealed any ties to the court or the aristocracy. Adélaïde had a basket of provisions at her feet, since she didn't know whether they'd be able to get any once they arrived, not that day at any rate.

As André slapped the reins against the horse's back, Gabrielle tapped Adélaïde on the shoulder. "I'm glad Marguerite never had to witness any of this."

Yes, Adélaïde thought. Her aristocratic student might have been in grave danger. She had no idea whether her family had fled or not. For their sakes, she hoped they'd emigrated from France.

The guard at the Porte Saint-Denis was sunk deep in his great-coat and turned away from them when André pulled the horses up to wait for permission to leave Paris. Although the toll booths had been pulled down in the uprisings of 1789, access to and from Paris still had to be through the gates.

"You there!" André called. Nothing.

"Do you suppose we can just go on? He will never know." Adélaïde whispered.

"He'd know a cart had been here. The cobbles are covered with mud. And we'd be labeled fugitives if we did, and they'd hunt us down. I'll wake him." He climbed down from the cart, walked over to the guard, and tapped his shoulder.

At first, the guard waved his arm at André as if swatting away a fly. When André persisted, the guard shook himself awake and stood.

Adélaïde gasped and quickly turned away. How could it be! She recognized Nicolas instantly, from the set of his shoulders and the frown on his face. What were the odds? She hadn't even known he had joined the citizen militia—although she'd heard nothing of him going abroad or being arrested, so she supposed it would have been his only option. His wealthy patroness must have vanished to the safety of England or Italy. Was it a good omen that their fate was in the hands of someone who once loved her? Or would he cause trouble out of spite? Better to be safe, she thought. If they were careful, he need not see who they were.

André had never met Adélaïde's estranged husband, so he had no way of recognizing him. "We are going to stay with our elderly aunt in Pontault," he said, repeating the story they thought was safest. "She is infirm and needs our help."

Adélaïde held her breath.

"What's the matter?" Gabrielle reached over from the back where she and Victoire sat on crates full of art supplies and touched Adélaïde's shoulder.

She shook her head and did not look around.

"And who are these lovely ladies you are taking with you, eh?"

"I am Marcel Henriot, here with my wife and two nieces," André said, another lie that would match the papers André had arranged for them.

A hard knot formed in Adélaïde's stomach. The sound of Nicolas's voice called up memories—painful, shameful, complicated memories. If only she could signal to André to beware! But it was dark, and she dared not make any gesture in his direction.

Boots scraped and crunched against the dirty cobbles as the two men approached the cart.

"Say nothing," Adélaïde whispered to Gabrielle and Victoire. The last thing she wanted was to leave them open to flirtation or harassment by Nicolas. She well knew that his rakish good looks were hard to resist if he put his mind to pleasing a woman. She held her breath.

As she suspected he would, Nicolas came right up close to Victoire and said, with a muted, seductive edge to his voice, "What service will you perform for this aging aunt?"

Without looking, Adélaïde knew he had touched Victoire's arm. She sensed the girl's slight movement away from him behind her.

"Whatever she needs," Victoire answered.

Yes, keep it vague. It was what they'd instructed the two students to do, if silence proved unwise.

"And what is this you have with you?" Nicolas had turned away from Victoire and spoke to André.

"Only the necessities of life," André said.

"So many necessities when you are going to someone else's household?" His tone of voice changed, becoming harder and more official, and he lifted up one of the rough pieces of canvas they'd tucked around the crates to protect them.

Before Adélaïde could stop her, Gabrielle said, "We must bring the tools of our trade as well. We are artists."

Artists. Poor Gabrielle could have no idea just how unfortunate her words had been. Adélaïde's veins turned to ice.

"Artists, eh?" He was thinking, Adélaïde knew, about just what a certain female artist had done to him, and now here, apparently, were three. "I must see your identity papers." He walked slowly but deliberately around the cart, pausing every now and again to fling off more of the coverings and hurl them to the ground. "Artists, you say. Not much use to the Revolution."

As he drew closer to Adélaïde, she steeled herself for a confrontation.

"I've a mind to make you wait until later and let the captain examine your papers, make sure everything is as you say. He has the list."

The list, Adélaïde knew, was the names of people who had been reported by neighbors and acquaintances to the Committee on Public Safety, and who had been singled out for arrest. She did not know if her name was on it, but she couldn't take any chances. The last thing she wanted was to show Nicolas the papers André had procured for them with false names. That would get them into more trouble than anything. She had only one card to play, and now would be her only opportunity to play it. She turned and faced Nicolas squarely, watching as recognition dawned in his eyes. "Yes. It's me."

There was just enough light from the torch at the guard post for Adélaïde to see her estranged husband's face darken at first, but the play of emotions on it that followed gave Adélaïde a glimmering of hope.

She looked away from him and swept her arm to encompass all of them. "Gabrielle, Victoire, André, allow me to introduce you to Monsieur Nicolas Guiard. Monsieur Guiard, my family, such as it is."

Gabrielle's sharp intake of breath was the only reaction. Adélaïde waited, in silence, for what Nicolas would say next.

"Well, then. I could have you arrested for lying about your identity."

"You could," Adélaïde said, thankful she had not actually shown him the false papers, which would give his threat real teeth. Their actual documents were buried in one of the crates behind her. She reached into her deepest resources of strength to stay calm and climbed down from the cart, approaching him with her hands outstretched, pouring every ounce of pleading she could into her eyes. "Please," she said, and touched his arm. She felt the muscle in his forearm tense and the barrel of the rifle he held against his shoulder quiver in sympathy. She lowered her voice. "Nicolas, you loved me once. You were right. It was all my fault. I shouldn't have treated you so unkindly."

Nicolas shifted his weight from one foot to the other and looked down at the ground, angling himself slightly away from Adélaïde.

She moved so she was once again in his direct line of sight and lifted his chin just enough so he could not avoid looking into her eyes. "Please, Nicolas. You may not know. I have ties to the court that could get me arrested."

"Hah," he said, but quietly, and without mirth. "I did know. I know everything about you. I know about your royal appointment and your grand commission from Provence—Provence that was, I mean. I know what you did to make money with Gallimard. And I know about your committees and your studio. And . . ."

His eyes shifted in André's direction. Was Nicolas still jealous? Had he in fact been the author of the pamphlet that sent her to the courts for redress, as she suspected? It seemed that the question of the erotic pastels was no longer relevant, or he might have been less circumspect in the way he mentioned them. Who knew what had happened to them anyway? And where was Nicolas's wealthy widow? She caught at the scraps of words that flew threw her mind, reaching for something, anything she could say. "I did not know you were in the militia. You're handsome in the uniform, you know. And neither of us too old to wish for comfort." She didn't know how he'd interpret her words and hoped she hadn't overplayed her hand.

With a jerk of his arm, Nicolas shook her off. Adélaïde stepped back, never taking her eyes from his, watching for a softening, some inkling of the man who had once cared for her.

"Nothing can change the past." Adélaïde took a tentative step towards him.

He stepped away again. "She left me too, you know."

Adélaïde's mind raced. A man doubly disappointed might wish to retaliate against the nearest object. A thought came to her. "Did she take everything with her? Then you must be in need of funds." Adélaïde hoped he would remember that she had neither sapped his finances nor made any claim to what had been jointly theirs. She reached into the pocket tied next to her inner petticoat, drew out the pouch of coins they'd brought to help them survive while they were in Pontault, and held it out in his direction. They would have to sell some paintings or get some students quickly once they were settled instead.

Nicolas took the pouch from her and weighed it in his hand. "And this is what you think I'm worth?"

Her face burned. She had insulted him. "Of course not. But it is all we have."

He tossed the pouch up in the air and caught it before holding it back out to her. "Then you had better keep it. And go. Now. Before I change my mind and decide to make you wait for the captain to examine your papers—which I have no doubt have been forged."

"Thank you," Adélaïde breathed, and on impulse stood on her tiptoes and kissed his cheek.

He put his hand up to the spot and touched it briefly. "You'd better not call attention to yourselves in Pontault. I know the officials there. I could tell enough tales to have you dragged back to Paris." He swiveled on his boot heels and faced the two girls and André, who had been watching the entire exchange with wide, frightened eyes. "All of you!"

André threw the cloths back over their cargo, helped Adélaïde to her seat, and climbed up to take the reins. Without another word, he clucked the horse to a walk and then a trot.

"Remember, I see you!" Nicolas called after them.

$$\backsim$$

They all remained silent until they arrived at the house in Pontault not long after sunrise. The small village was just awakening although the baker had been at his work before dawn, and the comforting smell of fresh bread made Adélaïde's stomach rumble. The smell was familiar enough, but everything else about the village felt foreign.

Adélaïde hadn't strayed from the neighborhood around the Louvre for three years, a neighborhood packed with four- and five-story houses broken up only by grand residences, where her view of the heavens was circumscribed by the abundant artifacts of humanity. Here, only a sprinkling of houses and a row of shops marked the center of town, along with a market square that was slowly filling with barrows and a larger house that might have been the mayor's. From there, the town thinned out into farms. The few people they saw gazed at them with idle curiosity as they passed down the main street. Adélaïde wondered how many other strangers had arrived to blend into the obscurity of a sleepy village and escape the uncertainties of Paris.

The house they had rented on the edge of town was modest, yet there was room enough for the four of them and one or two other students if they came, a kitchen separated from the house by a small yard, a large reception room and dining room, and an attic with ample, north-facing windows. A studio. Not capacious enough for ambitious history paintings, but suitable for teaching and creating works on a smaller scale.

"Will we ever go back to Paris?" Gabrielle said as they sat at the rough dining table eating the breakfast Adélaïde had taken out of the basket she'd brought.

"I hope so," Adélaïde said, noting the dark shadows under her students' eyes. "The important thing is just to be safe. And to get some rest! We have all been under great strain these last few months."

"Do you suppose Guiard will come after us?" André said.

Adélaïde thought for a while. "In allowing us to pass, he has implicated himself in our escape. I doubt he would be so foolish." She'd seen the look in his eyes, though. He hadn't forgiven her for the past and had been hurt by having to confront the man that—although she didn't leave Nicolas because of him—had taken his place in her bed. Did she really know what he would do or what story he might concoct to explain his role in it all?

Adélaïde had come to understand the fear that could make one desperate to preserve oneself no matter the cost. The Revolution had twisted everyone into partisans, and neighbors informed against neighbors in an effort to protect themselves. How could she think ill of anyone—including Madame Le Brun—for choosing to flee France for safety?

Still, Adélaïde would never leave France, simply because André would not. He would not emigrate, and she would not go without him. But again, she thought, she had no young child to protect, only her students, who were grown women capable of looking after themselves if anything happened to her. That was something, at least. She had not had the chance to experience the joys of motherhood, of raising a child of her own, but she was also preserved from its sorrows.

Tomorrow they would make a start on their new life in Pontault. She hoped it would be temporary but prepared herself to make the most of it. She would find drawing students, perhaps a few portrait commissions. Together they would weather whatever havoc Robespierre could inflict, out of sight and hopefully out of mind.

Twenty-Nine

They'd been in Pontault for a year. Adélaïde had managed to attract half a dozen students, most of them with little talent. They were the daughters of the town officials and minor functionaries who had newfound confidence that they had as much right as anyone to taste the finer pleasures of life. And why didn't they? Adélaïde believed that with her whole heart, yet the habits of her formative years were hard to shake.

As to habits, or mores, or whatever, the townspeople assumed she and André were married, and Adélaïde did nothing to disabuse them of that notion. It was hard enough to survive without provoking a mass exodus from her studio on moral grounds.

André had a few students as well, and one or two of the wealthier bourgeois commissioned small portraits. By these means they were able to scrape together an existence, uneasy though it was.

The one good outcome of those terrible times was that the new government had made divorce legal. Adélaïde quietly started proceedings, not wanting to make too much of it lest the neighbors discover that not only were she and André not married but that she was still legally tied to someone else. She had hope that within the year she would be a free woman again—free to marry André, if he asked. But they both agreed that the times were too turbulent to take such a step right away, even if the divorce did come through. And besides, she wasn't entirely certain it was what she wanted—to be known as the wife of the painter Vincent, rather than in her own right after all she'd struggled to achieve. If she could have shed her nominal association with Guiard and simply referred to herself as Adélaïde Labille, she would happily have done it. But the law would not permit it.

She couldn't shake the feeling that her own concerns seemed small compared to what was happening in Paris. They were grateful to be away from the city every time they heard of another victim of Robespierre's terror. The king had been a shock, but not a surprise. Nor was Marie Antoinette. So much of the people's rancor had been heaped upon her, it was hard to imagine that once heads began to roll, hers would not be among them. Adélaïde had never met the queen. But Madame Le Brun counted her not only a patron but a friend. Was her rival in deep mourning? Or just relieved that she had had the good sense to flee while she could?

As long as Robespierre's vengeance fell upon those close to the monarch, Adélaïde hadn't been overly fearful. But when the leaders of the Revolution turned their blood lust upon the deputies whose portraits Adélaïde had painted, she became more and more uneasy. And when the blade came down a few weeks ago on Gabrielle's heroine, Olympe de Gouges, even Gabrielle began to lose her enthusiasm for the Revolution.

"I remember Monsieur Robespierre so clearly," Adélaïde said over breakfast one dreary late-November morning. The short days were making it difficult to get any work done, and several students had left once the weather discouraged them from making the jaunt to the Vincent house on the outskirts of town. "He did not seem like a powerful man or one who could create such terror. He was rather vain— very concerned that I paint him at an angle that would emphasize his good features." He reminded her a bit, she thought, of David. She had heard that David had continued to go along with all Robespierre's ideals, voting for the execution of the king and queen.

David did not impinge upon their life in Pontault, however—at least, she saw no evidence that he had. But they had not been left entirely unmolested. Adélaïde had no way of knowing for sure, but she sometimes wondered if Nicolas had said something to his associates in Pontault that had caused them to levy complaints against the household that had no foundation but ensured that Adélaïde or André had to appear before the local magistrate on a regular basis. Frequently they had to pay a fine they could ill afford. The complaints were more nuisance than cause for alarm, and they continued to believe they were safe in Pontault. Only safety mattered now. No career was worth risking one's life, even though Adélaïde frequently sighed over how close she'd been to achieving her dreams when it had all come crashing down. At least, she thought, when the upheaval ended, she might go back and retrieve her paintings and try to resurrect what was left of her reputation as an artist. She had done very little work of her own in Pontault—a few sketches of her students and more portraits of André. He tried to encourage her to paint a new self-portrait, but she did not want to record her face at that time. She knew that worry would remain etched on her features no matter how determined she was to erase it.

The four of them sat lost in their own thoughts, staring out at the gray sky, when they were jolted to attention by pounding on the door. Victoire half stood up. André put his finger to his lips and motioned her to sit down again.

A moment later a gruff voice called out, "Open! In the name of the Revolution!"

Adélaïde shot to her feet, and her chair tipped backwards. Gabrielle put her hand over her mouth, eyes wide with fear.

"I'll go," André said, taking Adélaïde's hand.

"Both of us," she said and pulled him along with her.

The pounding continued. "Open, or we'll break down the door!"

"Do you suppose, Guiard . . ." André didn't finish his thought.

Adélaïde shook her head as they went to unbolt the door. "No. I don't think he would do such a thing." Although the actions of many during this turbulent time had surprised her, she refused to believe that Nicolas would knowingly endanger her life. Of course, the authorities may have discovered his role in letting them pass under false identities and they were now being called to pay the price.

The officer's fist was poised to pound again when André opened the door. Behind the one who was clearly in charge were four other guards on horseback, rifles with bayonets strapped across their backs, faces hard. They looked like young boys. Their commander had the square-jawed, narrow-eyed look of someone accustomed to being obeyed.

"Won't you come in?" Adélaïde said, forcing her most welcoming smile.

A glimmer of confusion leapt into the commanding officer's eyes before he had time to prevent it and reassume his authoritative glare. "This is not a social call, Madame Guiard."

Madame Guiard. She'd been called Madame Vincent by most of their neighbors since they came to the town. Perhaps it was Nicolas after all. Who else would have known who and where she was? "How may I help you, Citizen?" Adélaïde said.

"Your presence has been requested in Paris. We are to escort you there immediately." He nodded his head toward a rough conveyance behind the guards, drawn by one horse and just large enough to carry a single person.

André had gradually encircled her waist with his arm from behind. She could feel his heart beating faster and faster. "I shall accompany Madame Guiard," he said.

"It is Madame Guiard alone who is requested," the officer said.

Adélaïde turned to André and planted a quick kiss on his lips. "It's all right. You stay here with the children." A little lie might dispose the guards more kindly to her, she thought. "I'll just get my cloak. I'm sure it is a routine matter that will be quickly resolved. I have done nothing wrong." *Except travel under an assumed name*, she thought. They had shed their false identities once settled in Pontault, but the fact remained that they'd intended to flee without anyone knowing—and succeeded, thanks to Nicolas. Adélaïde wracked her brains, turning over a dozen possibilities, but the only thing that made any sense at all was that she had to appear before a magistrate because of something to do with the impending divorce.

Moments later Adélaïde was seated on a hard wooden bench in the open cart, facing backward, her mouth as dry as the dead leaves that eddied up behind them on the road. She had not been to Paris in over a year. She had no idea what to expect or how much had changed. Gabrielle had wanted to make the trip into the city, but with the tally of people they knew who had met their fates on the guillotine mounting daily, they hadn't dared, not even to retrieve much-needed supplies. They would have had to pass through the sentry point where Nicolas might be on duty, and the last thing Adélaïde wanted to do was remind him of how he had helped them—and possibly put himself in danger—during their flight.

Sure enough, as they approached the Porte Saint-Denis, Adélaïde recognized Nicolas's stance. When the driver pulled the cart up and presented his papers so they could pass, Nicolas glanced up for a moment and met her eyes, a look of genuine concern on his face. So it couldn't have been his doing, this summons to Paris, she thought. Apparently Nicolas, for all his show of zeal, did not wish destruction on those who had done no harm to the Revolution. She met his gaze and raised an eyebrow. He lifted one shoulder in the slightest shrug, and a ghost of a smile of encouragement altered his expression.

The guard in charge reached out to reclaim the papers. "I shall keep these until Madame Guiard returns," Nicolas said, not giving the other guard any chance to contradict him.

"*Eh bien, si tu veux.*"

The guard's easy answer was noncommittal. But to Adélaïde it signaled that she possibly was destined to return. Or did it mean it wouldn't matter because the papers would soon belong to a dead person? As they passed beyond the gate, Nicolas lifted his hand in a brief salute.

Their route into Paris took them past the place where the Bastille once stood. The ground had been picked nearly clean by those eager to carry away a souvenir of that fateful evening. Adélaïde shuddered to remember it.

As they continued along the Rue Saint-Antoine in the direction of what used to be the Place de l'Hôtel de Ville and was now dubbed the Place de la Revolution, Adélaïde's heart fluttered and she had to remind herself to breathe. If that were their destination, so be it. She prayed, briefly, to the Virgin, to give her courage, although having been such an irregular attendee at Mass, she figured her prayers would no doubt fall upon deaf ears. The scattered clusters of people followed her cart with curious gazes as they continued along the northern edge of the square. Adélaïde tried not to look at the guillotine, but it exerted such a pull on her that she could not turn her eyes away. So small a thing to deliver so much bloody vengeance. Thank God, she thought, there were no executions on that day. The clean, oblique blade glinted as it caught the afternoon sun, and Adélaïde shivered. Once they had passed beyond the point of danger, Adélaïde craned around to look forward, away from the guillotine's macabre attraction. Even if all this had something to do with the divorce, she would probably have had to go to the Hôtel de Ville. Clearly, that was not their destination.

And then, Adélaïde thought, perhaps they would go to the Louvre. Was she to be reprimanded for something she'd painted years ago? But they continued along the Rue Saint-Honoré, past the Louvre to the gardens of the Tuileries. It was there that the driver pulled up the horses, and the guard who had led the way slid down from his horse and approached the cart. "This way," he said, and offered his hand to help her step down. He conducted her to where a group of people huddled, facing a pile of wooden planks and dead branches. It was some kind of pyre. More guards with torches stood by. No one spoke.

A fanfare broke the stillness, and from the direction of the Louvre came a procession of soldiers carrying paintings—some in frames, some rolled up, some canvases dangled by a corner and flapping in the cold wind. The sight was so absurd, Adélaïde had to suppress the urge to laugh out loud. They were like children carrying toys, was all she could think.

She wanted to laugh, that was, until she recognized a series of pictures she knew were hers. The portraits of the deputies. And a few portraits of noblewomen. She swallowed down a cry of protest. How could an inanimate painting harm anyone? Adélaïde was about to turn to the others in the motley group to ask them why they were also there when three men carrying one enormous, rolled-up canvas issued from the doors of the palace. One of them stood at each end, and one made sure the middle did not sag and drag along the ground. From where she stood, the stitching that held the panels together became visible as they drew closer. She calculated the cost of so much canvas, and her heart thudded into her stomach.

Someone Adélaïde did not recognize climbed up on a platform and read from a proclamation bearing an official-looking seal. The chill breeze tore his words into fragments so that Adélaïde caught only their general meaning. These works of art were deemed contrary to the revolutionary spirit and would be destroyed. To send a message to those who had perpetrated them in less enlightened times, the artists who created them—at least, those still living—would have to watch, after which time they would be permitted to return to their homes and reflect upon what they had witnessed.

The man spoke of many notable artists, but Adélaïde saw no one she recognized standing with her or among those whose roles appeared official. At least, not at first. But then she caught sight of a slight man who had been out of sight to that point. He stood off to the side, directing those who were bringing the paintings to their destruction.

David.

Adélaïde clenched her teeth and dug her nails into her palms. How could he? How could a fellow artist, even one who disagreed with her artistic choices and who had been seduced by revolutionary ideas, preside over such desecration? She was so preoccupied with her anger that by the time she looked back at the pyre all the paintings had been laid on top of it—oils, watercolors, pastels. All except the massive canvas she had just completed before their flight to Pontault that they'd been forced to leave behind. With a flourish, the soldiers carrying it unfurled it before dragging it atop all the others, perhaps so it would ignite more quickly. The guards that held torches now touched them to the wood at the base of the pyre.

It took a while for the heavy canvas to catch. At first, tendrils of acrid smoke rose into the sky, the wind blowing it toward the onlookers. Adélaïde's eyes stung, but she kept them open. She wanted to see that picture for as long as possible, claim her own work until the very final second. Before long, the flames started leaping, higher and higher. The burning oil and charred linen released increasingly dense plumes of black smoke that made everyone around her cough and brought bile into Adélaïde's throat. Corners of paintings curled up first, then rolled rapidly into tubes of fire like so many tapers. How many hours of work, Adélaïde thought, were destroyed in a matter of minutes? How much pain and frustration was now worth nothing because there was nothing to show for it? Adélaïde stood close enough to feel the heat scorching her face and see the features of the Comte de Provence bubble and dissolve. Ten thousand livres of her own money, gone.

It's over, she thought. All those years. So much heartache and bitterness, so many triumphs and accolades, all reduced to ash. She would never be able to reach such a pinnacle again. The world would not let her. Everything Angiviller and Pierre and all those other nay-sayers wanted had come true. Here was proof that she'd been wrong to strive for so much, that what she did had no significance. She did not deserve her fame.

André's works had apparently been spared, however, as she had seen none in the procession to the pyre. Adélaïde supposed that the historical subjects did not glorify nobility as much, did not depend on vanity and patronage for their existence, as did the portraits she painted. And besides, David had never felt threatened by André the way he had by Adélaïde, although she couldn't quite understand why. André was more a rival to him than she was. But in her heart, she knew there was no logic in it. She forced herself to look once again at David. He watched the conflagration not with sadness or regret but with a look of satisfaction bordering on triumph.

When all that was left were smoldering ashes, the guard came and dragged Adélaïde back to the cart. She was numb through her body and soul and hardly noticed anything else. They must have retraced the same route, passed through the same gate, perhaps even gone right by Guiard. But she kept her eyes down, watching her own hands as she folded and unfolded them, imagining them holding the brushes and crayons that she had so lovingly used to create pictures that no one would ever see again. She remembered them all, from initial sketches to the final wash of glaze.

When she walked through the door of the house in Pontault, André and her two students rushed to her and moistened her shoulders and her hair with tears. André led her into the parlor, and Gabrielle brought her a cup of tea. "What happened?" André asked.

"Tomorrow. I can't talk about it now. I'll tell you tomorrow."

She left her cup of tea untouched and climbed the stairs to the bedroom she shared with André and went to bed.

Thirty

Paris, 1802

Adélaïde was perched on a ladder working on a large painting of a family, a companion piece to one she'd exhibited two years ago, when the invitation arrived. Gabrielle held it up to her, and she climbed down so she could lay her brush and palette aside and open it.

"It's from that American painter, Benjamin West," she said, handing it back to Gabrielle. "I think I'd rather not go." The thought of facing a crowd of strangers—even ones she knew by name or reputation—felt exhausting.

"Oh Maman! You need to go out more. I've heard that everyone important will be there. Perhaps you'll meet someone and get a portrait commission. And the invitation includes all three of us."

Adélaïde had no desire to go out. But ever since they'd returned to Paris from Pontault they'd stayed close to home, much to themselves, so relieved to be back where they truly belonged. It had been three years, and the last party or concert Adélaïde had attended was well over a year ago. *It must be a dull life for Gabrielle*, she thought, gazing at her tenderly. Gabrielle had been so attentive to her, especially in the past few months, perhaps sensing that all was not well. It would be selfish of her to consider only her own preference. "I haven't anything suitable to wear."

"You know that doesn't matter."

Yes, Adélaïde accepted that she'd never been a beauty, and nowadays, everyone except First Consul Napoleon's wife Josephine and her circle dressed simply. What she had was good enough. "Shall you tell André or shall I?" she said, before climbing up the ladder again to continue working.

The return to Paris after Robespierre's death had been full of joy and full of sorrow. So many of their friends and acquaintances were either dead or had emigrated. The art world was in shambles, with no established academies. Nonetheless, it had come as a pleasant surprise when Adélaïde had been awarded lodgings in the Louvre, so many years after she thought it was the most important thing in the world. She was sure David had had nothing to do with that. He was off fawning over Napoleon now. Still, the honor somewhat mitigated the pain of the loss of her paintings.

She didn't really need the lodgings, although the studio was magnificent. She didn't need a place to live anymore because two years ago, she and André had married at last. He finally persuaded her they must, for both their sakes, and with her career in tatters anyway, Adélaïde decided it didn't matter any more whether she had her own identity as an artist or not. Those who she really cared about knew—those who were left, at any rate.

Victoire had returned to her family, but Adélaïde and André made the decision to officially adopt Gabrielle after they wed, so she could inherit their estates. The thought gave Adélaïde comfort. Gabrielle had stayed by them, always steadfast, stepping gladly into the role of assistant once again upon their return to Paris, even though she now had students of her own. Now she was nurturing young talent and taking aspiring women artists under her wing. How she'd changed from that fervid young woman who traveled alone from Lyon for the sake of art! Changed—and grown.

When, a few days later, Adélaïde, André, and Gabrielle found themselves at a long banquet table seated near its head, among a pantheon of the most important native and visiting artists in Paris, Adélaïde regretted her decision to come. She regretted it mainly because she found herself an arm's reach away from Elisabeth Louise Vigée Le Brun, who was seated in the place of honor on the right side of the host. Madame Le Brun wore a necklace and earrings of diamonds that caught the light from the candles and sprinkled it over everyone near her. *She must be in her late forties*, Adélaïde thought, but she was still stunning—and she knew it. Her coquettish gestures drew all eyes to her even as she looked down in false modesty, pushed her food around her plate, and took the daintiest sips of wine. She regaled the table with tales of her sojourns in Italy, Austria, Russia, and Germany, and the names of nobles and aristocrats rolled off her tongue like water. Even André couldn't help gazing at her with admiration.

But hers was only one face and figure of interest to Adélaïde. She cast her eyes around the table, drinking in the entire scene. It all looked so different now compared to the old days. Men no longer hid their hair under itchy powdered wigs, and women had stopped pinning themselves into silk gowns with stays, tight bodices, and petticoats. Since the end of the Revolution, finery—among all but the wealthiest people—had gone out of fashion. While that was as it should be, Adélaïde thought, with everyone on a much more equal footing, she sometimes missed it. She missed the sparkle of jewels in torchlight as opera or theater goers descended from their carriages. She missed the gaudy gleam of satin, the intricate luxury of lace. Although she herself had never been one for ostentation, her artist's eye mourned the loss of so much visual interest, and she sometimes longed for the challenge of capturing the play of light and shadow on contrasting textures of velvet and silk or the witticism of dotting a scatter of hair powder on the shoulder of a gentleman whose portrait she was being paid thousands of livres to paint.

Adélaïde hardly attended to the conversation around her, only nodding now and again as someone spoke to her, letting her mind continue on its own journey. She considered what it would be like to paint this gathering of young and old, men and women, beautiful and ugly. How would she do it? The tableau would be difficult, more difficult than the Hospitalers portrait. She would have to foreshorten the perspective to capture the scene of people seated together at a table. And the expressions—changing constantly, flickering from joyful to pensive moment by moment, always in motion. One minute a face in profile, gazing at the person sitting next to her. The next a head thrown back in laughter so loud it rattled the china. And with each gesture, large or small, the colors would change.

Of course, many of the faces still bore evidence of trauma and sorrow in permanently etched lines down from the corners of their mouths or between their eyebrows. But there were also some who had not endured the Terror, those lucky enough to have been abroad or too young to have been affected by it. In some of the guests' eyes Adélaïde detected weariness, ennui; in others, the sparkle of keen interest.

What a pleasure it had been for those glorious years, even when she was struggling and barely able to pay her rent, to have no higher purpose than to fix the essence of a human being on canvas for posterity. She knew, now, that it had also been a great privilege—a privilege shared by Madame Le Brun, who, to Adélaïde's surprise, was now staring at her. A smile flicked across her former rival's lips, and then she looked away.

After dessert had been consumed and the guests were folding their napkins and preparing to leave the table, Madame Le Brun rose, tapped a delicate silver spoon against her plate, and lifted her glass. All eyes turned toward her, and the room went silent.

"We should all toast our wonderful host, Monsieur West, who has brought together many I would never have expected to see in the same room, let alone seated at the same table." A quiet chuckle rippled among the guests. Then she looked straight at Adélaïde. "I would like also to toast a fellow artist who has not had such good fortune as I have had, but whose artistry deserves the highest praise. I need everyone to know how much I admire and value Madame Vincent."

Everyone rose except Adélaïde. Was Madame Le Brun sincere? She couldn't tell. And why did she put it so? Why did she need others to know of her admiration? The chorus of "*Salut!*" echoed in her head and dizzied her for a moment. By the time André helped her up from her seat, everyone had already drifted away from the table to the reception room.

"Just find me a comfortable chair in a corner, my love," Adélaïde said, squeezing André's arm.

"Are you unwell?" André asked, looking down at her with unfocused eyes. He didn't like to wear his spectacles in company.

"Quite well, *mon trésor*. Please don't mind me. You and Gabrielle should go and enjoy yourselves. You know I'm content to be quiet and watch."

His brow still creased with worry, André nodded to her and went to join a group of former academicians arguing about the future of painting. Gabrielle, Adélaïde could see, had gone to talk to Anne Vallayer-Coster, who, although quite elderly, still painted her remarkable still lifes.

Madame Le Brun, of course, stood on the other side of the room surrounded by an admiring crowd of men. They bent to her like flowers toward the sun, following her movements and gestures as though they wanted to fix them in some corner of memory to examine at a later time. But although Madame Le Brun nodded and smiled and responded in ways that made her supplicants laugh and blush, Adélaïde couldn't help feeling that at her essence, she was hollowed out; a beautifully decorated eggshell whose insides had been sucked through a hole too tiny to see. How must that feel, to be empty at one's core? Something like pity welled up in Adélaïde and threatened to spill out of her eyes as tears. She blinked fast and fought them back before anyone could see. It was her illness making her more susceptible, that was all. But where did this unexpected feeling come from? Adélaïde had been inclined to hear a note of condescension in Madame Le Brun's toast, but now, as she thought of it again, could it rather have been envy?

Adélaïde wondered what it would have been like if things could have been different between the two of them—two talented and passionate woman artists, both struggling in a world that fought to keep them out. But no, it wouldn't have been possible. And perhaps not simply because of Madame Le Brun. Since the very beginning, since the salon at the Académie de Saint-Luc, Adélaïde had fixed Madame Le Brun in her mind as something to be overcome, the embodiment of everything Adélaïde desired but would never attain. She admired her as an artist—that came easily enough. But as a woman? It had never occurred to Adélaïde to give Madame Le Brun a heart, a passion, for anything other than art, to acknowledge that she could also be vulnerable and that she had faced her own trials and disappointments.

How must it have felt to hear that her husband had divorced her in absentia? He did it to avoid being sent to the guillotine, but still, it must have stung. And then, her young daughter—who apparently had shown great promise as a portraitist—ran wild and made a disastrous marriage to a Russian officer and cut off all ties with her family. There were rumors that Madame Le Brun had consoled herself with dozens of admirers, if not lovers. And yet, here she was, alone.

Adélaïde was still deep in contemplation when a voice nearby startled her. "Madame Vincent? Might I speak with you a while?"

She looked up. It was Madame Le Brun. She'd shed her hangers-on.

"Thank you for your kind words earlier," Adélaïde said, feeling she ought to say more but not knowing what.

"I'm glad we've finally met. I know we've seen each other, but . . . such a lot has happened since those days when we were rivals."

"Were we? Rivals?" Yes, Adélaïde knew it. The world was different then. It didn't matter now.

Madame Le Brun answered Adélaïde's question with a smile. "You stayed. I thought you were very brave to do so. What was it like here, during the Revolution?"

"Difficult. Impossible, really, especially when Robespierre . . ." Adélaïde's voice trailed off as she thought of the men and women who had perished for no good reason.

"Yes. I lost some very dear friends."

Adélaïde assumed Madame Le Brun meant the queen and her court. Even though they were no longer, she found it a bit presumptuous that someone only attached to them by employment would pretend to the relationship of friend. "I'm sorry. The news must have distressed you greatly."

Madame Le Brun drew herself up and forced a smile. "But we must go on, mustn't we? Did you finish the commission for Provence—Louis XVIII, as he is known in exile?"

It was Adélaïde's turn to smile. So she had known about it. "Yes."

"Where is it now? I should like to see it."

Did she not know? Was she deliberately tormenting her? How odd of her to ask such a question. "As you must be aware, like almost all my paintings from before the Revolution, it was destroyed. Tossed on a bonfire."

"I-I was not aware." Madame Le Brun lowered herself into the chair next to Adélaïde. "I don't know what to say."

Could it be that a fellow artist truly was ignorant of how much art had been destroyed in the chaos that transpired in her absence? But she had been very far away. "Have many of your paintings from before the Revolution survived?"

"Most of them, yes. And those that did not—I made many copies, you understand."

Adélaïde nodded, not knowing what other response to make. She had heard of how Madame Le Brun had been able to churn out duplicates of many of her most successful canvases. "How fortunate that you were able to do so and remain far away from the troubles here."

A hint of tears moistened the corners of Madame Le Brun's eyes. She gathered herself as if she were going to stand and leave.

Adélaïde reached out her hand and touched Madame Le Brun's arm. "I'm sorry. That was unkind." Of course she must feel guilty for having fled, having remained safe, when so many others saw it all through, for good or ill.

Madame Le Brun settled back into her chair and spoke without looking at Adélaïde. "I see you think me a coward. I fear if I had stayed I would have met the same fate as my dear friends, Rosalie and Émilie. You didn't have the ties to court that I had, or the vicious rumors to contend with."

"No. That is true." Of course Madame Le Brun must have been distraught to hear of Rosalie Bocquet Filleul's death. They had been friends since youth. Adélaïde could picture her now, perhaps the most beautiful creature she had ever seen in that brief moment at the Saint-Luc salon. "Which paintings have survived? Any of your pastels?"

"Some. Some were taken out of the country, and I have created more since the Revolution." Madame Le Brun folded and unfolded her hands as if she didn't quite know what to do with them. "I have two questions I've longed to ask you, things I've been pondering for more than a dozen years."

What could this successful, vibrant woman artist want to ask of someone like her, who had faded into the background and was now wracked with illness she had not even confessed to André or Gabrielle? "So, ask. I will answer if I can."

"First, at the Académie salon of 1783—the first for both of us, as I recall—I saw you. You had a beautiful fan which you fluttered as I passed you. Where did you get it?"

Ah, thought Adélaïde. The episode with the fan had hurt her. "I know your father painted it. My own father had just given it to me

an hour before, as a memento of my deceased mother. The fan was a
gift from him to her many years ago. It was thoughtless of me to use it
that night, but it was what I had, and the crush was intense and very
warm, as I recall."

Madame Le Brun looked away and sighed.

"You may not believe it now, but that moment has plagued my conscience ever since. Is it too late to say I'm sorry if it distressed you in
any way?" Adélaïde was relieved to have this chance to settle an old
wrong.

Madame Le Brun turned back to her with a sad smile. "Such
things are unimportant now."

She hadn't actually accepted Adélaïde's apology. But at least
Adélaïde's conscience was clear. "You said you had two questions for
me."

"Ah, yes. A long time ago—in a different world, really—I used to
have evenings at the Hôtel Le Brun. The Comte de Vaudreuil was a
frequent guest." The blush that suffused her cheeks made Adélaïde
suspect he had been more than a guest. Perhaps he had been Madame
Le Brun's great passion. "I overheard a conversation that I later asked
Joseph—Vaudreuil—about. It concerned some magnificent pastels in
a private collection."

Pastels in a private collection. Could it be? Adélaïde stifled a laugh
and pressed her lips together. Was this, then, the legacy of her erotic
works? "Why would such pastels concern me?"

"You were, without doubt, the most skilled pastellist working in
Paris at that time—even better than Rosalie." She looked away briefly.
"But no matter. The question I have wanted to ask is simply: Was it you
who produced those pastels, last heard of in the collection of Louis
XVIII when he was still Comte de Provence?"

"Did you see any of them?"

"Alas, no. But they were spoken of in such glowing terms, I just
wondered."

Adélaïde smiled. Should she admit to it and put Madame Le Brun out of her misery? Those pastels could not trouble her now. But still. She had her pride. "I am afraid, Madame Le Brun, I know nothing of these pastels you speak of."

"Oh. I see. I must confess I am relieved. I would have hated to think that anyone of your esteemed position could have exercised her talent on so base a subject." Her smile held more disappointment than relief.

"Will you stay in Paris?" Adélaïde asked, deciding to let the implied insult slide.

Madame Le Brun scanned the glittering crowd of the most celebrated artists in Europe, a crowd that had honored her as perhaps the finest among them, Adélaïde thought. But she didn't look content. "I think not. In my travels I met many English nobles and aristocrats who have invited me to visit them in London. And I have other friends there, who have also written to urge me to stay at their homes. I'm going tomorrow."

Again, Adélaïde thought she saw the faintest glimmer of moisture in Madame Le Brun's eyes.

"Paris is much changed from when we were both women artists aspiring to make our way in the world, against all the odds," Madame Le Brun said.

"Yes. Yes, it is."

The clock on the mantel chimed. André wandered over from where he'd been engaged in conversation and bowed politely to Madame Le Brun.

She smiled in response. "I hear I must congratulate you belatedly on your marriage. How wonderful that you are husband and wife at last. If you'll excuse me, it is time I went home. I have much to do before I depart in the morning." She stood and nodded to both of them.

Adélaïde watched the most popular lady portraitist in Europe don her mask of studied pleasantness and mingle once more with the guests, smiling, accepting the odd kiss on the hand, and edging toward the door. Where was home for her former rival?

∾

When at last they left the party to stroll back to the Louvre through the autumn twilight, Gabrielle and André on each of Adélaïde's arms, Gabrielle asked, "What were you and Madame Le Brun talking about?"

"Oh, this and that." And then, with a note of wonder, Adélaïde said, "She asked about a fan, which I still possess. I'd like you to have it, Gabrielle. It's a trifle. It was my mother's."

Gabrielle squeezed Adélaïde's arm and rested her head on her shoulder for a moment. "Thank you, Maman. I shall treasure it. But was that all? To occupy such a long conversation?"

"Not all. She wanted to know something about me."

"Did you tell her?"

"No."

"Why not?"

Adélaïde sighed. "It was not important, and a little too personal for a dinner party."

André nudged her with his elbow. "Would you tell us?"

She glanced up at him. It couldn't do any harm for him to know, she thought. But, still, she hesitated. She had grown so accustomed to her secret, having guarded it with such ferocity all these years. It had loomed over her like a threat at first, but over time, it had gained a kind of mythical power. If she shared it now, it would stop being important. It would stop being hers. She had given the rest of herself to André and done it willingly. Still, little as it was, she did not want him to know everything about her, to possess not just her body and her heart, but also her past. "I think not. It's nothing either of you should concern yourself with."

Gabrielle asked, "If it's of so little importance, why did Madame Le Brun want to know it?"

Why indeed? It couldn't possibly matter now. Or perhaps it does, Adélaïde thought. I—no, we—the artists who remain, are captives of another lifetime, capable only of leaving our ghostly presence behind on scraps of canvas and paper. Yet art pushes onward, changing as the world changes. We scramble along behind, trying to fix everything before our eyes in place as it is right now, but to what purpose? Those who come after us will never truly be able to understand what we saw. They will view the images through different eyes, eyes that know truths yet to be understood. Perhaps David—opportunist that he is—comprehended that in a way the rest of us didn't, or couldn't. He knew that it was our place as artists to bear witness in the moment, pouring every bit of ourselves into that one endeavor. That was the bargain we made, what we agreed to the first time we picked up a brush or a crayon. We pledged to put our vision on canvas, on paper, on ivory, on board, and preserve it for the gaze of those not yet born.

Therein lies my great sin, Adélaïde thought. *I have betrayed my art not by executing those pastels but by refusing to own them, admit to them.*

"You haven't answered my question," Gabrielle said, giving her arm a little pinch. "And why won't you tell us what it was?"

Adélaïde opened her mouth to speak and then closed it again and shrugged. Madame Le Brun would go to London tomorrow and who knew if she'd be back ever again. She would take her curiosity with her, along with all evidence that the pastels had ever existed. They would remain unseen, unknown. Even if Madame Le Brun returned one day, Adélaïde thought, she herself would no longer be here to satisfy her curiosity, if it still existed. Adélaïde knew that she was gravely ill. The doctor had advised her to get her affairs in order. As far as she was concerned, though, her affairs were in perfect order. All was as it should be.

And then, in that instant, Adélaïde understood everything completely. She pulled her husband and her adopted daughter to a standstill. "I will not tell you what Madame Le Brun asked me for one simple reason. What she wanted to know concerning my past matters less than why she wanted to know it."

"And why was that?" André asked.

Adélaïde smiled and looked back and forth between her husband and her adopted child, who was no child, but a full-grown woman with a great career ahead of her. "Because she knows that, for all her success and my failure, I possess something she doesn't, and never will, no matter how much she desires it."

They stood for a moment at the apex of the Pont de la Revolution gazing out over the Seine and the streets and buildings of Paris. A light breeze caressed Adélaïde's cheek, and the moon cast a reflection on the moving water that fractured into shards of light behind a passing barge. The Louvre huddled on the right bank as it always had, the center of Adélaïde's existence as long as she could remember, filled with triumphs, disappointments, and love.

After a moment, Adélaïde shivered. "Come. I'm chilled through."

They linked arms again and walked the rest of the way home in silence, feeling each other's warmth, listening to the comforting nighttime sounds of Paris at peace.

Author's Note

When I started to write this manuscript several years ago, I thought I would write about Elisabeth Louise Vigée Le Brun (1755–1842), who not only left a legacy of magnificent portraits scattered throughout galleries around the world but also left a three-volume memoir about her eventful life before, during, and after the French Revolution. At some point in the course of drafting the book, I realized that there was another woman artist, a rival, nowhere near as well known today and whose life—although in many ways parallel to Vigée Le Brun's—had followed a similar but markedly different trajectory. This, of course, was the woman who is the subject of this novel. What piqued my curiosity about her were two things: First, while volumes have been written about Vigée Le Brun, the available sources about Labille-Guiard are slim. The second—and possibly more interesting fact—was that in all of Madame Le Brun's voluminous memoirs, the name Labille-Guiard never appears. Vigée Le Brun makes an oblique reference or two to another woman painter whom she thought maligned her in the eyes of Mesdames but never mentions Labille-Guiard by name. This is in spite of the fact that they exhibited in the same salons, were elected to the Académie Royale de Peinture et Sculpture in the same year, and both had official appointments in the court of Louis XVI at the same time. This intrigued me.

Vigée Le Brun was wildly successful during her sometimes unhappy life. But Labille-Guiard had to struggle to achieve her fleeting successes. I have always been attracted to underdogs, and the more

275

I read, the more my sympathies gradually realigned themselves with Adélaïde. After a brief attempt to make the book about both of these captivating figures, I finally succumbed to the allure of bringing this one remarkable artist and her extraordinary life to a broader audience.

The paucity of material concerning the details of Labille-Guiard's biography was both a hindrance and a blessing. I am thankful for the superb work by Laura Auricchio, *Adélaïde Labille-Guiard: Artist in the Age of Revolution* (The J. Paul Getty Museum, 2009), which, although primarily a study of her art, provided many important details concerning her life and politics. Also useful was Roger Portalis's biography of Adélaïde from 1902, which added some details and the texts of several early documents. While Adélaïde has been mentioned in other books about women artists, those are the only two, to my knowledge, dedicated to her alone.

I have been able to fill in much detail concerning the art world of Paris in the eighteenth century by reading the sources dedicated to Elisabeth Vigée Le Brun. Among them, *Elisabeth Vigée Le Brun: The Odyssey of an Artist in an Age of Revolution* by Gita May (Yale University Press, 2005), and *The Exceptional Woman, Elisabeth Vigée Le Brun and the Cultural Politics of* Art by Mary D. Sheriff (University of Chicago Press, 1996). Another fabulous resource was the Metropolitan Museum of Art catalogue of the exhibition "Vigée Le Brun: Woman Artist in Revolutionary France," in 2016. For insight about the life and works of Jacques-Louis David, I referred to Anita Brookner's book about the artist, published in 1980.

While I have stayed true to whatever basic facts of my heroine's life were available, I have—as always—answered the demands of the novelist to create a compelling narrative, and invented or modified several key events. With the exception of Adélaïde's first student, Paulette, and the minor characters—Jacqueline, tradespeople and so on—all the characters in these pages lived at the time and were a part of Adélaïde's life. However, I have taken some liberties with them, in particular her father, Claude-Edmé Labille, and her husband, Nicolas Guiard.

Labille was indeed a *marchand des modes* whose atelier once boasted the future Madame du Barry as a shop girl. But by the time of the events in my book, he had sold the business and was a functionary of some sort at court. Nicolas Guiard was a secretary to the clergy, but he may well have been a family friend; possibly Adélaïde had been encouraged to marry him. Aside from the fact of his having been her husband, I could find no information about him, and thus invented the circumstances of their separation, his character as a somewhat abusive husband who discouraged Adélaïde, and his role as a guard in the Revolution.

Likewise, Adélaïde's mother is a shadowy figure in history. She died when Adélaïde was seventeen, and Adélaïde was the only surviving child of eight. Her mother's cause of death is unknown, and I have no knowledge of what the mother-daughter relationship—or the father-daughter relationship, for that matter—was like.

The events surrounding the various salons are accurate in essence, but there are no records of Adélaïde and Elisabeth ever meeting at that time, nor is there any evidence that Adélaïde possessed a fan decorated by Elisabeth's father. All Adélaïde's portrait commissions are verifiable, including the massive commission for the Hospitalers portrait. The destruction of much of her work on a bonfire is also a fact, but the exact circumstances and location is not recorded, nor is whether or not Jacques-Louis David had anything to do with it. However, his enmity toward Adélaïde is a matter of record, as is his vacillating loyalty to Robespierre and then to Napoleon.

Adélaïde's and Gabrielle's involvement in the politics of the Académie are based in history, as is the deputies' commissioning both Adélaïde and David to record the king signing the new constitution— and their never doing so because of events that overtook them.

I'm sad to say, though, that there is no evidence whatsoever that

Adélaïde produced erotic pastels. That said, such drawings were readily available in eighteenth-century Paris. It was a short leap of the imagination to have cash-strapped Adélaïde resort to that lucrative trade once in a while.

Remarkably, the meeting of Adélaïde and Elisabeth at a dinner party given by Benjamin West in 1802 really happened. It's the only documented meeting of these two rivals I could find anywhere.

Adélaïde died in 1803, about a year after the last scene in this book, at the age of 54. I could not discover where she was buried, although André Vincent is resting in Père Lachaise cemetery in Paris. He survived her by thirteen years, and when he died, his paintings were sold for a handsome sum. At the same time, the paintings in his possession by Adélaïde garnered mere pennies.

A note about names: At this time, many French people had double-barreled first names with family origins. Thus François-Élie Vincent was the father of François-André Vincent. To avoid confusion for the reader, I have chosen to use the names that are different as the first names of my characters here. Thus it is Élie and André Vincent, and Marie-Gabrielle Capet is Gabrielle while Marie-Marguerite Carreaux de Rosemonde is Marguerite.

The painting Adélaïde produced for the salon of 1785, of herself at work with Gabrielle and Marguerite looking on, is on permanent exhibit at the Metropolitan Museum of Art in New York City. A detail of that painting is on the cover of this book. It's worth a pilgrimage to the Met to see the entire work, however. I go whenever I can and marvel at the sheer brilliance of its painter, whose frank gaze and air of defiance inspired me to create her character in this book.

Acknowledgments

Writing a novel is both a lonely endeavor and one that requires a community of support and encouragement. I am so fortunate in my friends and colleagues in the world I inhabit. I am grateful for the ongoing opportunity to work with the talented writers at Writers in Progress in Florence, Massachusetts, including director Dori Ostermiller and assistant director Emily Lackey. Emily is an insightful editor, and her keen eye helped me take this book to the next level.

The Pioneer Valley is blessed with several organizations that foster writing craft and offer opportunities for writers to interact with each other and be inspired. The participants in the manuscript workshop led by Kate Senecal at Pioneer Valley Writers' Workshop were of invaluable aid in making me realize that I just couldn't make a book about both Elisabeth and Adélaïde work. And members of Straw Dog Writers Guild patiently listened while I read portions of this when it was a work in progress at their fun, supportive Writers' Nights Out—which became Writers' Nights In during the pandemic.

I'm also thankful for the community of book coaches at Author Accelerator, especially the remarkable Jennie Nash, whose programs have not only taught me a great deal about coaching others to write the best books they're capable of, but helped me strengthen my own work.

And as beta readers go, Margaret McNellis is the supreme champion. I am so grateful for her insightful and targeted comments, which helped me tighten and polish the manuscript.

Thank you as well to Brooke Warner, Lauren Wise, Julie Metz, and the team at She Writes Press who have made this book a work of art as well as literature.

About the Author

Susanne Dunlap is the author of twelve works of historical fiction for adults and teens, as well as an Author Accelerator Certified Book Coach. Her love of historical fiction arose partly from her PhD studies in music history at Yale University, partly from her lifelong interest in women in the arts as a pianist and non-profit performing arts executive. Her novel *The Paris Affair* was a first place CIBA award winner. *The Musician's Daughter* was a Junior Library Guild Selection and a Bank Street Children's Book of the Year, and was nominated for the Utah Book Award and the Missouri Gateway Reader's Prize. *In the Shadow of the Lamp* was an Eliot Rosewater Indiana High School Book Award nominee. Susanne earned her BA and an MA (musicology) from Smith College and lives in Biddeford, Maine, with her little dog, Betty.

SELECTED TITLES FROM SHE WRITES PRESS

She Writes Press is an independent publishing company founded to serve women writers everywhere. Visit us at www.shewritespress.com.

Estelle by Linda Stewart Henley. $16.95, 978-1-63152-791-3
From 1872 to '73, renowned artist Edgar Degas called New Orleans home. Here, the narratives of two women—Estelle, his Creole cousin and sister-in-law, and Anne Gautier, who in 1970 finds a journal written by a relative who knew Degas—intersect . . . and a painting Degas made of Estelle spells trouble.

Finding Napoleon: A Novel by Margaret Rodenberg
$16.95, 978-1-64742-016-1
In an intriguing adaptation of Napoleon Bonaparte's real attempt to write a novel, the defeated emperor and his little-known last love—the audacious, pregnant Albine de Montholon—plot to escape exile and free his young son. To succeed, Napoleon demands loyalty. To survive, Albine plunges into betrayal.

Portrait of a Woman in White by Susan Winkler. $16.95, 978-1-93831-483-4
When the Nazis steal a Matisse portrait from the eccentric, art-loving Rosenswigs, the Parisian family is thrust into the tumult of war and separation, their fates intertwined with that of their beloved portrait.

Talland House by Maggie Humm. $16.95, 978-1-63152-729-6
1919 London: When artist Lily Briscoe meets her old tutor, Louis Grier, by chance at an exhibition, he tells her of their mutual friend Mrs. Ramsay's mysterious death—an encounter that spurs Lily to investigate the death of this woman whom she loved and admired.

The Green Lace Corset by Jill G. Hall. $16.95, 978-1-63152-769-2
An artist buys a corset in a Flagstaff resale boutique and is forced to make the biggest decision of her life. A young midwestern woman is kidnapped on a train in 1885 and taken to the Wild West. Both women find the strength to overcome their fears and discover the true meaning of family—with a little push from a green lace corset.